# POKÉMON™

## THE COMPLETE POKÉMON POCKET GUIDE

#44
Gible to G

# A two-volume set that includes all 898 Pokémon!

All 898 Pokémon! *The Complete Pokémon Pocket Guide* consists of two volumes. This is volume 2, where you can learn about 456 Pokémon, from Gible to Calyrex.

## TABLE OF CONTENTS

The Pokémon with Pokédex numbers 001–442 can all be found in volume 1.

This series recognizes Pokémon up to Generation 8, Pokémon: Sword & Shield.

# GIGANTAMAX AND MEGA EVOLUTION POKÉMON

*The Mega Evolution forms are on the pages after the original forms.

# HOW TO READ THE POKÉMON POCKET GUIDE

This guide is in Pokédex order, so you'll be able to find the Pokémon you're looking for with ease. Check out how you should read this guide!

### CATEGORY

A Pokémon's unique characteristic.

### POKÉDEX NUMBER

The numerical listing of a Pokémon.

### TYPE

There are 18 types in all. Some Pokémon have two types. Type effectiveness is very important in a battle.

### ABILITY

A special ability that each Pokémon has that is useful in battle. If there are two abilities that a type of Pokémon can use, then each individual Pokémon will only be able to use one of those abilities.

### SIZE

The height and weight of a Pokémon.

### DESCRIPTION

The Pokémon's detailed description.

### EVOLUTION

A Pokémon may evolve under certain conditions, at which point its name and form will change. The name written in red is the Pokémon being explained on this page, so you can easily see what the Pokémon looks like before and after it evolves.

### POKÉDEX NUMBERING

The numerical section of the Pokémon within this guide.

### NAME

The Pokémon's name.

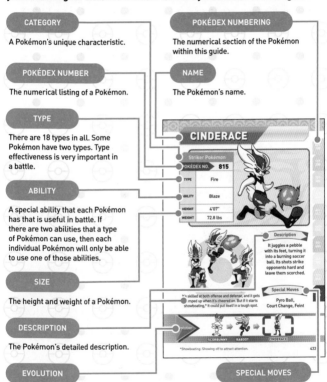

**CINDERACE**

Striker Pokémon

| POKÉDEX NO. | 815 |
| --- | --- |
| TYPE | Fire |
| ABILITY | Blaze |
| HEIGHT | 4'07" |
| WEIGHT | 72.8 lbs |

Description

It juggles a pebble with its feet, turning it into a burning soccer ball. Its shots strike opponents hard and leave them scorched.

It's skilled at both offense and defense, and it gets pumped up when it's cheered on. But if it starts showboating,* it could put itself in a tough spot.

Special Moves

Pyro Ball, Court Change, Feint

Evolution

SCORBUNNY    RABOOT    CINDERACE

*Showboating: Showing off to attract attention.

433

### SPECIAL MOVES

Moves that this Pokémon will learn. It may learn many other moves too.

# REGIONAL FORMS

Some regions like Galar and Alola have Pokémon with regional forms who have the same name but look different and have different features. These Pokémon will say "___ Form" below their names.

## GALARIAN FORM

Pokémon who have changed to adapt to the Galar region. "Galarian Form" will appear below their name.

## ALOLAN FORM

Pokémon who have changed to adapt to the Alola region. "Alolan Form" will appear below their name.

**SLOWKING**
GALARIAN FORM

Hexpert Pokémon

| POKÉDEX NO. | 199 |
| --- | --- |
| TYPE | Poison, Psychic |
| ABILITY | Own Tempo, Curious Medicine |
| HEIGHT | 5'11" |
| WEIGHT | 175.3 lbs |

**Description**
A combination of toxins and the shock of evolving has increased Shellder's* intelligence to the point that Shellder now controls Slowking.

While chanting strange spells, this Pokémon combines its internal toxins with what it's eaten, creating strange potions.

**Special Moves**
Eerie Spell, Acid, Curse

Evolution
SLOWPOKE → SLOWKING GALARIAN FORM

*Shellder: A Pokémon you'll find on page 137.

267

**EXEGGUTOR**
ALOLAN FORM

Coconut Pokémon

| POKÉDEX NO. | 103 |
| --- | --- |
| TYPE | Grass, Dragon |
| ABILITY | Frisk |
| HEIGHT | 35'09" |
| WEIGHT | 916.2 lbs |

**Description**
Blazing sunlight has brought out the true form and powers of this Pokémon.

This Pokémon's psychic powers aren't as strong as they once were. The head on this Exeggutor's tail scans surrounding areas with weak telepathy.

**Special Moves**
Dragon Hammer, Seed Bomb, Absorb

Evolution
EXEGGCUTE → EXEGGUTOR ALOLAN FORM

154

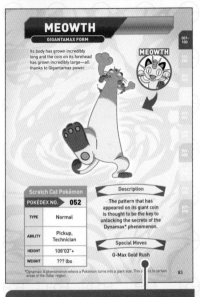

**MEOWTH**

GIGANTAMAX FORM

Its body has grown incredibly long and the coin on its forehead has grown incredibly large—all thanks to Gigantamax power.

MEOWTH

| Scratch Cat Pokémon | |
|---|---|
| POKÉDEX NO. | **052** |
| TYPE | Normal |
| ABILITY | Pickup, Technician |
| HEIGHT | 108'03"+ |
| WEIGHT | ??? lbs |

**Description**

The pattern that has appeared on its giant coin is thought to be the key to unlocking the secrets of the Dynamax* phenomenon.

**Special Moves**

G-Max Gold Rush

*Dynamax: A phenomenon where a Pokémon turns into a giant size. This occurs in certain areas of the Galar region.

83

"Gigantamax" is the phenomenon of the Pokémon growing in size and changing form. It is a unique phenomenon that only occurs in certain areas of Galar. So far, 32 Pokémon have been discovered that can Gigantamax.

## It can use G-Max Moves!

A very powerful move that only Gigantamax Pokémon can use.

## Its form and size change!

It is so huge that its weight is unknown. Its type and ability remain the same.

**MEOWTH**
(GIGANTAMAX FORM)

MEOWTH

# MEGA EVOLVED POKÉMON

## MEGA LUCARIO

Its aura has expanded due to Mega Evolution. Governed only by its combative instincts, it strikes enemies without mercy.

LUCARIO

### Aura Pokémon

| POKÉDEX NO. | **448** |
|---|---|
| TYPE | Fighting, Steel |
| ABILITY | Adaptability |
| HEIGHT | 4'03" |
| WEIGHT | 126.8 lbs |

**Description**

Bathed in explosive energy, its combative instincts have awakened. For its enemies, it has no mercy whatsoever.

**Special Moves**

Aura Sphere, Close Combat, Bone Rush

17

Mega Evolution is a phenomenon of the Pokémon evolving during a battle to wield incredible power. Its type, height, and weight may change, so you might want to compare them with the original Pokémon. So far, 48 Pokémon have been discovered to be able to Mega Evolve.

## When a Pokémon Mega Evolves, its form and stats change!

Its attack and speed will increase, making it become even more powerful in battle. The abilities of some Pokémon will change too.

LUCARIO

MEGA LUCARIO

*The Mega Evolution forms are on the pages after the original forms.

7

# TYPE EFFECTIVENESS IS THE KEY TO A BATTLE

Type effectiveness is very important in a Pokémon battle. The effectiveness of a move will change depending on the type of the move used by the Pokémon and the type of the Pokémon defending itself from the attack. Check the chart below and memorize the type effectiveness!

## MOVE/TYPE EFFECTIVENESS CHART

| TYPE OF POKÉMON MOVE USED BY THE ATTACKER ↓ / TYPE OF POKÉMON DEFENDING → | Normal | Fire | Water | Electric | Grass | Ice | Fighting | Poison | Ground | Flying | Psychic | Bug | Rock | Ghost | Dragon | Dark | Steel | Fairy |
|---|---|---|---|---|---|---|---|---|---|---|---|---|---|---|---|---|---|---|
| Normal |  |  |  |  |  |  |  |  |  |  |  |  | ▲ | ✕ |  |  | ▲ |  |
| Fire |  | ▲ | ▲ |  | ● | ● |  |  |  |  |  | ● | ▲ |  | ▲ |  | ● |  |
| Water |  | ● | ▲ |  | ▲ |  |  |  | ● |  |  |  | ● |  | ▲ |  |  |  |
| Electric |  |  | ● | ▲ | ▲ |  |  |  | ✕ | ● |  |  |  |  | ▲ |  |  |  |
| Grass |  | ▲ | ● |  | ▲ |  |  | ▲ | ● | ▲ |  | ▲ | ● |  | ▲ |  | ▲ |  |
| Ice |  | ▲ | ▲ |  | ● | ▲ |  |  | ● | ● |  |  |  |  | ● |  | ▲ |  |
| Fighting | ● |  |  |  |  | ● |  | ▲ |  | ▲ | ▲ | ▲ | ● | ✕ |  | ● | ● | ▲ |
| Poison |  |  |  |  | ● |  |  | ▲ | ▲ |  |  |  | ▲ | ▲ |  |  | ✕ | ● |
| Ground |  | ● | ● |  | ▲ |  |  | ● | ✕ |  |  | ▲ | ● |  |  |  | ● |  |
| Flying |  |  |  | ▲ | ● |  | ● |  |  |  |  | ● | ▲ |  |  |  | ▲ |  |
| Psychic |  |  |  |  |  |  | ● | ● |  |  | ▲ |  |  |  |  | ✕ | ▲ |  |
| Bug |  | ▲ |  |  | ● |  | ▲ | ▲ |  | ▲ | ● |  |  | ▲ |  | ● | ▲ | ▲ |
| Rock |  | ● |  |  |  | ● | ▲ |  | ▲ | ● |  | ● |  |  |  |  | ▲ |  |
| Ghost | ✕ |  |  |  |  |  |  |  |  |  | ● |  |  | ● | ▲ |  |  |  |
| Dragon |  |  |  |  |  |  |  |  |  |  |  |  |  |  | ● |  | ▲ | ✕ |
| Dark |  |  |  |  |  |  | ▲ |  |  |  | ● |  |  | ● | ▲ | ▲ |  | ▲ |
| Steel |  | ▲ | ▲ | ▲ |  | ● |  |  |  |  |  |  | ● |  |  |  | ▲ | ● |
| Fairy |  | ▲ |  |  |  |  | ● | ▲ |  |  |  |  |  |  | ● | ● | ▲ |  |

| MARK DESCRIPTIONS | ● Super Effective | ▲ Not Very Effective |
|---|---|---|
|  | ✕ No Effect | ☐ Normal Effect |

# AIM FOR "SUPER EFFECTIVE"!

Learn the combinations to a "Super Effective" attack! For example, Rowlet excels in Grass-type moves, so it is strong against Oshawott, which is a Water-type Pokémon. But Rowlet is weak against Cyndaquil using a Fire-type move.

**ROWLET**
GRASS TYPE

Fire-type moves are **Super Effective!**

Grass-type moves are **Super Effective!**

Water-type moves are **Super Effective!**

CYNDAQUIL FIRE TYPE  OSHAWOTT WATER TYPE

# GIBLE

Gible attacks anything that moves, and it drags whatever it catches into the crevice that is its lair. Despite its big mouth, Gible's stomach is small.

## Land Shark Pokémon

| POKÉDEX NO. | 443 |
| --- | --- |
| TYPE | Dragon, Ground |
| ABILITY | Sand Veil |
| HEIGHT | 2'04" |
| WEIGHT | 45.2 lbs |

### Description

Gible prefers to stay in narrow holes on the sides of caves heated by geothermal energy. This way, Gible can stay warm even during a blizzard.

### Special Moves

Sand Tomb, Dragon Breath, Dig

### Evolution

GIBLE → GABITE → GARCHOMP

# GABITE

| Cave Pokémon | |
|---|---|
| **POKÉDEX NO.** | **444** |
| **TYPE** | Dragon, Ground |
| **ABILITY** | Sand Veil |
| **HEIGHT** | 4'07" |
| **WEIGHT** | 123.5 lbs |

This Pokémon emits ultrasonic waves from protrusions on either side of its head to probe pitch-dark caves.

### Description

Jewels are buried in the caves these Pokémon nest in, but you'll be torn apart by claws and fangs the moment you enter one of these caves.

### Special Moves

Dragon Breath, Bite, Sandstorm

001-100
101-200
201-300
401-442
443-500
501-600
701-900
801-898

**Evolution**

GIBLE

GABITE

GARCHOMP

# GARCHOMP

## Mach Pokémon

| POKÉDEX NO. | **445** |
| --- | --- |
| **TYPE** | Dragon, Ground |
| **ABILITY** | Sand Veil |
| **HEIGHT** | 6'03" |
| **WEIGHT** | 209.4 lbs |

Garchomp is fast both underground and above. It can bring down prey and return to its den before its body has chilled from being outside.

### Description

Garchomp makes its home in volcanic mountains. It flies through the sky as fast as a jet airplane, hunting down as much prey as it can.

### Special Moves

Dragon Rush, Dual Chop, Bulldoze

**Evolution**

GIBLE

GABITE

GARCHOMP

12

# MEGA GARCHOMP

Its disposition is more vicious than before its Mega Evolution. Garchomp carves its opponents up with the scythes on both arms.

GARCHOMP

001-100

101-200

201-300

401-442

443-500

501-600

701-800

801-898

## Mach Pokémon

| POKÉDEX NO. | **445** |
|---|---|
| TYPE | Dragon, Ground |
| ABILITY | Sand Force |
| HEIGHT | 6'03" |
| WEIGHT | 209.4 lbs |

### Description

Its arms and wings melted into something like scythes. Mad with rage, it rampages on and on.

### Special Moves

Dragon Rush, Dual Chop, Dragon Rage

# MUNCHLAX

| Big Eater Pokémon | |
|---|---|
| **POKÉDEX NO.** | **446** |
| **TYPE** | Normal |
| **ABILITY** | Pickup, Thick Fat |
| **HEIGHT** | 2'00" |
| **WEIGHT** | 231.5 lbs |

It stores food beneath its fur.
It might share just one bite,
but only if it really trusts you.

### Description

Stuffing itself with
vast amounts of food
is its only concern.
Whether the food is
rotten or fresh, yummy
or tasteless—it does
not care.

### Special Moves

Body Slam,
Belly Drum, Stockpile

**Evolution**

MUNCHLAX → SNORLAX

# RIOLU

### Emanation Pokémon

| | |
|---|---|
| **POKÉDEX NO.** | **447** |
| **TYPE** | Fighting |
| **ABILITY** | Inner Focus, Steadfast |
| **HEIGHT** | 2'04" |
| **WEIGHT** | 44.5 lbs |

It can use waves called auras to gauge how others are feeling. These same waves can also tell this Pokémon about the state of the environment.

### Description

It's exceedingly energetic, with enough stamina to keep running all through the night. Taking it for walks can be a challenging experience.

### Special Moves

Force Palm, Metal Claw, Swords Dance

**Evolution**

RIOLU → LUCARIO

001-100
101-200
201-300
401-442
443-500
501-600
701-800
801-898

# LUCARIO

| Aura Pokémon | |
|---|---|
| **POKÉDEX NO.** | **448** |
| TYPE | Fighting, Steel |
| ABILITY | Inner Focus, Steadfast |
| HEIGHT | 3'11" |
| WEIGHT | 119.0 lbs |

It controls waves known as auras, which are powerful enough to pulverize huge rocks. It uses these waves to take down its prey.

## Description

It can tell what people are thinking. Only Trainers who have justice in their hearts can earn this Pokémon's trust.

## Special Moves

Aura Sphere, Power-Up Punch, Bone Rush

---

**Evolution**

RIOLU

LUCARIO

# MEGA LUCARIO

Its aura has expanded due to Mega Evolution. Governed only by its combative instincts, it strikes enemies without mercy.

LUCARIO

| Aura Pokémon | |
|---|---|
| **POKÉDEX NO.** | **448** |
| **TYPE** | Fighting, Steel |
| **ABILITY** | Adaptability |
| **HEIGHT** | 4'03" |
| **WEIGHT** | 126.8 lbs |

### Description

Bathed in explosive energy, its combative instincts have awakened. For its enemies, it has no mercy whatsoever.

### Special Moves

Aura Sphere, Close Combat, Bone Rush

001-100
101-200
201-300
401-442
443-500
501-600
701-800
801-898

# HIPPOPOTAS

This Pokémon is active during the day and passes the cold desert nights burrowed snugly into the sand.

| Hippo Pokémon | |
|---|---|
| POKÉDEX NO. | **449** |
| TYPE | Ground |
| ABILITY | Sand Stream |
| HEIGHT | 2'07" |
| WEIGHT | 109.1 lbs |

### Description

It moves through the sands with its mouth open, swallowing sand along with its prey. It gets rid of the sand by spouting it from its nose.

### Special Moves

Sand Attack, Dig, Double-Edge

Evolution

HIPPOPOTAS → HIPPOWDON

# HIPPOWDON

001-100

101-200

201-300

401-442

443-500

501-600

701-890

801-898

Stones can get stuck in the ports on their bodies. Dwebble* help dislodge such stones, so Hippowdon look after those Pokémon.

| Heavyweight Pokémon | |
|---|---|
| POKÉDEX NO. | 450 |
| TYPE | Ground |
| ABILITY | Sand Stream |
| HEIGHT | 6'07" |
| WEIGHT | 661.4 lbs |

### Description

When roused to violence by its rage, it spews out the quantities of sand it has swallowed and whips up a sandstorm.

### Special Moves

Sandstorm, Sand Tomb, Double-Edge

**Evolution**

HIPPOPOTAS → HIPPOWDON

---

*Dwebble: A Pokémon you'll find on page 143.

# SKORUPI

After burrowing into the sand, it waits patiently for prey to come near. This Pokémon and Sizzlipede* share common descent.

| Scorpion Pokémon | |
| --- | --- |
| POKÉDEX NO. | **451** |
| TYPE | Poison, Bug |
| ABILITY | Sniper, Battle Armor |
| HEIGHT | 2'07" |
| WEIGHT | 26.5 lbs |

### Description

It attacks using the claws on its tail. Once locked in its grip, its prey is unable to move as this Pokémon's poison seeps in.

### Special Moves

Poison Sting, Venoshock, Knock Off

### Evolution

SKORUPI → DRAPION

*Sizzlipede: A Pokémon you'll find on page 481.

# DRAPION

001-100
101-200
201-300
401-442
443-500
501-600
701-800
801-898

Its poison is potent, but it rarely sees use. This Pokémon prefers to use physical force instead, going on rampages with its car-crushing strength.

## Ogre Scorpion Pokémon

| POKÉDEX NO. | 452 |
|---|---|
| TYPE | Poison, Dark |
| ABILITY | Sniper, Battle Armor |
| HEIGHT | 4'03" |
| WEIGHT | 135.6 lbs |

### Description

It's so vicious that it's called the Sand Demon. Yet when confronted by Hippowdon,* Drapion keeps a low profile and will never pick a fight.

### Special Moves

Toxic Spikes, Pin Missile, Poison Fang

**Evolution**

SKORUPI → DRAPION

*Hippowdon: A Pokémon you'll find on page 19.

21

# CROAGUNK

## Toxic Mouth Pokémon

| POKÉDEX NO. | **453** |
| --- | --- |
| TYPE | Poison, Fighting |
| ABILITY | Dry Skin, Anticipation |
| HEIGHT | 2'04" |
| WEIGHT | 50.7 lbs |

Once diluted, its poison becomes medicinal. This Pokémon came into popularity after a pharmaceutical company chose it as a mascot.

### Description

It makes frightening noises with its poison-filled cheek sacs. When opponents flinch, Croagunk hits them with a poison jab.

### Special Moves

Poison Sting, Nasty Plot, Sludge Bomb

Evolution

CROAGUNK → TOXICROAK

# TOXICROAK

It booms out a victory croak when its prey goes down in defeat. This Pokémon and Seismitoad* are related species.

001-100
101-200
201-300
401-442
443-500
501-600
701-800
801-898

| Toxic Mouth Pokémon | |
|---|---|
| POKÉDEX NO. | 454 |
| TYPE | Poison, Fighting |
| ABILITY | Dry Skin, Anticipation |
| HEIGHT | 4'03" |
| WEIGHT | 97.9 lbs |

## Description

It bounces toward opponents and gouges them with poisonous claws. No more than a scratch is needed to knock out its adversaries.

## Special Moves

Poison Jab, Venoshock, Sludge Bomb

**Evolution**

CROAGUNK → TOXICROAK

---

*Seismitoad: A Pokémon you'll find on page 118.

# CARNIVINE

It attracts prey with its sweet-smelling saliva, then chomps down. It takes a whole day to eat its prey.

| Bug Catcher Pokémon | |
|---|---|
| POKÉDEX NO. | **455** |
| TYPE | Grass |
| ABILITY | Levitate |
| HEIGHT | 4'07" |
| WEIGHT | 59.5 lbs |

## Description

It binds itself to trees in marshes. It attracts prey with its sweet-smelling drool and gulps them down.

## Special Moves

Leaf Tornado, Sweet Scent, Ingrain

**Evolution**

CARNIVINE

Does not evolve

# FINNEON

## Wing Fish Pokémon

| POKÉDEX NO. | 456 |
|---|---|

| TYPE | Water |
|---|---|
| ABILITY | Swift Swim, Storm Drain |
| HEIGHT | 1'04" |
| WEIGHT | 15.4 lbs |

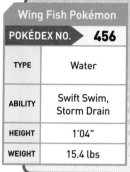

It lures in prey with its shining tail fins. It stays near the surface during the day and moves to the depths when night falls.

### Description

When night falls, their pink patterns begin to shine. They're popular with divers, so there are resorts that feed them to keep them close.

### Special Moves

Rain Dance, Water Gun, Aqua Ring

**Evolution**

FINNEON

LUMINEON

001-100
101-200
201-300
401-442
443-500
501-600
701-800
801-898

# LUMINEON

They traverse the deep waters as if crawling over the seafloor. The fantastic lights of its fins shine like stars in the night sky.

| Neon Pokémon | |
|---|---|
| POKÉDEX NO. | 457 |
| TYPE | Water |
| ABILITY | Swift Swim, Storm Drain |
| HEIGHT | 3'11" |
| WEIGHT | 52.9 lbs |

### Description

Deep down at the bottom of the ocean, prey is scarce. Lumineon get into fierce disputes with Lanturn* over food.

### Special Moves

Whirlpool, Water Pulse, Silver Wind

Evolution

FINNEON

LUMINEON

*Lanturn: A Pokémon you'll find in volume 1.

# MANTYKE

## Kite Pokémon

| | |
|---|---|
| **POKÉDEX NO.** | **458** |

| | |
|---|---|
| **TYPE** | Water, Flying |
| **ABILITY** | Water Absorb, Swift Swim |
| **HEIGHT** | 3'03" |
| **WEIGHT** | 143.3 lbs |

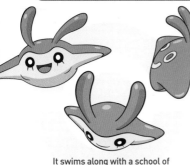

### Description

Mantyke living in Galar seem to be somewhat sluggish. The colder waters of the seas in this region may be the cause.

It swims along with a school of Remoraid*, and they'll all fight together to repel attackers.

### Special Moves

Water Gun, Bounce, Bubble Beam

001-100
101-200
201-300
401-442
443-500
501-600
701-800
801-898

**Evolution**

MANTYKE → MANTINE

*Remoraid: A Pokémon you'll find in volume 1.

# SNOVER

| Frost Tree Pokémon | |
|---|---|
| **POKÉDEX NO.** | **459** |
| **TYPE** | Grass, Ice |
| **ABILITY** | Snow Warning |
| **HEIGHT** | 3'03" |
| **WEIGHT** | 111.3 lbs |

### Description

The berries that grow around its belly are like ice pops. Galarian Darumaka* absolutely love these berries.

It lives on snowy mountains. It sinks its legs into the snow to absorb water and keep its own temperature down.

### Special Moves

Powder Snow, Icy Wind, Ice Shard

**Evolution**

SNOVER → ABOMASNOW

*Darumaka: A Pokémon you'll find on page 136.

# ABOMASNOW

001-100
101-200
201-300
401-442
443-500
501-600
701-800
801-898

This Pokémon is known to bring blizzards. A shake of its massive body is enough to cause whiteout conditions.

## Frost Tree Pokémon

| POKÉDEX NO. | 460 |
|---|---|
| TYPE | Grass, Ice |
| ABILITY | Snow Warning |
| HEIGHT | 7'03" |
| WEIGHT | 298.7 lbs |

## Description

If it sees any packs of Darumaka* going after Snover, it chases them off, swinging its sizable arms like hammers.

## Special Moves

Ice Punch, Sheer Cold, Blizzard

**Evolution**

  →

SNOVER ⟶ ABOMASNOW

*Darumaka: A Pokémon you'll find on page 136.

29

# MEGA ABOMASNOW

It blankets wide areas in snow by whipping up blizzards. It is also known as the Ice Monster.

**ABOMASNOW**

| Frost Tree Pokémon | |
|---|---|
| **POKÉDEX NO.** | **460** |
| TYPE | Grass, Ice |
| ABILITY | Snow Warning |
| HEIGHT | 8'10" |
| WEIGHT | 407.9 lbs |

### Description

They appear when the snow flowers bloom. When the petals fall, they retreat to places unknown again.

### Special Moves

Ice Punch, Sheer Cold, Wood Hammer

# WEAVILE

## Sharp Claw Pokémon

| | |
|---|---|
| **POKÉDEX NO.** | **461** |
| **TYPE** | Dark, Ice |
| **ABILITY** | Pressure |
| **HEIGHT** | 3'07" |
| **WEIGHT** | 75.0 lbs |

001-100
101-200
201-300
401-442
443-500
501-600
701-800
801-898

### Description

They attack their quarry in packs. Prey as large as Mamoswine easily fall to the teamwork of a group of Weavile.

With its claws, it leaves behind signs for its friends to find. The number of distinct signs is said to be over 500.

### Special Moves

Metal Claw, Icy Wind, Dark Pulse

**Evolution**

 →

SNEASEL          WEAVILE

# MAGNEZONE

It's thought that a special magnetic field changed the molecular structure of this Pokémon's body, and that's what caused the Pokémon's evolution.

| Magnet Area Pokémon | |
|---|---|
| POKÉDEX NO. | **462** |
| TYPE | Electric, Steel |
| ABILITY | Sturdy, Magnet Pull |
| HEIGHT | 3'11" |
| WEIGHT | 396.8 lbs |

## Description

Some say Magnezone receives signals from space via the antenna on its head and that it's being controlled by some mysterious being.

## Special Moves

Flash Cannon, Tri Attack, Discharge

Evolution  ➡  ➡

MAGNEMITE        MAGNETON        MAGNEZONE

# LICKILICKY

**Licking Pokémon**

| POKÉDEX NO. | **463** |
|---|---|
| TYPE | Normal |
| ABILITY | Oblivious, Own Tempo |
| HEIGHT | 5'07" |
| WEIGHT | 308.6 lbs |

Lickilicky's strange tongue can stretch to many times the length of its body. No one has figured out how Lickilicky's tongue can stretch so far.

### Description

Lickilicky can do just about anything with its tongue, which is as dexterous as the human hand. In contrast, Lickilicky's use of its fingers is clumsy.

### Special Moves

Lick, Belly Drum, Power Whip

**Evolution**

LICKITUNG → LICKILICKY

001-100
101-200
201-300
401-442
443-500
501-600
701-800
801-898

# RHYPERIOR

## Drill Pokémon

| | |
|---|---|
| **POKÉDEX NO.** | **464** |
| **TYPE** | Ground, Rock |
| **ABILITY** | Lightning Rod, Solid Rock |
| **HEIGHT** | 7'10" |
| **WEIGHT** | 623.5 lbs |

It relies on its carapace to deflect incoming attacks and throw its enemy off-balance. As soon as that happens, it drives its drill into the foe.

### Description

It can load up to three projectiles per arm into the holes in its hands. What launches out of those holes could be either rocks or Roggenrola.*

### Special Moves

Drill Run, Horn Attack, Rock Wrecker

**Evolution**

RHYHORN → RHYDON → RHYPERIOR

*Roggenrola: A Pokémon you'll find on page 104.

# TANGROWTH

001-100
101-200
201-300
401-442
443-500
501-600
701-800
801-898

Tangrowth has two arms that it can extend as it pleases. Recent research has shown that these arms are, in fact, bundles of vines.

## Vine Pokémon

| POKÉDEX NO. | **465** |
|---|---|
| TYPE | Grass |
| ABILITY | Chlorophyll, Leaf Guard |
| HEIGHT | 6'07" |
| WEIGHT | 283.5 lbs |

## Description

Vine growth is accelerated for Tangrowth living in warm climates. If the vines grow long, Tangrowth shortens them by tearing parts of them off.

## Special Moves

Power Whip, Vine Whip, Giga Drain

**Evolution**

TANGELA → TANGROWTH

# ELECTIVIRE

## Thunderbolt Pokémon

| POKÉDEX NO. | 466 |
|---|---|
| **TYPE** | Electric |
| **ABILITY** | Motor Drive |
| **HEIGHT** | 5'11" |
| **WEIGHT** | 305.6 lbs |

In terms of electrical-energy output, Electivire is one of the best among all electric Pokémon. It discharges high-voltage currents from its tails.

### Description

The amount of electrical energy this Pokémon produces is proportional to the rate of its pulse. The voltage jumps while Electivire is battling.

### Special Moves

Shock Wave, Thunderbolt, Thunder

**Evolution**

ELEKID → ELECTABUZZ → ELECTIVIRE

# MAGMORTAR

## Blast Pokémon

| POKÉDEX NO. | **467** |
|---|---|
| TYPE | Fire |
| ABILITY | Flame Body |
| HEIGHT | 5'03" |
| WEIGHT | 149.9 lbs |

001-100
101-200
201-300
401-442
443-500
501-600
701-800
801-898

When Magmortar inhales deeply, the fire burning in its belly intensifies, rising in temperature to over 3,600 degrees Fahrenheit.

### Description

Living in the crater of a volcano has caused this Pokémon's body to resemble its environment—it has an organ similar to a magma chamber.

### Special Moves

Lava Plume, Clear Smog, Flamethrower

**Evolution**

MAGBY → MAGMAR → MAGMORTAR

# TOGEKISS

## Jubilee Pokémon

| POKÉDEX NO. | 468 |
| --- | --- |
| TYPE | Fairy, Flying |
| ABILITY | Serene Grace, Hustle |
| HEIGHT | 4'11" |
| WEIGHT | 83.8 lbs |

### Description

These Pokémon are never seen anywhere near conflict or turmoil. In recent times, they've hardly been seen at all.

### Special Moves

Air Slash, Wish, Sky Attack

Known as a bringer of blessings, it's been depicted on good-luck charms since ancient times.

Evolution

TOGEPI → TOGETIC → TOGEKISS

# YANMEGA

It prefers to battle by biting apart foes' heads instantly while flying by at high speed.

001-100

101-200

201-300

401-442

443-500

501-600

701-800

801-898

## Ogre Darner Pokémon

| POKÉDEX NO. | **469** |
|---|---|
| TYPE | Bug, Flying |
| ABILITY | Tinted Lens, Speed Boost |
| HEIGHT | 6'03" |
| WEIGHT | 113.5 lbs |

### Description

This six-legged Pokémon is easily capable of transporting an adult in flight. The wings on its tail help it stay balanced.

### Special Moves

Sonic Boom, Bug Buzz, Pursuit

Evolution

YANMA ➡ YANMEGA

# LEAFEON

### Verdant Pokémon

| POKÉDEX NO. | 470 |
|---|---|
| TYPE | Grass |
| ABILITY | Leaf Guard |
| HEIGHT | 3'03" |
| WEIGHT | 56.2 lbs |

This Pokémon's tail is blade sharp, with a fantastic cutting edge that can slice right through large trees.

### Description

Galarians favor the distinctive aroma that drifts from this Pokémon's leaves. There's a popular perfume made using that scent.

### Special Moves

Leaf Blade, Magical Leaf, Take Down

### Evolution

EEVEE → LEAFEON

# GLACEON

001-100
101-200
201-300
401-442
443-500
501-600
701-900
801-898

**Fresh Snow Pokémon**

| POKÉDEX NO. | 471 |
| --- | --- |
| TYPE | Ice |
| ABILITY | Snow Cloak |
| HEIGHT | 2'07" |
| WEIGHT | 57.1 lbs |

The coldness emanating from Glaceon causes powdery snow to form, making it quite a popular Pokémon at ski resorts.

### Description

Any who become captivated by the beauty of the snowfall that Glaceon creates will be frozen before they know it.

### Special Moves

Icy Wind, Freeze-Dry, Blizzard

**Evolution**

EEVEE ➡

GLACEON

41

# GLISCOR

## Fang Scorpion Pokémon

| POKÉDEX NO. | 472 |
| --- | --- |

| TYPE | Ground, Flying |
| --- | --- |
| ABILITY | Sand Veil, Hyper Cutter |
| HEIGHT | 6'07" |
| WEIGHT | 93.7 lbs |

### Description

It observes prey while hanging inverted from branches. When the chance presents itself, it swoops!

Its flight is soundless. It uses its lengthy tail to carry off its prey... Then its elongated fangs do the rest.

### Special Moves

Sky Uppercut, Guillotine, Poison Jab

Evolution

GLIGAR → GLISCOR

# MAMOSWINE

It looks strong, and that's exactly what it is. As the weather grows colder, its ice tusks grow longer, thicker, and more impressive.

001-100
101-200
201-300
401-442
443-500
501-600
701-800
801-898

## Twin Tusk Pokémon

| POKÉDEX NO. | 473 |
|---|---|
| TYPE | Ice, Ground |
| ABILITY | Oblivious, Snow Cloak |
| HEIGHT | 8'02" |
| WEIGHT | 641.5 lbs |

### Description

This Pokémon can be spotted in wall paintings from as far back as 10,000 years ago. For a while, it was thought to have gone extinct.

### Special Moves

Double Hit, Icy Wind, Earthquake

### Evolution

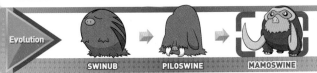

SWINUB → PILOSWINE → MAMOSWINE

# PORYGON-Z

Porygon-Z had a program installed to allow it to move between dimensions, but the program also caused instability in Porygon-Z's behavior.

| Virtual Pokémon | |
|---|---|
| POKÉDEX NO. | **474** |
| TYPE | Normal |
| ABILITY | Adaptability, Download |
| HEIGHT | 2'11" |
| WEIGHT | 75.0 lbs |

### Description

Some say an additional program made this Pokémon evolve, but even academics can't agree on whether Porygon-Z is really an evolution.

### Special Moves

Conversion 2, Zap Cannon, Recover

Evolution

PORYGON

PORYGON2

PORYGON-Z

# GALLADE

| Blade Pokémon | |
|---|---|
| **POKÉDEX NO.** | **475** |
| **TYPE** | Psychic, Fighting |
| **ABILITY** | Steadfast |
| **HEIGHT** | 5'03" |
| **WEIGHT** | 114.6 lbs |

Sharply attuned to others' wishes for help, this Pokémon seeks out those in need and aids them in battle.

### Description

True to its honorable-warrior image, it uses the blades on its elbows only in defense of something or someone.

### Special Moves

Psycho Cut,
Close Combat, Slash

**Evolution**

RALTS    KIRLIA (MALE)    GALLADE

001-100
101-200
201-300
401-442
443-500
501-600
701-800
801-898

# MEGA GALLADE

A master of courtesy and swordsmanship, it fights using the extending swords on its elbows.

**GALLADE**

| Blade Pokémon | |
|---|---|
| **POKÉDEX NO.** | **475** |
| TYPE | Psychic, Fighting |
| ABILITY | Inner Focus |
| HEIGHT | 5'03" |
| WEIGHT | 124.3 lbs |

### Description

Because it can sense what its foe is thinking, its attacks burst out first, fast, and fierce.

### Special Moves

Psycho Cut, Close Combat, Leaf Blade

# PROBOPASS

It uses three small units to catch prey and battle enemies. The main body mostly just gives orders.

001-100
101-200
201-300
401-442
443-500
501-600
701-800
801-898

## Compass Pokémon

| POKÉDEX NO. | 476 |
| --- | --- |
| TYPE | Rock, Steel |
| ABILITY | Sturdy, Magnet Pull |
| HEIGHT | 4'07" |
| WEIGHT | 749.6 lbs |

### Description

Although it can control its units, known as Mini-Noses, they sometimes get lost and don't come back.

### Special Moves

Tri Attack, Zap Cannon, Block

### Evolution

NOSEPASS

PROBOPASS

# DUSKNOIR

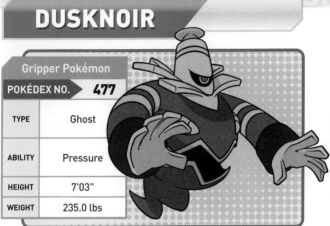

## Gripper Pokémon

| POKÉDEX NO. | 477 |
| --- | --- |

| TYPE | Ghost |
| --- | --- |
| ABILITY | Pressure |
| HEIGHT | 7'03" |
| WEIGHT | 235.0 lbs |

With the mouth on its belly, Dusknoir swallows its target whole. The soul is the only thing eaten—Dusknoir disgorges the body before departing.

### Description

At the bidding of transmissions from the spirit world, it steals people and Pokémon away. No one knows whether it has a will of its own.

### Special Moves

Shadow Ball, Confuse Ray, Destiny Bond

Evolution

DUSKULL → DUSCLOPS → DUSKNOIR

# FROSLASS

After a woman met her end on a snowy mountain, her regrets lingered on. From them, this Pokémon was born. Its favorite food is frozen souls.

## Snow Land Pokémon

| POKÉDEX NO. | **478** |
| --- | --- |
| TYPE | Ice, Ghost |
| ABILITY | Snow Cloak |
| HEIGHT | 4'03" |
| WEIGHT | 58.6 lbs |

### Description

It spits out cold air of nearly -60 degrees Fahrenheit to freeze its quarry. It brings frozen prey back to its lair and neatly lines them up.

### Special Moves

Hex, Frost Breath, Icy Shard

**Evolution**

 ➡

SNORUNT        FROSLASS

001-100
101-200
201-300
401-442
443-500
501-600
701-800
801-898

| | |
|---|---|
| **Plasma Pokémon** | |
| **POKÉDEX NO.** | **479** |
| **TYPE** | Electric, Ghost |
| **ABILITY** | Levitate |
| **HEIGHT** | 1'00" |
| **WEIGHT** | 0.7 lbs |

### Description

One boy's invention led to the development of many different machines that take advantage of Rotom's unique capabilities.

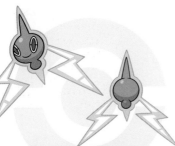

With a body made of plasma, it can inhabit all sorts of machines. It loves to surprise others.

### Special Moves

Thunder Shock, Electro Ball, Shock Wave

**Evolution**

Does not evolve

ROTOM

# ROTOM

**WASH ROTOM**

| Plasma Pokémon | |
|---|---|
| **POKÉDEX NO.** | **479** |
| **TYPE** | Electric, Water |
| **ABILITY** | Levitate |
| **HEIGHT** | 1'00" |
| **WEIGHT** | 0.7 lbs |

This form of Rotom enjoys coming up with water-based pranks. Be careful with it if you don't want your room flooded.

### Description

This Rotom has possessed a washing machine that uses a special motor. It blasts out water to get enemies to back down.

### Special Moves

Hydro Pump, Electro Ball, Shock Wave

**Evolution**  Does not evolve

ROTOM
(WASH ROTOM)

001-100
101-200
01-00
401-442
443-500
501-600
701-800
801-898

# ROTOM

## Plasma Pokémon

| | |
|---|---|
| **POKÉDEX NO.** | **479** |
| **TYPE** | Electric, Grass |
| **ABILITY** | Levitate |
| **HEIGHT** | 1'00" |
| **WEIGHT** | 0.7 lbs |

### Description

This is Rotom after it's seized control of a lawn mower that has a special motor. As it mows down grass, it scatters the clippings everywhere.

In this form, Rotom focuses its antics on plants. Any flowers you were growing are going to get mowed down.

### Special Moves

Leaf Storm, Electro Ball, Shock Wave

**Evolution** — Does not evolve

ROTOM
(MOW ROTOM)

52

# ROTOM

### FAN ROTOM

| Plasma Pokémon | |
|---|---|
| **POKÉDEX NO.** | **479** |
| **TYPE** | Electric, Flying |
| **ABILITY** | Levitate |
| **HEIGHT** | 1'00" |
| **WEIGHT** | 0.7 lbs |

001-100

101-200

201-300

401-442

443-500

501-600

701-800

801-898

### Description

This Rotom has taken over a fan that has a special motor. Its gusts of wind blow its opponent away!

In this form, Rotom applies its new power over wind to its love of pranks. It will happily blow away any important documents it can find.

### Special Moves

Air Slash, Electro Ball, Shock Wave

**Evolution**

Does not evolve

ROTOM
(FAN ROTOM)

# ROTOM

## HEAT ROTOM

### Plasma Pokémon

| POKÉDEX NO. | 479 |
|---|---|
| TYPE | Electric, Fire |
| ABILITY | Levitate |
| HEIGHT | 1'00" |
| WEIGHT | 0.7 lbs |

This form of Rotom enjoys making mischief by turning up the heat. It will gleefully burn your favorite outfit.

### Description

This Rotom has possessed a convection microwave oven that uses a special motor. It also has a flair for manipulating flames.

### Special Moves

Overheat, Electro Ball, Shock Wave

Evolution

Does not evolve

ROTOM
[HEAT ROTOM]

# ROTOM

**FROST ROTOM**

## Plasma Pokémon

| | |
|---|---|
| **POKÉDEX NO.** | **479** |
| **TYPE** | Electric, Ice |
| **ABILITY** | Levitate |
| **HEIGHT** | 1'00" |
| **WEIGHT** | 0.7 lbs |

When it's like this, Rotom likes to play pranks that are freezing cold. You may find it's turned the bath you just filled to solid ice!

### Description

Rotom assumes this form when it takes over a refrigerator powered by a special motor. It battles by spewing cold air.

### Special Moves

Blizzard, Electro Ball, Shock Wave

**Evolution**

ROTOM
(FROST ROTOM)

Does not evolve

001-100
101-200
201-300
401-442
443-500
501-600
701-800
801-898

# UXIE

### Knowledge Pokémon

| POKÉDEX NO. | 480 |
| --- | --- |
| TYPE | Psychic |
| ABILITY | Levitate |
| HEIGHT | 1'00" |
| WEIGHT | 0.7 lbs |

It is said that its emergence gave humans the intelligence to improve their quality of life.

### Description

Known as the Being of Knowledge. It is said that it can wipe out the memory of those who see its eyes.

### Special Moves

Future Sight, Psychic, Extrasensory

Evolution  Does not evolve

UXIE

# MESPRIT

**Emotion Pokémon**

| POKÉDEX NO. | 481 |
|---|---|

| TYPE | Psychic |
|---|---|
| ABILITY | Levitate |
| HEIGHT | 1'00" |
| WEIGHT | 0.7 lbs |

001-100
101-200
201-300
401-442
443-500
501-600
701-800
801-898

### Description

Known as the Being of Emotion. It taught humans the nobility of sorrow, pain, and joy.

It sleeps at the bottom of a lake. Its spirit is said to leave its body to fly on the lake's surface.

### Special Moves

Healing Wish, Psybeam, Imprison

**Evolution**

Does not evolve

MESPRIT

57

# AZELF

## Willpower Pokémon

| POKÉDEX NO. | 482 |
| --- | --- |
| TYPE | Psychic |
| ABILITY | Levitate |
| HEIGHT | 1'00" |
| WEIGHT | 0.7 lbs |

It is known as the Being of Willpower. It sleeps at the bottom of a lake to keep the world in balance.

### Description

It is thought that Uxie,* Mesprit,** and Azelf all came from the same egg.

### Special Moves

Explosion, Extrasensory, Future Sight

**Evolution**

AZELF

Does not evolve

*Uxie: A Pokémon you'll find on page 56. **Mesprit: A Pokémon you'll find on page 57.

# DIALGA

## Temporal Pokémon

| | |
|---|---|
| **POKÉDEX NO.** | **483** |
| **TYPE** | Steel, Dragon |
| **ABILITY** | Pressure |
| **HEIGHT** | 17'09" |
| **WEIGHT** | 1505.8 lbs |

### Description

This Pokémon is spoken of in legend. It is said that time began moving when Dialga was born.

It has the power to control time. It appears in Sinnoh-region myths as an ancient deity.

### Special Moves

Roar of Time, Aura Sphere, Metal Claw

**Evolution**

DIALGA

Does not evolve

001-100
101-200
201-300
401-442
443-500
501-600
701-800
801-898

# PALKIA

## Spatial Pokémon

| POKÉDEX NO. | 484 |
| --- | --- |

| TYPE | Water, Dragon |
| --- | --- |
| ABILITY | Pressure |
| HEIGHT | 13'09" |
| WEIGHT | 740.8 lbs |

It is said to live in a gap in the spatial dimension parallel to ours. Palkia appears in mythology.

### Description

It has the ability to distort space. It is described as a deity in Sinnoh-region mythology.

### Special Moves

Special Rend, Aqua Tail, Aura Sphere

Evolution  Does not evolve

PALKIA

# HEATRAN

### Lava Dome Pokémon

| POKÉDEX NO. | **485** |
|---|---|
| **TYPE** | Fire, Steel |
| **ABILITY** | Flash Fire |
| **HEIGHT** | 5'07" |
| **WEIGHT** | 948.0 lbs |

001-100

101-200

201-300

442

443-500

501-600

701-800

801-898

### Description

Boiling blood, like magma, circulates through its body. It makes its dwelling place in volcanic caves.

It dwells in volcanic caves. It digs in with its cross-shaped feet to crawl on ceilings and walls.

### Special Moves

Magma Storm, Lava Plume, Iron Head

**Evolution**

Does not evolve

**HEATRAN**

# REGIGIGAS

## Colossal Pokémon

| POKÉDEX NO. | **486** |
|---|---|
| TYPE | Normal |
| ABILITY | Slow Start |
| HEIGHT | 12'02" |
| WEIGHT | 925.9 lbs |

### Description

It is said to have made Pokémon that look like itself from a special ice mountain, rocks, and magma.

There is an enduring legend that states this Pokémon towed continents with ropes.

### Special Moves

Crush Grip,
Giga Impact, Stomp

Evolution  Does not evolve

REGIGIGAS

# GIRATINA

### ALTERED FORME

## Renegade Pokémon

| POKÉDEX NO. | **487** |
|---|---|
| TYPE | Ghost, Dragon |
| ABILITY | Pressure |
| HEIGHT | 14'09" |
| WEIGHT | 1653.5 lbs |

### Description

It was banished for its violence. It silently gazed upon the old world from the Distortion World.

A Pokémon that is said to live in a world on the reverse side of ours. It appears in an ancient cemetery.

### Special Moves

Shadow Force, Earth Power, Destiny Bond

**Evolution**  Does not evolve

GIRATINA
(ALTERED FORME)

001-100
101-200
201-300
401-442
443-500
501-600
701-800
801-898

# GIRATINA

## ORIGIN FORME

### Renegade Pokémon

| POKÉDEX NO. | **487** |
|---|---|
| TYPE | Ghost, Dragon |
| ABILITY | Levitate |
| HEIGHT | 22'08" |
| WEIGHT | 1433.0 lbs |

### Description

It was banished for its violence. It silently gazed upon the old world from the Distortion World.

This Pokémon is said to live in a world on the reverse side of ours, where common knowledge is distorted and strange.

### Special Moves

Shadow Force, Shadow Sneak, Dragon Claw

**Evolution**

**GIRATINA**
(ORIGIN FORME)

Does not evolve

# CRESSELIA

When it flies, it releases shiny particles from its veil-like wings.

001-100

101-200

201-300

401-442

443-500

501-600

701-600

801-898

| Lunar Pokémon | |
|---|---|
| **POKÉDEX NO.** | **488** |
| TYPE | Psychic |
| ABILITY | Levitate |
| HEIGHT | 4'11" |
| WEIGHT | 188.7 lbs |

### Description

Those who sleep holding Cresselia's feather are assured of joyful dreams. It is said to represent the crescent moon.

### Special Moves

Lunar Dance, Aurora Beam, Slash

**Evolution**  Does not evolve

CRESSELIA

65

# PHIONE

## Sea Drifter Pokémon

| POKÉDEX NO. | 489 |
|---|---|

| TYPE | Water |
|---|---|
| ABILITY | Hydration |
| HEIGHT | 1'04" |
| WEIGHT | 6.8 lbs |

### Description

It drifts in warm seas. It always returns to where it was born, no matter how far it may have drifted.

When the water warms, they inflate the floatation sac on their heads and drift languidly on the sea in packs.

### Special Moves

Aqua Ring, Water Pulse, Dive

Evolution  Does not evolve

PHIONE

# MANAPHY

## Seafaring Pokémon

| POKÉDEX NO. | **490** |
|---|---|

| TYPE | Water |
|---|---|
| ABILITY | Hydration |
| HEIGHT | 1'00" |
| WEIGHT | 3.1 lbs |

Water makes up 80 percent of its body. This Pokémon is easily affected by its environment.

### Description

It is born with a wondrous power that lets it bond with any kind of Pokémon.

### Special Moves

Heart Swap, Water Pulse, Whirlpool

**Evolution**

Does not evolve

MANAPHY

001-100
101-200
201-300
401-442
443-500
501-600
601-700
701-800
801-898

# DARKRAI

## Pitch-Black Pokémon

| POKÉDEX NO. | **491** |
| --- | --- |

| TYPE | Dark |
| --- | --- |
| **ABILITY** | Bad Dreams |
| **HEIGHT** | 4'11" |
| **WEIGHT** | 111.3 lbs |

Description

To protect itself, it afflicts those around it with nightmares. However, it means no harm.

It chases people and Pokémon from its territory by causing them to experience deep, nightmarish slumbers.

Special Moves

Dark Void, Nightmare, Dark Pulse

Evolution

DARKRAI

Does not evolve

# SHAYMIN
## LAND FORME

| Gratitude Pokémon | |
|---|---|
| **POKÉDEX NO.** | **492** |
| TYPE | Grass |
| ABILITY | Natural Cure |
| HEIGHT | 0'08" |
| WEIGHT | 4.6 lbs |

001-100

101-200

201-300

401-442

443-500

501-600

701-800

801-898

### Description

The flowers all over its body burst into bloom if it is lovingly hugged and senses gratitude.

It can dissolve toxins in the air to instantly transform ruined land into a lush field of flowers.

### Special Moves

Seed Flare,
Natural Gift, Growth

**Evolution**

SHAYMIN
(LAND FORME)

Does not evolve

# SHAYMIN

## SKY FORME

| Gratitude Pokémon | |
|---|---|
| **POKÉDEX NO.** | **492** |
| TYPE | Grass, Flying |
| ABILITY | Serene Grace |
| HEIGHT | 1'04" |
| WEIGHT | 11.5 lbs |

### Description

The blooming of Gracidea flowers confers the power of flight upon it. Feelings of gratitude are the message it delivers.

It can dissolve toxins in the air to instantly transform ruined land into a lush field of flowers.

### Special Moves

Air Slash, Seed Flare, Growth

Evolution  Does not evolve

SHAYMIN
(SKY FORME)

# ARCEUS

## Alpha Pokémon

| POKÉDEX NO. | 493 |
|---|---|
| TYPE | Normal |
| ABILITY | Multitype |
| HEIGHT | 10'06" |
| WEIGHT | 705.5 lbs |

001-100
101-200
201-300
401-442
443-500
501-600
701-800
801-898

### Description

According to the legends of Sinnoh, this Pokémon emerged from an egg and shaped all there is in this world.

It is told in mythology that this Pokémon was born before the universe even existed.

### Special Moves

Judgment, Hyper Beam, Extreme Speed

Evolution

Does not evolve

**ARCEUS**

## FORM CHANGE

Arceus has the Multitype ability and is capable of changing its type and body color by holding a Plate.

**Dark Type**
Dread Plate

**Rock Type**
Stone Plate

**Psychic Type**
Mind Plate

**Fighting Type**
Fist Plate

**Grass Type**
Meadow Plate

**Ghost Type**
Spooky Plate

**Ice Type**
Icicle Plate

**Ground Type**
Earth Plate

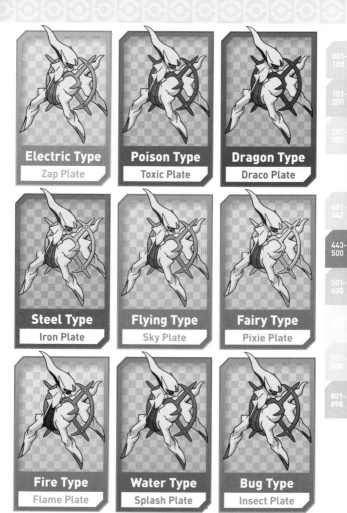

**Electric Type**
Zap Plate

**Poison Type**
Toxic Plate

**Dragon Type**
Draco Plate

**Steel Type**
Iron Plate

**Flying Type**
Sky Plate

**Fairy Type**
Pixie Plate

**Fire Type**
Flame Plate

**Water Type**
Splash Plate

**Bug Type**
Insect Plate

001-100
101-200
201-300
401-442
443-500
501-600
701-800
801-898

# VICTINI

| | |
|---|---|
| **Victory Pokémon** | |
| **POKÉDEX NO.** | **494** |
| **TYPE** | Psychic, Fire |
| **ABILITY** | Victory Star |
| **HEIGHT** | 1'04" |
| **WEIGHT** | 8.8 lbs |

When it shares the infinite energy it creates, with a being, that being's entire body will be overflowing with power.

**Description**

This Pokémon brings victory. It is said that Trainers with Victini always win, regardless of the type of encounter.

**Special Moves**

V-create, Flare Blitz, Inferno

**Evolution**   Does not evolve

VICTINI

# SNIVY

### Grass Snake Pokémon

| POKÉDEX NO. | 495 |
|---|---|
| TYPE | Grass |
| ABILITY | Overgrow |
| HEIGHT | 2'00" |
| WEIGHT | 17.9 lbs |

001-100
101-200
201-300
401-442
443-500
501-600
701-800
801-898

They photosynthesize by bathing their tails in sunlight. When they are not feeling well, their tails droop.

### Description

Being exposed to sunlight makes its movements swifter. It uses vines more adeptly than its hands.

### Special Moves

Vine Whip, Mega Drain, Leech Seed

**Evolution**

SNIVY → SERVINE → SERPERIOR

# SERVINE

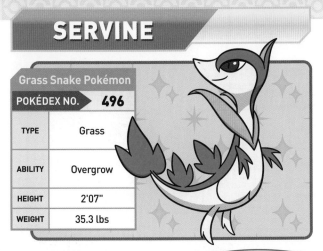

**Grass Snake Pokémon**

| POKÉDEX NO. | 496 |
| --- | --- |
| **TYPE** | Grass |
| **ABILITY** | Overgrow |
| **HEIGHT** | 2'07" |
| **WEIGHT** | 35.3 lbs |

When it gets dirty, its leaves can't be used in photosynthesis, so it always keeps itself clean.

### Description

It moves along the ground as if sliding. Its swift movements befuddle its foes, and it then attacks with a vine whip.

### Special Moves

Leaf Tornado, Coil, Vine Whip

**Evolution**

SNIVY → SERVINE → SERPERIOR

# SERPERIOR

| Regal Pokémon | |
|---|---|
| **POKÉDEX NO.** | **497** |
| **TYPE** | Grass |
| **ABILITY** | Overgrow |
| **HEIGHT** | 10'10" |
| **WEIGHT** | 138.9 lbs |

## Description

It only gives its all against strong opponents who are not fazed by the glare from Serperior's noble eyes.

## Special Moves

Leaf Storm, Leaf Tornado, Wrap

It can stop its opponents' movements with just a glare. It takes in solar energy and boosts it internally.

**Evolution**

 ➡  ➡

SNIVY     SERVINE     SERPERIOR

001-100
101-200
201-300
401-442
443-500
501-600
701-800
801-898

# TEPIG

## Fire Pig Pokémon

| POKÉDEX NO. | 498 |
| --- | --- |
| TYPE | Fire |
| ABILITY | Blaze |
| HEIGHT | 1'08" |
| WEIGHT | 21.8 lbs |

It loves to eat roasted berries, but sometimes it gets too excited and burns them to a crisp.

### Description

It can deftly dodge its foe's attacks while shooting fireballs from its nose. It roasts berries before it eats them.

### Special Moves

Ember, Flame Charge, Tail Whip

Evolution

TEPIG ➡ PIGNITE ➡ EMBOAR

# PIGNITE

### Fire Pig Pokémon

| | |
|---|---|
| **POKÉDEX NO.** | **499** |
| **TYPE** | Fire, Fighting |
| **ABILITY** | Blaze |
| **HEIGHT** | 3'03" |
| **WEIGHT** | 122.4 lbs |

When its internal fire flares up, its movements grow sharper and faster. When in trouble, it emits smoke.

### Description

The more it eats, the more fuel it has to make the fire in its stomach stronger. This fills it with even more power.

### Special Moves

Arm Thrust, Heat Crash, Flame Charge

**Evolution**

TEPIG

PIGNITE

EMBOAR

001-100
101-200
201-300
401-442
443-500
501-600
701-800
801-898

# EMBOAR

Mega Fire Pig Pokémon

| POKÉDEX NO. | **500** |
| --- | --- |

| TYPE | Fire, Fighting |
| --- | --- |
| ABILITY | Blaze |
| HEIGHT | 5'03" |
| WEIGHT | 330.7 lbs |

### Description

It has mastered fast and powerful fighting moves. It grows a beard of fire.

It can throw a fire punch by setting its fists on fire with its fiery chin. It cares deeply about its friends.

### Special Moves

Hammer Arm, Flamethrower, Take Down

Evolution

TEPIG ➡ PIGNITE ➡ EMBOAR

# OSHAWOTT

### Sea Otter Pokémon

| | |
|---|---|
| **POKÉDEX NO.** | **501** |
| **TYPE** | Water |
| **ABILITY** | Torrent |
| **HEIGHT** | 1'08" |
| **WEIGHT** | 13.0 lbs |

The scalchop on its stomach isn't just used for battle—it can be used to break open hard berries as well.

001-100

101-200

201-300

401-442

443-600

501-600

701-900

801-898

### Description

It fights using the scalchop on its stomach. In response to an attack, it retaliates immediately by slashing.

### Special Moves

Water Gun, Fury Cutter, Water Sport

**Evolution**

OSHAWOTT ➡ DEWOTT ➡ SAMUROTT

# DEWOTT

### Discipline Pokémon

| | |
|---|---|
| **POKÉDEX NO.** | **502** |
| **TYPE** | Water |
| **ABILITY** | Torrent |
| **HEIGHT** | 2'07" |
| **WEIGHT** | 54.0 lbs |

As a result of strict training,
each Dewott learns different forms
for using the scalchops.

### Description

Strict training is how
it learns its flowing
double-scalchop
technique.

### Special Moves

Razor Shell, Water Pulse,
Focus Energy

**Evolution**

OSHAWOTT　　DEWOTT　　SAMUROTT

# SAMUROTT

### Formidable Pokémon

| POKÉDEX NO. | 503 |
|---|---|
| **TYPE** | Water |
| **ABILITY** | Torrent |
| **HEIGHT** | 4'11" |
| **WEIGHT** | 208.6 lbs |

001-100

101-200

201-300

401-442

443-500

501-600

601-700

701-800

801-898

### Description

One swing of the sword that's part of its armor can fell an opponent. A simple glare from one of them quiets everybody.

### Special Moves

Hydro Pump, Swords Dance, Slash

Part of the armor on its anterior legs becomes a giant sword. Its cry alone is enough to intimidate most enemies.

**Evolution**

OSHAWOTT → DEWOTT → SAMUROTT

# PATRAT

Using food stored in cheek pouches, they can keep watch for days. They use their tails to communicate with others.

| Scout Pokémon | |
|---|---|
| POKÉDEX NO. | **504** |
| TYPE | Normal |
| ABILITY | Keen Eye, Run Away |
| HEIGHT | 1'08" |
| WEIGHT | 25.6 lbs |

## Description

Extremely cautious, one of them will always be on the lookout, but it won't notice a foe coming from behind.

## Special Moves

Crunch, Nasty Plot, Hypnosis

## Evolution

PATRAT → WATCHOG

# WATCHOG

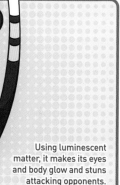

Using luminescent matter, it makes its eyes and body glow and stuns attacking opponents.

| Lookout Pokémon | |
|---|---|
| POKÉDEX NO. | **505** |
| TYPE | Normal |
| ABILITY | Keen Eye, Illuminate |
| HEIGHT | 3'07" |
| WEIGHT | 59.5 lbs |

001-100
101-200
201-300
401-442
443-500
501-600
601-700
701-800
801-898

## Description

When they see an enemy, their tails stand high, and they spit the seeds of berries stored in their cheek pouches.

## Special Moves

Hyper Fang, Rototiller, Confuse Ray

**Evolution**

PATRAT → WATCHOG

# LILLIPUP

This Pokémon is courageous but also cautious. It uses the soft fur covering its face to collect information about its surroundings.

| Puppy Pokémon | |
|---|---|
| POKÉDEX NO. | **506** |
| TYPE | Normal |
| ABILITY | Pickup, Vital Spirit |
| HEIGHT | 1'04" |
| WEIGHT | 9.0 lbs |

### Description

This Pokémon is far brighter than the average child, and Lillipup won't forget the love it receives or any abuse it suffers.

### Special Moves

Tackle, Bite, Baby-Doll Eyes

**Evolution**

LILLIPUP → HERDIER → STOUTLAND

# HERDIER

The black fur that covers this Pokémon's body is dense and springy. Even sharp fangs bounce right off.

001-100

101-200

201-300

401-442

443-500

501-600

601-700

701-800

801-898

## Loyal Dog Pokémon

| | |
|---|---|
| POKÉDEX NO. | **507** |
| TYPE | Normal |
| ABILITY | Intimidate, Sand Rush |
| HEIGHT | 2'11" |
| WEIGHT | 32.4 lbs |

### Description

Herdier is a very smart and friendly Pokémon. So much so that there's a theory that Herdier was the first Pokémon to partner with people.

### Special Moves

Crunch, Take Down, Baby-Doll Eyes

Evolution

LILLIPUP          HERDIER          STOUTLAND

# STOUTLAND

Stoutland is immensely proud of its impressive moustache. It's said that moustache length is what determines social standing among this species.

| Big-Hearted Pokémon | |
|---|---|
| **POKÉDEX NO.** | **508** |
| TYPE | Normal |
| ABILITY | Intimidate, Sand Rush |
| HEIGHT | 3'11" |
| WEIGHT | 134.5 lbs |

### Description

These Pokémon seem to enjoy living with humans. Even a Stoutland caught in the wild will warm up to people in about three days.

### Special Moves

Giga Impact, Ice Fang, Crunch

**Evolution**

LILLIPUP → HERDIER → STOUTLAND

# PURRLOIN

001-100
101-200
201-390
491-442
443-500
501-600
701-800
801-898

### Devious Pokémon

| POKÉDEX NO. | 509 |
|---|---|
| TYPE | Dark |
| ABILITY | Limber, Unburden |
| HEIGHT | 1'04" |
| WEIGHT | 22.3 lbs |

### Description

Opponents that get drawn in by its adorable behavior come away with stinging scratches from its claws and stinging pride from its laughter.

It steals things from people just to amuse itself with their frustration. A rivalry exists between this Pokémon and Nickit.*

### Special Moves

Fury Swipes, Nasty Plot, Play Rough

Evolution

PURRLOIN → LIEPARD

*Nickit: A Pokémon you'll find on page 449.

# LIEPARD

This stealthy Pokémon sneaks up behind prey without making any sound at all. It competes with Thievul* for territory.

## Cruel Pokémon

| POKÉDEX NO. | 510 |
| --- | --- |
| TYPE | Dark |
| ABILITY | Limber, Unburden |
| HEIGHT | 3'07" |
| WEIGHT | 82.7 lbs |

### Description

Don't be fooled by its gorgeous and elegant figure. This is a moody and vicious Pokémon.

### Special Moves

Night Slash, Fake Out, Fury Swipes

### Evolution

PURRLOIN →  LIEPARD

*Thievul: A Pokémon you'll find on page 450.

# PANSAGE

001-100
101-200
201-300
401-442
443-500
501-600
601-700
701-800
801-898

| Grass Monkey Pokémon | |
|---|---|
| POKÉDEX NO. | 511 |
| TYPE | Grass |
| ABILITY | Gluttony |
| HEIGHT | 2'00" |
| WEIGHT | 23.1 lbs |

It's good at finding berries and gathers them from all over. It's kind enough to share them with friends.

### Description

It shares the leaf on its head with weary-looking Pokémon. These leaves are known to relieve stress.

### Special Moves

Fury Swipes,
Vine Whip, Grass Knot

Evolution

PANSAGE → SIMISAGE

# SIMISAGE

Ill-tempered, it fights by swinging its barbed tail around wildly. The leaf growing on its head is very bitter.

| Thorn Monkey Pokémon | |
|---|---|
| POKÉDEX NO. | 512 |
| TYPE | Grass |
| ABILITY | Gluttony |
| HEIGHT | 3'07" |
| WEIGHT | 67.2 lbs |

### Description

It attacks enemies with strikes of its thorn-covered tail. This Pokémon is wild-tempered.

### Special Moves

Seed Bomb, Leer, Lick

### Evolution

PANSAGE

SIMISAGE

# PANSEAR

| High Temp Pokémon | |
|---|---|
| POKÉDEX NO. | **513** |
| TYPE | Fire |
| ABILITY | Gluttony |
| HEIGHT | 2'00" |
| WEIGHT | 24.3 lbs |

Very intelligent, it roasts berries before eating them. It likes to help people.

### Description

This Pokémon lives in caves in volcanoes. The fire within the tuft on its head can reach 600 degrees Fahrenheit.

### Special Moves

Flame Burst, Acrobatics, Bite

001-100
101-200
201-300
401-442
443-500
501-600
601-700
701-800
801-898

Evolution

PANSEAR    SIMISEAR

# SIMISEAR

When it gets excited, embers rise from its head and tail and it gets hot. For some reason, it loves sweets.

| Ember Pokémon | |
|---|---|
| POKÉDEX NO. | **514** |
| TYPE | Fire |
| ABILITY | Gluttony |
| HEIGHT | 3'03" |
| WEIGHT | 61.7 lbs |

**Description**

It loves sweets because they become energy for the fire burning inside its body.

**Special Moves**

Flame Burst, Fury Swipes, Leer

Evolution

PANSEAR → SIMISEAR

# PANPOUR

### Spray Pokémon

| | |
|---|---|
| **POKÉDEX NO.** | **515** |
| TYPE | Water |
| ABILITY | Gluttony |
| HEIGHT | 2'00" |
| WEIGHT | 29.8 lbs |

It does not thrive in dry environments. It keeps itself damp by shooting water stored in its head tuft from its tail.

### Description

The water stored inside the tuft on its head is full of nutrients. Plants that receive its water grow large.

### Special Moves

Water Gun, Water Sport, Fury Swipes

**Evolution**

PANPOUR

➡

SIMIPOUR

001-100

101-200

201-300

401-442

443-500

501-600

601-700

701-800

801-898

# SIMIPOUR

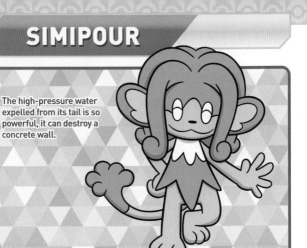

The high-pressure water expelled from its tail is so powerful, it can destroy a concrete wall.

| Geyser Pokémon | |
|---|---|
| **POKÉDEX NO.** | **516** |
| TYPE | Water |
| ABILITY | Gluttony |
| HEIGHT | 3'03" |
| WEIGHT | 63.9 lbs |

### Description

It prefers places with clean water. When its tuft runs low, it replenishes it by siphoning up water with its tail.

### Special Moves

Scald, Leer,
Fury Swipes

Evolution

PANPOUR → SIMIPOUR

# MUNNA

001-100
101-200
201-300
401-442
443-500
501-600
701-800
801-898

### Dream Eater Pokémon

| POKÉDEX NO. | 517 |
|---|---|

| TYPE | Psychic |
|---|---|
| ABILITY | Synchronize, Forewarn |
| HEIGHT | 2'00" |
| WEIGHT | 51.4 lbs |

Late at night, it appears beside people's pillows. As it feeds on dreams, the pattern on its body gives off a faint glow.

### Description

It eats dreams and releases mist. The mist is pink when it's eating a good dream, and black when it's eating a nightmare.

### Special Moves

Defense Curl, Hypnosis, Dream Eater

---

Evolution

  ➡

**MUNNA**  **MUSHARNA**

# MUSHARNA

### Drowsing Pokémon

| | |
|---|---|
| POKÉDEX NO. | **518** |
| TYPE | Psychic |
| ABILITY | Synchronize, Forewarn |
| HEIGHT | 3'07" |
| WEIGHT | 133.4 lbs |

### Description

It drowses and dreams all the time. It's best to leave it be if it's just woken up, as it's a terrible grump when freshly roused from sleep.

When dark mists emanate from its body, don't get too near. If you do, your nightmares will become reality.

### Special Moves

Moonblast, Psychic, Calm Mind

Evolution

MUNNA → MUSHARNA

# PIDOVE

Where people go, these Pokémon follow. If you're scattering food for them, be careful—several hundred of them can gather at once.

## Tiny Pigeon Pokémon

| POKÉDEX NO. | 519 |
| --- | --- |
| TYPE | Normal, Flying |
| ABILITY | Super Luck, Big Pecks |
| HEIGHT | 1'00" |
| WEIGHT | 4.6 lbs |

### Description

It's forgetful and not very bright, but many Trainers love it anyway for its friendliness and sincerity.

### Special Moves

Gust, Tailwind, Quick Attack

001-100

101-200

201-300

401-442

443-500

501-600

601-700

701-800

801-898

Evolution

PIDOVE     TRANQUILL     UNFEZANT

# TRANQUILL

These bright Pokémon have acute memories. Apparently delivery workers often choose them as their partners.

| Wild Pigeon Pokémon | |
|---|---|
| **POKÉDEX NO.** | **520** |
| **TYPE** | Normal, Flying |
| **ABILITY** | Super Luck, Big Pecks |
| **HEIGHT** | 2'00" |
| **WEIGHT** | 33.1 lbs |

## Description

It can fly moderately quickly. No matter how far it travels, it can always find its way back to its master and its nest.

## Special Moves

Feather Dance, Air Cutter, Roost

**Evolution**

PIDOVE → TRANQUILL → UNFEZANT

# UNFEZANT

| | |
|---|---|
| **Proud Pokémon** | |
| **POKÉDEX NO.** | **521** |
| **TYPE** | Normal, Flying |
| **ABILITY** | Super Luck, Big Pecks |
| **HEIGHT** | 3'11" |
| **WEIGHT** | 63.9 lbs |

Male

Female

### Description

This Pokémon is intelligent and intensely proud. People will sit up and take notice if you become the Trainer of one.

Unfezant are exceptional fliers. The females are known for their stamina, while the males outclass them in terms of speed.

### Special Moves

Dragon Claw, Agility, Thrash

001-100
101-200
201-300
401-442
443-500
501-600
601-700
701-800
801-898

**Evolution**

PIDOVE    TRANQUILL    UNFEZANT

# BLITZLE

When thunderclouds cover the sky, it will appear. It can catch lightning with its mane and store the electricity.

## Electrified Pokémon

| POKÉDEX NO. | 522 |
|---|---|
| TYPE | Electric |
| ABILITY | Lightning Rod, Motor Drive |
| HEIGHT | 2'07" |
| WEIGHT | 65.7 lbs |

### Description

Its mane shines when it discharges electricity. They use the frequency and rhythm of these flashes to communicate.

### Special Moves

Quick Attack, Discharge, Wild Charge

### Evolution

BLITZLE → ZEBSTRIKA

# ZEBSTRIKA

They have lightning-like movements. When Zebstrika run at full speed, the sound of thunder reverberates.

| Thunderbolt Pokémon | |
|---|---|
| **POKÉDEX NO.** | **523** |
| TYPE | Electric |
| ABILITY | Lightning Rod, Motor Drive |
| HEIGHT | 5'03" |
| WEIGHT | 175.3 lbs |

### Description

When this ill-tempered Pokémon runs wild, it shoots lightning from its mane in all directions.

### Special Moves

Ion Deluge, Shock Wave, Thrash

**Evolution**

  **BLITZLE** ➡  **ZEBSTRIKA**

001-100
101-200
201-300
401-442
443-500
501-600
701-800
801-898

# ROGGENROLA

### Mantle Pokémon

| | |
|---|---|
| POKÉDEX NO. | **524** |
| TYPE | Rock |
| ABILITY | Sturdy, Weak Armor |
| HEIGHT | 1'04" |
| WEIGHT | 39.7 lbs |

When it detects a noise, it starts to move. The energy core inside it makes this Pokémon slightly warm to the touch.

### Description

It's as hard as steel, but apparently a long soak in water will cause it to soften a bit.

### Special Moves

Sand Attack, Rock Slide, Stealth Rock

Evolution

ROGGENROLA ➡ BOLDORE ➡ GIGALITH

# BOLDORE

If you see its orange crystals start to glow, be wary. It's about to fire off bursts of energy.

## Ore Pokémon

| POKÉDEX NO. | 525 |
| --- | --- |
| TYPE | Rock |
| ABILITY | Sturdy, Weak Armor |
| HEIGHT | 2'11" |
| WEIGHT | 224.9 lbs |

### Description

It relies on sound in order to monitor what's in its vicinity. When angered, it will attack without ever changing the direction it's facing.

### Special Moves

Power Gem, Iron Defense, Stone Edge

001-100

101-200

201-300

401-442

443-500

501-600

701-800

801-898

**Evolution**

ROGGENROLA    BOLDORE    GIGALITH

# GIGALITH

This hardy Pokémon can often be found on construction sites and in mines, working alongside people and Copperajah.*

| Compressed Pokémon | |
|---|---|
| **POKÉDEX NO.** | **526** |
| TYPE | Rock |
| ABILITY | Sturdy, Sand Stream |
| HEIGHT | 5'07" |
| WEIGHT | 573.2 lbs |

### Description

Although its energy blasts can blow away a dump truck, they have a limitation— they can only be fired when the sun is out.

### Special Moves

Explosion, Rock Blast, Smack Down

**Evolution**

ROGGENROLA    BOLDORE    GIGALITH

*Copperajah: A Pokémon you'll find on page 521.

# WOOBAT

It emits ultrasonic waves as it flutters about, searching for its prey—bug Pokémon.

| Bat Pokémon | |
|---|---|
| **POKÉDEX NO.** | **527** |
| TYPE | Psychic, Flying |
| ABILITY | Unaware, Klutz |
| HEIGHT | 1'04" |
| WEIGHT | 4.6 lbs |

### Description

While inside a cave, if you look up and see lots of heart-shaped marks lining the walls, it's evidence that Woobat live there.

### Special Moves

Gust, Confusion, Simple Beam

**Evolution**

WOOBAT → SWOOBAT

001-100
101-200
201-300
401-442
443-600
501-600
601-700
701-800
801-898

# SWOOBAT

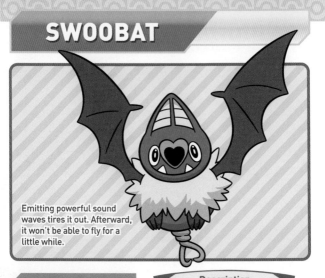

Emitting powerful sound waves tires it out. Afterward, it won't be able to fly for a little while.

| Courting Pokémon | |
|---|---|
| **POKÉDEX NO.** | **528** |
| TYPE | Psychic, Flying |
| ABILITY | Unaware, Klutz |
| HEIGHT | 2'11" |
| WEIGHT | 23.1 lbs |

### Description

The auspicious shape of this Pokémon's nose apparently leads some regions to consider Swoobat a symbol of good luck.

### Special Moves

Air Cutter, Psychic, Future Sight

Evolution

WOOBAT → SWOOBAT

# DRILBUR

## Mole Pokémon

| POKÉDEX NO. | 529 |
| --- | --- |
| **TYPE** | Ground |
| **ABILITY** | Sand Rush, Sand Force |
| **HEIGHT** | 1'00" |
| **WEIGHT** | 18.7 lbs |

It's a digger, using its claws to burrow through the ground. It causes damage to vegetable crops, so many farmers have little love for it.

### Description

It brings its claws together and whirls around at high speed before rushing toward its prey.

### Special Moves

Mud-Slap, Rapid Spin, Dig

**Evolution**

DRILBUR

EXCADRILL

109

# EXCADRILL

Known as the Drill King, this Pokémon can tunnel through the terrain at speeds of over 90 mph.

## Subterrene Pokémon

| POKÉDEX NO. | 530 |
| --- | --- |
| TYPE | Ground, Steel |
| ABILITY | Sand Rush, Sand Force |
| HEIGHT | 2'04" |
| WEIGHT | 89.1 lbs |

### Description

It's not uncommon for tunnels that appear to have formed naturally to actually be a result of Excadrill's rampant digging.

### Special Moves

Horn Drill, Drill Run, Metal Claw

### Evolution

DRILBUR

EXCADRILL

# AUDINO

**Hearing Pokémon**

| POKÉDEX NO. | 531 |
|---|---|

| TYPE | Normal |
|---|---|
| ABILITY | Healer, Regenerator |
| HEIGHT | 3'07" |
| WEIGHT | 68.3 lbs |

This Pokémon has a kind heart. By touching with its feelers, Audino can gauge other creatures' feelings and physical conditions.

## Description

Audino's sense of hearing is superb. Not even a pebble rolling along over a mile away will escape Audino's ears.

## Special Moves

Life Dew, Heal Pulse, Helping Hand

**Evolution**

AUDINO — Does not evolve

001-100
101-200
201-300
401-442
643-600
501-600
601-700
701-800
801-898

# MEGA AUDINO

**AUDINO**

It touches others with the feelers on its ears, using the sound of their heartbeats to tell how they are feeling.

## Hearing Pokémon

| POKÉDEX NO. | **531** |
| --- | --- |
| TYPE | Normal, Fairy |
| ABILITY | Healer |
| HEIGHT | 4'11" |
| WEIGHT | 70.5 lbs |

### Description

Its auditory sense is astounding. It has a radar-like ability to understand its surroundings through slight sounds.

### Special Moves

Double Slap, Hyper Voice, Misty Terrain

# TIMBURR

Muscular Pokémon

| POKÉDEX NO. | 532 |
|---|---|

| TYPE | Fighting |
|---|---|
| ABILITY | Guts, Sheer Force |
| HEIGHT | 2'00" |
| WEIGHT | 27.6 lbs |

001-100
101-200
201-300
401-442
443-500
501-600
701-800
801-898

It loves helping out with construction projects. It loves it so much that if rain causes work to halt, it swings its log around and throws a tantrum.

### Description

Timburr that have started carrying logs that are about three times their sizes are nearly ready to evolve.

### Special Moves

Low Kick, Rock Slide, Stone Edge

Evolution

TIMBURR → GURDURR → CONKELDURR

# GURDURR

Gurdurr excels at demolition—construction is not its forte. In any case, there's skill in the way this Pokémon wields its metal beam.

## Muscular Pokémon

| POKÉDEX NO. | 533 |
|---|---|
| TYPE | Fighting |
| ABILITY | Guts, Sheer Force |
| HEIGHT | 3'11" |
| WEIGHT | 88.2 lbs |

### Description

It shows off its muscles to Machoke* and other Gurdurr. If it fails to measure up to the other Pokémon, it lies low for a little while.

### Special Moves

Slam, Focus Energy, Bulk Up

### Evolution

TIMBURR → GURDURR → CONKELDURR

*Machoke: A Pokémon you'll find in volume 1.

# CONKELDURR

Concrete mixed by Conkeldurr is much more durable than normal concrete, even when the compositions of the two materials are the same.

| Muscular Pokémon | |
|---|---|
| POKÉDEX NO. | **534** |
| TYPE | Fighting |
| ABILITY | Guts, Sheer Force |
| HEIGHT | 4'07" |
| WEIGHT | 191.8 lbs |

### Description

When going all out, this Pokémon throws aside its concrete pillars and leaps at opponents to pummel them with its fists.

### Special Moves

Superpower, Dynamic Punch, Focus Punch

**Evolution**

TIMBURR

GURDURR

CONKELDURR

# TYMPOLE

Graceful ripples running across the water's surface are a sure sign that Tympole are singing in high-pitched voices below.

| Tadpole Pokémon | |
|---|---|
| POKÉDEX NO. | **535** |
| TYPE | Water |
| ABILITY | Hydration, Swift Swim |
| HEIGHT | 1'08" |
| WEIGHT | 9.9 lbs |

### Description

It uses sound waves to communicate with others of its kind. People and other Pokémon species can't hear its cries of warning.

### Special Moves

Growl, Echoed Voice, Acid

Evolution

TYMPOLE     PALPITOAD     SEISMITOAD

# PALPITOAD

On occasion, their cries are sublimely pleasing to the ear. Palpitoad with larger lumps on their bodies can sing with a wider range of sounds.

## Vibration Pokémon

| POKÉDEX NO. | 536 |
|---|---|
| TYPE | Water, Ground |
| ABILITY | Hydration, Swift Swim |
| HEIGHT | 2'07" |
| WEIGHT | 37.5 lbs |

### Description

It weakens its prey with sound waves intense enough to cause headaches, then entangles them with its sticky tongue.

### Special Moves

Bubble Beam, Supersonic, Round

001-100
101-200
201-300
401-442
443-500
501-600
601-700
701-800
801-898

Evolution

TYMPOLE → PALPITOAD → SEISMITOAD

# SEISMITOAD

The vibrating of the bumps all over its body causes earthquake-like tremors. Seismitoad and Croagunk* are similar species.

| Vibration Pokémon | |
|---|---|
| **POKÉDEX NO.** | **537** |
| TYPE | Water, Ground |
| ABILITY | Swift Swim, Poison Touch |
| HEIGHT | 4'11" |
| WEIGHT | 136.7 lbs |

### Description

This Pokémon is popular among the elderly, who say the vibrations of its lumps are great for massages.

### Special Moves

Drain Punch, Hyper Voice, Rain Dance

**Evolution**

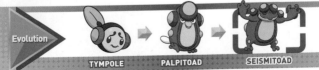

TYMPOLE → PALPITOAD → SEISMITOAD

*Croagunk: A Pokémon you'll find on page 22.

# THROH

001-100
101-200
201-300
401-442
443-500
501-600
701-800
801-898

It performs throwing moves with first-rate skill. Over the course of many battles, Throh's belt grows darker as it absorbs its wearer's sweat.

### Judo Pokémon

| POKÉDEX NO. | 538 |
|---|---|
| TYPE | Fighting |
| ABILITY | Guts, Inner Focus |
| HEIGHT | 4'03" |
| WEIGHT | 122.4 lbs |

### Description

They train in groups of five. Any member that can't keep up will discard its belt and leave the group.

### Special Moves

Seismic Throw, Circle Throw, Storm Throw

Evolution  Does not evolve

THROH

119

# SAWK

The karate chops of a Sawk that's trained itself to the limit can cleave the ocean itself.

## Karate Pokémon

| POKÉDEX NO. | 539 |
| --- | --- |
| TYPE | Fighting |
| ABILITY | Inner Focus, Sturdy |
| HEIGHT | 4'07" |
| WEIGHT | 112.4 lbs |

### Description

If you see a Sawk training in the mountains in its single-minded pursuit of strength, it's best to quietly pass by.

### Special Moves

Close Combat, Low Sweep, Brick Break

Evolution

SAWK

Does not evolve

# SEWADDLE

This Pokémon makes clothes for itself. It chews up leaves and sews them with sticky thread extruded from its mouth.

| Sewing Pokémon | |
|---|---|
| **POKÉDEX NO.** | **540** |
| TYPE | Bug, Grass |
| ABILITY | Swarm, Chlorophyll |
| HEIGHT | 1'00" |
| WEIGHT | 5.5 lbs |

## Description

Since this Pokémon makes its own clothes out of leaves, it is a popular mascot for fashion designers.

## Special Moves

String Shot, Bug Bite, Bug Buzz

Evolution

SEWADDLE → SWADLOON → LEAVANNY

001-100
101-200
201-300
401-442
443-500
501-600
701-800
801-898

# SWADLOON

**Leaf-Wrapped Pokémon**

| POKÉDEX NO. | **541** |
|---|---|
| TYPE | Bug, Grass |
| ABILITY | Chlorophyll, Leaf Guard |
| HEIGHT | 1'08" |
| WEIGHT | 16.1 lbs |

### Description

Forests where Swadloon live have superb foliage because the nutrients they make from fallen leaves nourish the plant life.

It protects itself from the cold by wrapping up in leaves. It stays on the move, eating leaves in forests.

### Special Moves

Razor Leaf, Grass Whistle, String Shot

**Evolution**

SEWADDLE → SWADLOON →  LEAVANNY

# LEAVANNY

001-100
101-200
201-300
401-442
443-500
501-600
601-700
701-800
801-898

It keeps its eggs warm with heat from fermenting leaves. It also uses leaves to make warm wrappings for Sewaddle.

| Nurturing Pokémon | |
|---|---|
| POKÉDEX NO. | **542** |
| TYPE | Bug, Grass |
| ABILITY | Swarm, Chlorophyll |
| HEIGHT | 3'11" |
| WEIGHT | 45.2 lbs |

### Description

Upon finding a small Pokémon, it weaves clothing for it from leaves by using the sticky silk secreted from its mouth.

### Special Moves

Slash, Leaf Blade, X-Scissor

Evolution

SEWADDLE → SWADLOON → 

LEAVANNY

# VENIPEDE

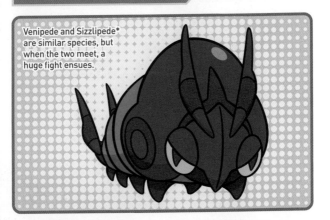

Venipede and Sizzlipede* are similar species, but when the two meet, a huge fight ensues.

## Centipede Pokémon

| POKÉDEX NO. | 543 |
|---|---|
| TYPE | Bug, Poison |
| ABILITY | Swarm, Poison Point |
| HEIGHT | 1'04" |
| WEIGHT | 11.7 lbs |

### Description

Its fangs are highly venomous. If this Pokémon finds prey it thinks it can eat, it leaps for them without any thought for how things might turn out.

### Special Moves

Poison Sting, Venoshock, Agility

**Evolution**

VENIPEDE

WHIRLIPEDE

SCOLIPEDE

 *Sizzlipede: A Pokémon you'll find on page 481.

# WHIRLIPEDE

001-100
101-200
201-300
401-442
463-500
501-600
601-700
701-800
801-898

This Pokémon spins itself rapidly and charges into its opponents. Its top speed is just over 60 mph.

| Curlipede Pokémon | |
|---|---|
| POKÉDEX NO. | **544** |
| TYPE | Bug, Poison |
| ABILITY | Swarm, Poison Point |
| HEIGHT | 3'11" |
| WEIGHT | 129.0 lbs |

## Description

Whirlipede protects itself with a sturdy shell and poisonous spikes while it stores up the energy it'll need for evolution.

## Special Moves

Iron Defense, Double-Edge, Venom Drench

**Evolution**

VENIPEDE → WHIRLIPEDE → SCOLIPEDE

125

# SCOLIPEDE

Scolipede latches on to its prey with the claws on its neck before slamming them into the ground and jabbing them with its claws' toxic spikes.

## Megapede Pokémon

| | |
|---|---|
| POKÉDEX NO. | **545** |
| TYPE | Bug, Poison |
| ABILITY | Swarm, Poison Point |
| HEIGHT | 8'02" |
| WEIGHT | 442.0 lbs |

### Description

Scolipede engage in fierce territorial battles with Centiskorch.* At the end of one of these battles, the victor makes a meal of the loser.

### Special Moves

Poison Tail, Megahorn, Take Down

### Evolution

VENIPEDE → WHIRLIPEDE → SCOLIPEDE

*Centiskorch: A Pokémon you'll find on page 482.

# COTTONEE

It shoots cotton from its body to protect itself. If it gets caught up in hurricane-strength winds, it can get sent to the other side of the world.

001-100
101-200
201-300
401-442
443-500
501-600
601-700
701-800
801-898

## Cotton Puff Pokémon

| POKÉDEX NO. | 546 |
|---|---|
| TYPE | Grass, Fairy |
| ABILITY | Prankster, Infiltrator |
| HEIGHT | 1'00" |
| WEIGHT | 1.3 lbs |

### Description

Weaving together the cotton from both Cottonee and Eldegoss* produces an exquisite cloth that's highly prized by many luxury brands.

### Special Moves

Absorb, Energy Ball, Razor Leaf

**Evolution**

COTTONEE →
WHIMSICOTT

*Eldegoss: A Pokémon you'll find on page 452.

# WHIMSICOTT

**Windveiled Pokémon**

| POKÉDEX NO. | 547 |
|---|---|
| TYPE | Grass, Fairy |
| ABILITY | Prankster, Infiltrator |
| HEIGHT | 2'04" |
| WEIGHT | 14.6 lbs |

### Description

As long as this Pokémon bathes in sunlight, its cotton keeps growing. If too much cotton fluff builds up, Whimsicott tears it off and scatters it.

It scatters cotton all over the place as a prank. If it gets wet, it'll become too heavy to move and have no choice but to answer for its mischief.

### Special Moves

Cotton Guard, Solar Beam, Hurricane

Evolution

COTTONEE → WHIMSICOTT

# PETILIL

001-100
101-200
201-300
401-442
443-600
501-600
701-800
801-898

| Bulb Pokémon | |
| --- | --- |
| **POKÉDEX NO.** | **548** |
| **TYPE** | Grass |
| **ABILITY** | Chlorophyll, Own Tempo |
| **HEIGHT** | 1'08" |
| **WEIGHT** | 14.6 lbs |

## Description

The leaves on its head grow right back even if they fall out. These bitter leaves refresh those who eat them.

## Special Moves

Absorb, Leech Seed, Sleep Powder

If the leaves on its head are pruned with regularity, this Pokémon can be grown into a fine plump shape.

**Evolution**

PETILIL →
LILLIGANT

129

# LILLIGANT

**Flowering Pokémon**

| POKÉDEX NO. | 549 |
|---|---|
| TYPE | Grass |
| ABILITY | Chlorophyll, Own Tempo |
| HEIGHT | 3'07" |
| WEIGHT | 35.9 lbs |

It's believed that even first-rate gardeners have a hard time getting the flower on a Lilligant's head to bloom.

### Description

Essential oils made from Lilligant flowers have a sublime scent, but they're also staggeringly expensive.

### Special Moves

Petal Blizzard, Petal Dance, Giga Drain

Evolution

PETILIL ➡ LILLIGANT

# BASCULIN

BLUE-STRIPED FORM

001-100
101-200
201-300
401-442
443-500
501-600
601-700
701-800
801-898

Known for their violence, these Pokémon have the most fights with schools of red-striped Basculin.

| Hostile Pokémon | |
|---|---|
| POKÉDEX NO. | **550** |
| TYPE | Water |
| ABILITY | Rock Head, Adaptability |
| HEIGHT | 3'03" |
| WEIGHT | 39.7 lbs |

### Description

Some people call it "the thug of the lake." Whether the differences in color are meaningful is not yet known.

### Special Moves

Double-Edge, Thrash, Aqua Jet

Evolution

BASCULIN
(BLUE-STRIPED FORM)

Does not evolve

# BASCULIN

**RED-STRIPED FORM**

Anglers love the fight this Pokémon puts up on the hook. And there are always more to catch—many people release them into lakes illicitly.

| Hostile Pokémon | |
|---|---|
| **POKÉDEX NO.** | **550** |
| **TYPE** | Water |
| **ABILITY** | Reckless, Adaptability |
| **HEIGHT** | 3'03" |
| **WEIGHT** | 39.7 lbs |

## Description

When a school of Basculin appears in a lake, everything else disappears, except for Corphish* and Crawdaunt.** That's how violent Basculin are.

## Special Moves

Head Smash, Thrash, Aqua Jet

**Evolution**

**BASCULIN (RED-STRIPED FORM)**

Does not evolve

*Corphish: A Pokémon you'll find in volume 1. **Crawdaunt: A Pokémon you'll find in volume 1.

# SANDILE

Sandile is small, but its legs and lower body are powerful. Pushing sand aside as it goes, Sandile moves through the desert as if it's swimming.

| Desert Croc Pokémon | |
|---|---|
| **POKÉDEX NO.** | **551** |
| TYPE | Ground, Dark |
| ABILITY | Intimidate, Moxie |
| HEIGHT | 2'04" |
| WEIGHT | 33.5 lbs |

### Description

The desert gets cold at night, so when the sun sets, this Pokémon burrows deep into the sand and sleeps until sunrise.

### Special Moves

Quick Attack, Wing Attack, Rock Slide

**Evolution**

SANDILE → KROKOROK → KROOKODILE

001-100
101-200
201-300
401-442
443-500
501-600
601-700
701-800
801-898

# KROKOROK

They live in groups of a few individuals. Protective membranes shield their eyes from sandstorms.

| Desert Croc Pokémon | |
|---|---|
| POKÉDEX NO. | **552** |
| TYPE | Ground, Dark |
| ABILITY | Intimidate, Moxie |
| HEIGHT | 3'03" |
| WEIGHT | 73.6 lbs |

### Description

Krokorok has specialized eyes that enable it to see in the dark. This ability lets Krokorok hunt in the dead of night without getting lost.

### Special Moves

Leer, Crunch, Sandstorm

**Evolution**

SANDILE

KROKOROK

KROOKODILE

# KROOKODILE

001-100

101-200

201-300

401-442

643-500

501-600

701-800

801-898

While terribly aggressive, Krookodile also has the patience to stay hidden under sand for days, lying in wait for prey.

## Intimidation Pokémon

| | |
|---|---|
| POKÉDEX NO. | **553** |
| TYPE | Ground, Dark |
| ABILITY | Intimidate, Moxie |
| HEIGHT | 4'11" |
| WEIGHT | 212.3 lbs |

### Description

This Pokémon is known as the Bully of the Sands. Krookodile's mighty jaws can bite through heavy plates of iron with almost no effort at all.

### Special Moves

Sand Tomb, Torment, Leer

## Evolution

SANDILE ➡ KROKOROK ➡ KROOKODILE

# DARUMAKA

## Zen Charm Pokémon

| POKÉDEX NO. | 554 |
|---|---|
| TYPE | Fire |
| ABILITY | Hustle |
| HEIGHT | 2'00" |
| WEIGHT | 82.7 lbs |

### Description

This popular symbol of good fortune will never fall over in its sleep, no matter how it's pushed or pulled.

It derives its power from fire burning inside its body. If the fire dwindles, this Pokémon will immediately fall asleep.

### Special Moves

Ember, Fire Fang, Fire Punch

Evolution

DARUMAKA → DARMANITAN

# DARUMAKA

### GALARIAN FORM

| Zen Charm Pokémon | |
|---|---|
| **POKÉDEX NO.** | **554** |
| TYPE | Ice |
| ABILITY | Hustle |
| HEIGHT | 2'04" |
| WEIGHT | 88.2 lbs |

001-100

101-200

201-300

401-442

443-500

501-600

601-700

701-800

801-898

### Description

It lived in snowy areas for so long that its fire sac cooled off and atrophied. It now has an organ that generates cold instead.

The colder they get, the more energetic they are. They freeze their breath to make snowballs, using them as ammo for playful snowball fights.

### Special Moves

Powder Snow, Work Up, Ice Punch

**Evolution**

DARUMAKA
(GAL'ARIAN FORM)

DARMANITAN
(GALARIAN FORM)

# DARMANITAN

| | |
|---|---|
| **Blazing Pokémon** | |
| **POKÉDEX NO.** | **555** |
| **TYPE** | Fire |
| **ABILITY** | Sheer Force |
| **HEIGHT** | 4'03" |
| **WEIGHT** | 204.8 lbs |

This Pokémon's power level rises along with the temperature of its fire, which can reach 2,500 degrees Fahrenheit.

### Description

The thick arms of this hot-blooded Pokémon can deliver punches capable of obliterating a dump truck.

### Special Moves

Hammer Arm, Belly Drum, Incinerate

**Evolution**

DARUMAKA → DARMANITAN

# DARMANITAN

ZEN MODE*

Through meditation, it calms its raging spirit and hones its psychic powers.

| Blazing Pokémon | |
|---|---|
| POKÉDEX NO. | **555** |
| TYPE | Fire, Psychic |
| ABILITY | Zen Mode |
| HEIGHT | 4'03" |
| WEIGHT | 204.8 lbs |

### Description

When wounded, it stops moving. It goes as still as stone to meditate, sharpening its mind and spirit.

### Special Moves

Incinerate, Flare Blitz, Fire Fang

Evolution

DARUMAKA

DARMANITAN

*Zen Mode: Some Darmanitan will temporarily enter this state when they face a difficult situation in battle.

001-100
101-200
201-300
401-442
443-500
501-600
601-700
701-800
801-898

# DARMANITAN

## GALARIAN FORM

### Zen Charm Pokémon

| POKÉDEX NO. | **555** |
|---|---|
| **TYPE** | Ice |
| **ABILITY** | Gorilla Tactics |
| **HEIGHT** | 5'07" |
| **WEIGHT** | 264.6 lbs |

Though it has a gentle disposition, it's also very strong. It will quickly freeze the snowball on its head before going for a headbutt.

### Description

On days when blizzards blow through, it comes down to where people live. It stashes food in the snowball on its head, taking it home for later.

### Special Moves

Icicle Crash, Ice Punch, Powder Snow

**Evolution**

**DARUMAKA**
(GALARIAN FORM)

➡

**DARMANITAN**
(GALARIAN FORM)

# DARMANITAN

**GALARIAN FORM / ZEN MODE\***

## Zen Charm Pokémon

| POKÉDEX NO. | 555 |
|---|---|
| **TYPE** | Ice, Fire |
| **ABILITY** | Zen Mode |
| **HEIGHT** | 5'07" |
| **WEIGHT** | 264.6 lbs |

001-100

101-200

201-300

401-442

443-500

501-600

601-700

701-800

801-898

### Description

Darmanitan takes this form when enraged. It won't stop spewing flames until its rage has settled, even if its body starts to melt.

Anger has reignited its atrophied flame sac. This Pokémon spews fire everywhere as it rampages indiscriminately.

### Special Moves

Bite, Belly Drum, Thrash

**Evolution**

DARUMAKA (GALARIAN FORM) → DARMANITAN (GALARIAN FORM)

\*Zen Mode: Some Darmanitan will temporarily enter this state when they face a difficult situation in battle.

# MARACTUS

## Cactus Pokémon

| POKÉDEX NO. | **556** |
|---|---|

| | |
|---|---|
| **TYPE** | Grass |
| **ABILITY** | Chlorophyll, Water Absorb |
| **HEIGHT** | 3'03" |
| **WEIGHT** | 61.7 lbs |

### Description

With noises that could be mistaken for the rattles of maracas, it creates an upbeat rhythm, startling bird Pokémon and making them fly off in a hurry.

Once each year, this Pokémon scatters its seeds. They're jam-packed with nutrients, making them a precious food source out in the desert.

### Special Moves

Spiky Shield, Petal Blizzard, Pin Missile

**Evolution**  Does not evolve

MARACTUS

# DWEBBLE

It first tries to find a rock to live in, but if there are no suitable rocks to be found, Dwebble may move in to the ports of a Hippowdon.*

D01-100
101-200
201-300
401-442
443-500
501-600
601-700
701-800
801-898

## Rock Inn Pokémon

| POKÉDEX NO. | 557 |
|---|---|
| TYPE | Bug, Rock |
| ABILITY | Sturdy, Shell Armor |
| HEIGHT | 1'00" |
| WEIGHT | 32.0 lbs |

### Description

When it finds a stone appealing, it creates a hole inside it and uses it as its home. This Pokémon is the natural enemy of Roggenrola** and Rolycoly.***

### Special Moves

Fury Cutter, Rock Slide, Bug Bite

**Evolution**

DWEBBLE → CRUSTLE

*Hippowdon: A Pokémon you'll find on page 19. **Roggenrola: A Pokémon you'll find on page 104.***Rolycoly: A Pokémon you'll find on page 460.

# CRUSTLE

This highly territorial Pokémon prefers dry climates. It won't come out of its boulder on rainy days.

| Stone Home Pokémon | |
|---|---|
| POKÉDEX NO. | **558** |
| TYPE | Bug, Rock |
| ABILITY | Sturdy, Shell Armor |
| HEIGHT | 4'07" |
| WEIGHT | 440.9 lbs |

## Description

Its thick claws are its greatest weapons. They're mighty enough to crack Rhyperior's* carapace.

## Special Moves

Stealth Rock, Rock Wrecker, Slash

**Evolution**

DWEBBLE → CRUSTLE

*Rhyperior: A Pokémon you'll find on page 34.

# SCRAGGY

**Shedding Pokémon**

| POKÉDEX NO. | **559** |
|---|---|
| **TYPE** | Dark, Fighting |
| **ABILITY** | Shed Skin, Moxie |
| **HEIGHT** | 2'00" |
| **WEIGHT** | 26.0 lbs |

It protects itself with its durable skin. It's thought that this Pokémon will evolve once its skin has completely stretched out.

## Description

If it locks eyes with you, watch out! Nothing and no one is safe from the reckless headbutts of this troublesome Pokémon.

## Special Moves

Leer, High Jump Kick, Brick Break

**Evolution**

SCRAGGY → SCRAFTY

001-100
101-200
201-300
401-442
443-500
501-600
701-800
801-898

# SCRAFTY

While mostly known for having the temperament of an aggressive ruffian, this Pokémon takes very good care of its family, friends, and territory.

## Hoodlum Pokémon

| POKÉDEX NO. | 560 |
|---|---|
| TYPE | Dark, Fighting |
| ABILITY | Shed Skin, Moxie |
| HEIGHT | 3'07" |
| WEIGHT | 66.1 lbs |

### Description

As halfhearted as this Pokémon's kicks may seem, they pack enough power to shatter Conkeldurr's* concrete pillars.

### Special Moves

Focus Punch, Head Smash, Swagger

### Evolution

 →

SCRAGGY → SCRAFTY

*Conkeldurr: A Pokémon you'll find on page 115.

# SIGILYPH

A discovery was made in the desert where Sigilyph fly. The ruins of what may have been an ancient city were found beneath the sands.

001-100
101-200
201-300
401-442
443-500
501-600
601-700
701-800
801-898

## Avianoid Pokémon

| POKÉDEX NO. | **561** |
|---|---|
| TYPE | Psychic, Flying |
| ABILITY | Magic Guard, Wonder Skin |
| HEIGHT | 4'07" |
| WEIGHT | 30.9 lbs |

### Description

Psychic power allows these Pokémon to fly. Some say they were the guardians of an ancient city. Others say they were the guardians' emissaries.

### Special Moves

Air Cutter, Psychic, Tailwind

**Evolution**

SIGILYPH

Does not evolve

# YAMASK

The spirit of a person from a bygone age became this Pokémon. It rambles through ruins, searching for someone who knows its face.

## Spirit Pokémon

| POKÉDEX NO. | 562 |
| --- | --- |
| TYPE | Ghost |
| ABILITY | Mummy |
| HEIGHT | 1'08" |
| WEIGHT | 3.3 lbs |

### Description

It wanders through ruins by night, carrying a mask that's said to have been the face it had when it was still human.

### Special Moves

Will-O-Wisp, Shadow Ball, Mean Look

Evolution  ➡

YAMASK    COFAGRIGUS

# YAMASK

## GALARIAN FORM

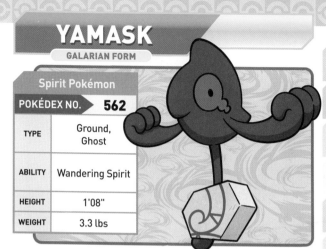

**Spirit Pokémon**

| POKÉDEX NO. | 562 |
| --- | --- |

| TYPE | Ground, Ghost |
| --- | --- |
| **ABILITY** | Wandering Spirit |
| **HEIGHT** | 1'08" |
| **WEIGHT** | 3.3 lbs |

### Description

A clay slab with cursed engravings took possession of a Yamask. The slab is said to be absorbing the Yamask's dark power.

It's said that this Pokémon was formed when an ancient clay tablet was drawn to a vengeful spirit.

### Special Moves

Earthquake, Shadow Ball, Crafty Shield

**Evolution**

YAMASK
(GALARIAN FORM) → RUNERIGUS

001-100
101-200
201-300
401-442
443-500
501-600
701-800
801-898

# COFAGRIGUS

| | |
|---|---|
| **Coffin Pokémon** | |
| **POKÉDEX NO.** | **563** |
| **TYPE** | Ghost |
| **ABILITY** | Mummy |
| **HEIGHT** | 5'07" |
| **WEIGHT** | 168.7 lbs |

This Pokémon has a body of sparkling gold. People say it no longer remembers that it was once human.

### Description

There are many depictions of Cofagrigus decorating ancient tombs. They're symbols of wealth that kings of bygone eras had.

### Special Moves

Shadow Claw, Curse, Dark Pulse

**Evolution**

YAMASK → COFAGRIGUS

# TIRTOUGA

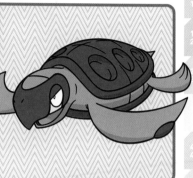

### Prototurtle Pokémon

| POKÉDEX NO. | 564 |
| --- | --- |
| **TYPE** | Water, Rock |
| **ABILITY** | Sturdy, Solid Rock |
| **HEIGHT** | 2'04" |
| **WEIGHT** | 36.4 lbs |

Tirtouga is considered to be the ancestor of many turtle Pokémon. It was restored to life from a fossil.

### Description

This Pokémon inhabited ancient seas. Although it can only crawl, it still comes up onto land in search of prey.

### Special Moves

Water Gun, Withdraw, Rock Slide

**Evolution**

TIRTOUGA → CARRACOSTA

001-100
101-200
201-300
401-442
443-500
501-600
601-700
701-800
801-898

# CARRACOSTA

This Pokémon emerges from the water in search of prey despite the fact that it moves more slowly on land.

| Prototurtle Pokémon | |
|---|---|
| **POKÉDEX NO.** | **565** |
| **TYPE** | Water, Rock |
| **ABILITY** | Sturdy, Solid Rock |
| **HEIGHT** | 3'11" |
| **WEIGHT** | 178.6 lbs |

## Description

Carracosta completely devours its prey—bones, shells, and all. Because of this, Carracosta's own shell grows thick and sturdy.

## Special Moves

Ancient Power, Hydro Pump, Brine

**Evolution**

TIRTOUGA → CARRACOSTA

# ARCHEN

Archen is said to be the ancestor of bird Pokémon. It lived in treetops, eating berries and bug Pokémon.

001-100
101-200
201-300
401-442
443-500
501-600
701-808
801-898

| First Bird Pokémon | |
| --- | --- |
| POKÉDEX NO. | **566** |
| TYPE | Rock, Flying |
| ABILITY | Defeatist |
| HEIGHT | 1'08" |
| WEIGHT | 20.9 lbs |

## Description

This Pokémon was successfully restored from a fossil. As research suggested, Archen is unable to fly. But it's very good at jumping.

## Special Moves

Quick Attack, Wing Attack, Rock Slide

**Evolution**

ARCHEN

ARCHEOPS

# ARCHEOPS

Though capable of flight, Archeops was apparently better at hunting on the ground.

| First Bird Pokémon | |
|---|---|
| POKÉDEX NO. | 567 |
| TYPE | Rock, Flying |
| ABILITY | Defeatist |
| HEIGHT | 4'07" |
| WEIGHT | 70.5 lbs |

## Description

It needs a running start to take off. If Archeops wants to fly, it first needs to run nearly 25 mph, building speed over a course of 2.5 miles.

## Special Moves

Dragon Claw, Agility, Thrash

Evolution

ARCHEN → ARCHEOPS

# TRUBBISH

001-100
101-200
201-300
401-442
443-500
501-600
601-700
701-800
801-898

Its favorite places are unsanitary ones. If you leave trash lying around, you could even find one of these Pokémon living in your room.

## Trash Bag Pokémon

| POKÉDEX NO. | 568 |
|---|---|
| TYPE | Poison |
| ABILITY | Stench, Sticky Hold |
| HEIGHT | 2'00" |
| WEIGHT | 68.3 lbs |

### Description

This Pokémon was born from a bag stuffed with trash. Galarian Weezing* relish the fumes belched by Trubbish.

### Special Moves

Poison Gas, Sludge Bomb, Gunk Shot

### Evolution

TRUBBISH → GARBODOR

*Weezing (Galarian Form): A Pokémon you'll find in volume 1.

# GARBODOR

The toxic liquid it launches from its right arm is so virulent that it can kill a weakened creature instantly.

| Trash Heap Pokémon | |
|---|---|
| **POKÉDEX NO.** | **569** |
| TYPE | Poison |
| ABILITY | Stench, Weak Armor |
| HEIGHT | 6'03" |
| WEIGHT | 236.6 lbs |

### Description

This Pokémon eats trash, which turns into poison inside its body. The main component of the poison depends on what sort of trash was eaten.

### Special Moves

Sludge, Explosion, Toxic Spikes

### Evolution

TRUBBISH → GARBODOR

# GARBODOR

It sprays toxic gas from its mouth and fingers. If the gas engulfs you, the toxins will seep in all the way down to your bones.

**GARBODOR**

001-100

101-200

201-300

401-442

443-500

501-600

701-600

801-898

| Trash Heap Pokémon | |
|---|---|
| **POKÉDEX NO.** | **569** |
| **TYPE** | Poison |
| **ABILITY** | Stench, Weak Armor |
| **HEIGHT** | 68'11"+ |
| **WEIGHT** | ??? lbs |

### Description

Due to Gigantamax energy, this Pokémon's toxic gas has become much thicker, congealing into masses shaped like discarded toys.

### Special Moves

G-Max Malodor

157

# ZORUA

| Tricky Fox Pokémon | |
|---|---|
| **POKÉDEX NO.** | **570** |
| TYPE | Dark |
| ABILITY | Illusion |
| HEIGHT | 2'04" |
| WEIGHT | 27.6 lbs |

Zorua is a timid Pokémon. This disposition seems to be what led to the development of Zorua's ability to take on the forms of other creatures.

## Description

Zorua sometimes transforms into a person and goes into cities to search for food. When Zorua does this, it usually takes on the form of a child.

## Special Moves

Nasty Plot, Foul Play, Fury Swipes

Evolution

ZORUA → ZOROARK

# ZOROARK

| Illusion Fox Pokémon | |
|---|---|
| **POKÉDEX NO.** | **571** |
| TYPE | Dark |
| ABILITY | Illusion |
| HEIGHT | 5'03" |
| WEIGHT | 178.8 lbs |

This Pokémon cares deeply about others of its kind, and it will conjure terrifying illusions to keep its den and pack safe.

## Description

Seeking to ease the burden of solitude, lonely Trainers tell Zoroark to show illusions to them.

## Special Moves

Night Slash, Night Daze, Fury Swipes

**Evolution**

  →

ZORUA    ZOROARK

001-100
101-00
201-300
401-442
443-500
501-600
701-800
801-898

# MINCCINO

| | | |
|---|---|---|
| **Chinchilla Pokémon** | | |
| **POKÉDEX NO.** | | **572** |
| TYPE | Normal | |
| ABILITY | Cute Charm, Technician | |
| HEIGHT | 1'04" | |
| WEIGHT | 12.8 lbs | |

The way it brushes away grime with its tail can be helpful when cleaning. But its focus on spotlessness can make cleaning more of a hassle.

### Description

They pet each other with their tails as a form of greeting. Of the two, the one whose tail is fluffier is a bit more boastful.

### Special Moves

Swift, Baby-Doll Eyes, Charm

**Evolution**

 →

MINCCINO          CINCCINO

160

# CINCCINO

A special oil that seeps through their fur helps them avoid attacks. The oil fetches a high price at market.

001-100
101-200
201-300
401-442
443-500
501-600
601-700
701-800
801-898

## Scarf Pokémon

| POKÉDEX NO. | 573 |
|---|---|
| TYPE | Normal |
| ABILITY | Cute Charm, Technician |
| HEIGHT | 1'08" |
| WEIGHT | 16.5 lbs |

### Description

Its body secretes oil that this Pokémon spreads over its nest as a coating to protect it from dust. Cinccino won't tolerate even a speck of the stuff.

### Special Moves

Tail Slap, Echoed Voice, Sing

### Evolution

MINCCINO
→

CINCCINO

161

# GOTHITA

| Fixation Pokémon | |
|---|---|
| POKÉDEX NO. | **574** |
| TYPE | Psychic |
| ABILITY | Frisk, Competitive |
| HEIGHT | 1'04" |
| WEIGHT | 12.8 lbs |

Even when nobody seems to be around, Gothita can still be heard making a muted cry. Many believe it's speaking to something only it can see.

### Description

Though they're still only babies, there's psychic power stored in their ribbonlike feelers, and sometimes they use that power to fight.

### Special Moves

Psybeam, Fake Tears, Hypnosis

Evolution

GOTHITA → GOTHORITA → GOTHITELLE

# GOTHORITA

001-100

101-200

201-300

401-442

443-500

501-600

601-700

701-800

801-898

On nights when the stars shine in the night sky, this Pokémon's psychic power is at its strongest. It's unknown just what link Gothorita has to the greater universe.

| Manipulate Pokémon | |
|---|---|
| POKÉDEX NO. | 575 |
| TYPE | Psychic |
| ABILITY | Frisk, Competitive |
| HEIGHT | 2'04" |
| WEIGHT | 39.7 lbs |

## Description

It's said that when stars shine in the night sky, this Pokémon will spirit away sleeping children. Some call it the Witch of Punishment.

## Special Moves

Psychic, Future Sight, Play Nice

Evolution

GOTHITA    GOTHORITA    GOTHITELLE

# GOTHITELLE

## Astral Body Pokémon

| POKÉDEX NO. | 576 |
| --- | --- |
| TYPE | Psychic |
| ABILITY | Frisk, Competitive |
| HEIGHT | 4'11" |
| WEIGHT | 97.0 lbs |

A criminal who was shown his fate by a Gothitelle went missing that same day and was never seen again.

### Description

It has tremendous psychic power, but it dislikes conflict. It's also able to predict the future based on the movement of the stars.

### Special Moves

Dragon Claw, Agility, Thrash

Evolution

GOTHITA

GOTHORITA

GOTHITELLE

# SOLOSIS

Many say that the special liquid covering this Pokémon's body would allow it to survive in the vacuum of space.

001-100
101-200
201-300
401-442
443-500
501-600
601-700
701-800
801-898

## Cell Pokémon

| POKÉDEX NO. | 577 |
|---|---|
| TYPE | Psychic |
| ABILITY | Magic Guard, Overcoat |
| HEIGHT | 1'00" |
| WEIGHT | 2.2 lbs |

### Description

It communicates with others telepathically. Its body is encapsulated in liquid, but if it takes a heavy blow, the liquid will leak out.

### Special Moves

Confusion, Psybeam, Light Screen

### Evolution

SOLOSIS → DUOSION → REUNICLUS

# DUOSION

Its brain has split into two, and the two halves rarely think alike. Its actions are utterly unpredictable.

## Mitosis Pokémon

| | |
|---|---|
| POKÉDEX NO. | **578** |
| TYPE | Psychic |
| ABILITY | Magic Guard, Overcoat |
| HEIGHT | 2'00" |
| WEIGHT | 17.6 lbs |

### Description

Its psychic power can supposedly cover a range of more than half a mile—but only if its two brains can agree with each other.

### Special Moves

Recover, Psychic, Charm

Evolution

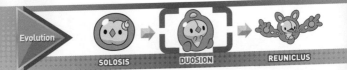

SOLOSIS → DUOSION → REUNICLUS

# REUNICLUS

While it could use its psychic abilities in battle, this Pokémon prefers to swing its powerful arms around to beat opponents into submission.

## Multiplying Pokémon

| POKÉDEX NO. | 579 |
|---|---|
| TYPE | Psychic |
| ABILITY | Magic Guard, Overcoat |
| HEIGHT | 3'03" |
| WEIGHT | 44.3 lbs |

### Description

When Reuniclus shake hands, a network forms between their brains, increasing their psychic power.

### Special Moves

Hammer Arm, Psyshock, Protect

**Evolution**

 ➡  ➡

SOLOSIS      DUOSION      REUNICLUS

# DUCKLETT

When attacked, it uses its feathers to splash water, escaping under cover of the spray.

## Water Bird Pokémon

| POKÉDEX NO. | 580 |
| --- | --- |
| TYPE | Water, Flying |
| ABILITY | Keen Eye, Big Pecks |
| HEIGHT | 1'08" |
| WEIGHT | 12.1 lbs |

### Description

They are better at swimming than flying, and they happily eat their favorite food, peat moss, as they dive underwater.

### Special Moves

Water Gun, Wing Attack, Rain Dance

Evolution

DUCKLETT → SWANNA

# SWANNA

Despite their elegant appearance, they can flap their wings strongly and fly for thousands of miles.

## White Bird Pokémon

| POKÉDEX NO. | **581** |
| --- | --- |
| TYPE | Water, Flying |
| ABILITY | Keen Eye, Big Pecks |
| HEIGHT | 4'03" |
| WEIGHT | 53.4 lbs |

### Description

Swanna start to dance at dusk. The one dancing in the middle is the leader of the flock.

### Special Moves

Brave Bird, Water Pulse, Roost

001-100
101-200
201-300
401-442
443-500
501-600
601-700
701-800
801-898

**Evolution**

DUCKLETT

SWANNA

# VANILLITE

Unable to survive in hot areas, it makes itself comfortable by breathing out air cold enough to cause snow. It burrows into the snow to sleep.

## Fresh Snow Pokémon

| POKÉDEX NO. | 582 |
|---|---|
| TYPE | Ice |
| ABILITY | Snow Cloak, Ice Body |
| HEIGHT | 1'04" |
| WEIGHT | 12.6 lbs |

### Description

Supposedly, this Pokémon was born from an icicle. It spews out freezing air at –58 degrees Fahrenheit to make itself more comfortable.

### Special Moves

Icy Wind, Icicle Spear, Harden

**Evolution**

VANILLITE

VANILLISH

VANILLUXE

# VANILLISH

It blasts enemies with cold air reaching –148 degrees Fahrenheit, freezing them solid. But it spares their lives afterward—it's a kind Pokémon.

## Icy Snow Pokémon

| | |
|---|---|
| **POKÉDEX NO.** | **583** |
| **TYPE** | Ice |
| **ABILITY** | Snow Cloak, Ice Body |
| **HEIGHT** | 3'07" |
| **WEIGHT** | 90.4 lbs |

### Description

By drinking pure water, it grows its icy body. This Pokémon can be hard to find on days with warm, sunny weather.

### Special Moves

Ice Beam, Avalanche, Icicle Spear

**Evolution**

 →  →

VANILLITE          VANILLISH          VANILLUXE

001-100
101-200
201-300
401-442
443-500
501-600
401-700
701-800
801-898

# VANILLUXE

When its anger reaches a breaking point, this Pokémon unleashes a fierce blizzard that freezes every creature around it, be they friend or foe.

## Snowstorm Pokémon

| POKÉDEX NO. | 584 |
|---|---|
| TYPE | Ice |
| ABILITY | Ice Body, Snow Warning |
| HEIGHT | 4'03" |
| WEIGHT | 126.8 lbs |

### Description

People believe this Pokémon formed when two Vanillish stuck together. Its body temperature is roughly 21 degrees Fahrenheit.

### Special Moves

Sheer Cold, Freeze-Dry, Acid Armor

### Evolution

VANILLITE → VANILLISH → VANILLUXE

# DEERLING

## Season Pokémon

| POKÉDEX NO. | **585** |
| --- | --- |
| **TYPE** | Normal, Grass |
| **ABILITY** | Chlorophyll, Sap Sipper |
| **HEIGHT** | 2'00" |
| **WEIGHT** | 43.0 lbs |

Spring Form

Summer Form

Winter Form

Autumn Form

The turning of the seasons changes the color and scent of this Pokémon's fur. People use it to mark the seasons.

### Description

Their coloring changes according to the season and can be slightly affected by the temperature and humidity as well.

### Special Moves

Tackle, Energy Ball, Double Kick

**Evolution**

DEERLING → SAWSBUCK

001-100
101-200
201-300
401-442
443-500
501-600
401-498
701-800
801-898

# SAWSBUCK

## Season Pokémon

| POKÉDEX NO. | 586 |
| --- | --- |
| **TYPE** | Normal, Grass |
| **ABILITY** | Chlorophyll, Sap Sipper |
| **HEIGHT** | 6'03" |
| **WEIGHT** | 203.9 lbs |

Spring Form

Summer Form

Winter Form

Autumn Form

They migrate according to seasons, so some people call Sawsbuck the harbingers of spring.

### Description

They migrate according to the seasons. People can tell the season by looking at Sawsbuck's horns.

### Special Moves

Horn Leech, Solar Beam, Megahorn

**Evolution**

DEERLING → SAWSBUCK

# EMOLGA

## Sky Squirrel Pokémon

| POKÉDEX NO. | **587** |
|---|---|
| TYPE | Electric, Flying |
| ABILITY | Static |
| HEIGHT | 1'04" |
| WEIGHT | 11.0 lbs |

### Description

This Pokémon absolutely loves sweet berries. Sometimes it stuffs its cheeks full of so much food that it can't fly properly.

As Emolga flutters through the air, it crackles with electricity. This Pokémon is cute, but it can cause a lot of trouble.

### Special Moves

Thunder Shock, Nuzzle, Spark

Evolution  Does not evolve

EMOLGA

001-100
101-200
201-300
401-442
443-590
501-600
701-800
801-898

# KARRABLAST

It spits a liquid from its mouth to melt through Shelmet's* shell. Karrablast doesn't eat the shell—it only eats the contents.

## Clamping Pokémon

| | |
|---|---|
| POKÉDEX NO. | **588** |
| TYPE | Bug |
| ABILITY | Shed Skin, Swarm |
| HEIGHT | 1'08" |
| WEIGHT | 13.0 lbs |

### Description

Its strange physiology reacts to electrical energy in interesting ways. The presence of a Shelmet will cause this Pokémon to evolve.

### Special Moves

False Swipe, Bug Buzz, Double-Edge

**Evolution**

 →

KARRABLAST    ESCAVALIER

*Shelmet: A Pokémon you'll find on page 204.

# ESCAVALIER

It charges its enemies, lances at the ready. An image of one of its duels is captured in a famous painting of Escavalier clashing with Sirfetch'd.*

## Cavalry Pokémon

| POKÉDEX NO. | 589 |
| --- | --- |
| TYPE | Bug, Steel |
| ABILITY | Swarm, Shell Armor |
| HEIGHT | 3'03" |
| WEIGHT | 72.8 lbs |

### Description

They use shells they've stolen from Shelmet** to arm and protect themselves. They're very popular Pokémon in the Galar region.

### Special Moves

X-Scissor, Metal Burst, Iron Defense

## Evolution

KARRABLAST → ESCAVALIER

*Sirfetch'd: A Pokémon you'll find on page 501. **Shelmet: A Pokémon you'll find on page 204.

001-100
101-200
201-300
401-442
443-500
501-600
701-800
801-898

# FOONGUS

## Mushroom Pokémon

| POKÉDEX NO. | **590** |
|---|---|
| TYPE | Grass, Poison |
| ABILITY | Effect Spore |
| HEIGHT | 0'08" |
| WEIGHT | 2.2 lbs |

### Description

No one knows what the Poké Ball–like pattern on Foongus means or why Foongus has it.

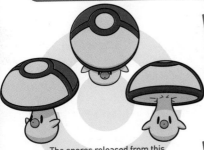

The spores released from this Pokémon's hands are highly poisonous, but when thoroughly dried, the spores can be used as stomach medicine.

### Special Moves

Astonish, Rage Powder, Spore

Evolution

FOONGUS → AMOONGUSS

# AMOONGUSS

| | |
|---|---|
| **Mushroom Pokémon** | |
| **POKÉDEX NO.** | **591** |
| **TYPE** | Grass, Poison |
| **ABILITY** | Effect Spore |
| **HEIGHT** | 2'00" |
| **WEIGHT** | 23.1 lbs |

This Pokémon puffs poisonous spores at its foes. If the spores aren't washed off quickly, they'll grow into mushrooms wherever they land.

### Description

Amoonguss generally doesn't move much. It tends to stand still near Poké Balls that have been dropped on the ground.

### Special Moves

Toxic, Solar Beam, Spore

**Evolution**

**FOONGUS**

**AMOONGUSS**

001-100
101-200
201-300
401-442
443-500
501-600
701-800
801-898

# FRILLISH

Male

Female

Legend has it that the residents of a sunken ancient city changed into these Pokémon.

| Floating Pokémon | |
|---|---|
| **POKÉDEX NO.** | **592** |
| **TYPE** | Water, Ghost |
| **ABILITY** | Water Absorb, Cursed Body |
| **HEIGHT** | 3'11" |
| **WEIGHT** | 72.8 lbs |

### Description

ts thin, veillike arms have tens of thousands of poisonous stingers. Females have slightly longer stingers

### Special Moves

Rain Dance, Water Pulse, Shadow Ball

**Evolution**

FRILLISH       JELLICENT

# JELLICENT

Male

Female

These Pokémon have body compositions that are mostly identical to seawater. They make their lairs from sunken ships.

## Floating Pokémon

| POKÉDEX NO. | **593** |
|---|---|
| TYPE | Water, Ghost |
| ABILITY | Water Absorb, Cursed Body |
| HEIGHT | 7'03" |
| WEIGHT | 297.6 lbs |

## Description

Whenever a full moon hangs in the night sky, schools of Jellicent gather near the surface of the sea, waiting for their prey to appear. The crown on its head gets bigger and bigger as it absorbs more and more of the life force of other creatures.

## Special Moves

Hydro Pump, Recover, Destiny Bond

Evolution

FRILLISH → JELLICENT

# ALOMOMOLA

The reason it helps Pokémon in a weakened condition is that any Pokémon coming after it may also attack Alomomola.

## Caring Pokémon

| POKÉDEX NO. | 594 |
|---|---|
| TYPE | Water |
| ABILITY | Hydration, Healer |
| HEIGHT | 3'11" |
| WEIGHT | 69.7 lbs |

### Description

Fishermen take them along on long voyages, because if they have an Alomomola with them, there'll be no need for a doctor or medicine.

### Special Moves

Water Sport, Healing Wish, Aqua Ring

Evolution

ALOMOMOLA

Does not evolve

# JOLTIK

Joltik that live in cities have learned a technique for sucking electricity from the outlets in houses.

## Attaching Pokémon

| POKÉDEX NO. | 595 |
|---|---|
| TYPE | Bug, Electric |
| ABILITY | Compound Eyes, Unnerve |
| HEIGHT | 0'04" |
| WEIGHT | 1.3 lbs |

### Description

Joltik can be found clinging to other Pokémon. It's soaking up static electricity because it can't produce a charge on its own.

### Special Moves

String Shot, Electroweb, Bug Buzz

001-100
101-200
201-300
401-442
443-500
501-600
701-800
801-898

Evolution

  ➡

JOLTIK          GALVANTULA

# GALVANTULA

It lays traps of electrified threads near the nests of bird Pokémon, aiming to snare chicks that are not yet good at flying.

## EleSpider Pokémon

| | |
|---|---|
| POKÉDEX NO. | **596** |
| TYPE | Bug, Electric |
| ABILITY | Compound Eyes, Unnerve |
| HEIGHT | 2'07" |
| WEIGHT | 31.5 lbs |

### Description

It launches electrified fur from its abdomen as a means of attack. Opponents hit by the fur could be in for three full days and nights of paralysis.

### Special Moves

Sticky Web, Electro Ball, Discharge

### Evolution

JOLTIK → GALVANTULA

# FERROSEED

**Thorn Seed Pokémon**

| POKÉDEX NO. | **597** |
|---|---|
| **TYPE** | Grass, Steel |
| **ABILITY** | Iron Barbs |
| **HEIGHT** | 2'00" |
| **WEIGHT** | 41.4 lbs |

## Description

It defends itself by launching spikes, but its aim isn't very good at first. Only after a lot of practice will it improve.

Mossy caves are their preferred dwellings. Enzymes contained in mosses help Ferroseed's spikes grow big and strong.

## Special Moves

Harden, Tackle, Metal Claw

**Evolution**

FERROSEED

FERROTHORN

001-100
101-200
201-300
401-442
443-500
501-600
701-800
801-898

# FERROTHORN

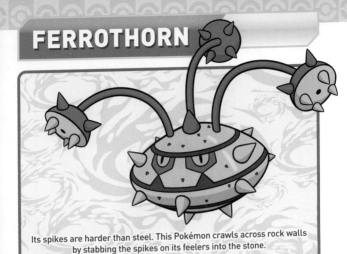

Its spikes are harder than steel. This Pokémon crawls across rock walls by stabbing the spikes on its feelers into the stone.

| Thorn Pod Pokémon | |
|---|---|
| **POKÉDEX NO.** | **598** |
| TYPE | Grass, Steel |
| ABILITY | Iron Barbs |
| HEIGHT | 3'03" |
| WEIGHT | 242.5 lbs |

### Description

This Pokémon scrapes its spikes across rocks, and then uses the tips of its feelers to absorb the nutrients it finds within the stone.

### Special Moves

Power Whip, Pin Missile, Iron Defense

**Evolution**

 →

FERROSEED    FERROTHORN

# KLINK

It's suspected that Klink were the inspiration behind ancient people's invention of the first gears.

001-100
101-200
201-300
401-442
443-500
501-600
701-800
801-898

## Gear Pokémon

| POKÉDEX NO. | 599 |
|---|---|
| TYPE | Steel |
| ABILITY | Plus, Minus |
| HEIGHT | 1'00" |
| WEIGHT | 46.3 lbs |

### Description

The two minigears that compose this Pokémon are closer than twins. They mesh well only with each other.

### Special Moves

Thunder Shock, Charge, Metal Sound

**Evolution**

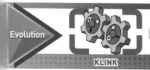 ➡  ➡

KLINK          KLANG          KLINKLANG

# KLANG

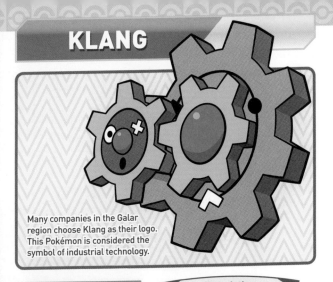

Many companies in the Galar region choose Klang as their logo. This Pokémon is considered the symbol of industrial technology.

| Gear Pokémon | |
|---|---|
| **POKÉDEX NO.** | **600** |
| TYPE | Steel |
| ABILITY | Plus, Minus |
| HEIGHT | 2'00" |
| WEIGHT | 112.4 lbs |

### Description

When Klang goes all out, the minigear links up perfectly with the outer part of the big gear, and this Pokémon's rotation speed increases sharply.

### Special Moves

Gear Grind, Discharge, Charge Beam

Evolution

KLINK     KLANG     KLINKLANG

# KLINKLANG

The three gears that compose this Pokémon spin at high speed. Its new spiked gear isn't a living creature.

001-100
101-200
201-300
401-442
443-500
501-600
601-700
701-800
801-898

## Gear Pokémon

| POKÉDEX NO. | 601 |
| --- | --- |
| TYPE | Steel |
| ABILITY | Plus, Minus |
| HEIGHT | 2'00" |
| WEIGHT | 178.6 lbs |

### Description

From its spikes, it launches powerful blasts of electricity. Its red core contains an enormous amount of energy.

### Special Moves

Gear Grind, Shift Gear, Zap Cannon

### Evolution

KLINK → KLANG → KLINKLANG

# TYNAMO

One alone can emit only a trickle of electricity, so a group of them gathers to unleash a powerful electric shock.

## EleFish Pokémon

| POKÉDEX NO. | **602** |
|---|---|
| TYPE | Electric |
| ABILITY | Levitate |
| HEIGHT | 0'08" |
| WEIGHT | 0.7 lbs |

### Description

While one alone doesn't have much power, a chain of many Tynamo can be as powerful as lightning.

### Special Moves

Thunder Wave, Spark, Charge Beam

Evolution

TYNAMO → EELEKTRIK → EELEKTROSS

# EELEKTRIK

These Pokémon have a big appetite. When they spot their prey, they attack it and paralyze it with electricity.

| EleFish Pokémon | |
|---|---|
| **POKÉDEX NO.** | **603** |
| TYPE | Electric |
| ABILITY | Levitate |
| HEIGHT | 3'11" |
| WEIGHT | 48.5 lbs |

## Description

It wraps itself around its prey and paralyzes it with electricity from the round spots on its sides. Then it chomps.

## Special Moves

Wild Charge, Acid, Crunch

**Evolution**

TYNAMO → EELEKTRIK → EELEKTROSS

001-100
101-200
201-300
401-442
443-500
501-600
601-700
701-800
801-898

# EELEKTROSS

They crawl out of the ocean using their arms. They will attack prey on shore and immediately drag it into the ocean.

| EleFish Pokémon | |
| --- | --- |
| POKÉDEX NO. | 604 |
| TYPE | Electric |
| ABILITY | Levitate |
| HEIGHT | 6'11" |
| WEIGHT | 177.5 lbs |

## Description

With their sucker mouths, they suck in prey. Then they use their fangs to shock the prey with electricity.

## Special Moves

Ion Deluge, Zap Cannon, Thrash

Evolution

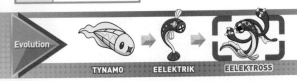

TYNAMO → EELEKTRIK → EELEKTROSS

# ELGYEM

This Pokémon was discovered about 50 years ago. Its highly developed brain enables it to exert its psychic powers.

## Cerebral Pokémon

| POKÉDEX NO. | 605 |
| --- | --- |
| TYPE | Psychic |
| ABILITY | Synchronize, Telepathy |
| HEIGHT | 1'08" |
| WEIGHT | 19.8 lbs |

### Description

If this Pokémon stands near a TV, strange scenery will appear on the screen. That scenery is said to be from its home.

### Special Moves

Confusion, Wonder Room, Teleport

Evolution

ELGYEM

BEHEEYEM

001-100
101-200
201-300
401-442
443-500
501-600
601-700
701-800
801-898

# BEHEEYEM

Sometimes found drifting above wheat fields, this Pokémon can control the memories of its opponents.

## Cerebral Pokémon

| POKÉDEX NO. | 606 |
| --- | --- |
| TYPE | Psychic |
| ABILITY | Synchronize, Telepathy |
| HEIGHT | 3'03" |
| WEIGHT | 76.1 lbs |

### Description

Whenever a Beheeyem visits a farm, a Dubwool* mysteriously disappears.

### Special Moves

Psybeam, Recover, Calm Mind

**Evolution**

 ➡

ELGYEM     BEHEEYEM

194   *Dubwool: A Pokémon you'll find on page 454.

# LITWICK

The younger the life this Pokémon absorbs, the brighter and eerier the flame on its head burns.

| Candle Pokémon | |
|---|---|
| **POKÉDEX NO.** | **607** |
| **TYPE** | Ghost, Fire |
| **ABILITY** | Flash Fire, Flame Body |
| **HEIGHT** | 1'00" |
| **WEIGHT** | 6.8 lbs |

## Description

The flame on its head keeps its body slightly warm. This Pokémon takes lost children by the hand to guide them to the spirit world.

## Special Moves

Smog, Fire Spin, Confuse Ray

Evolution

LITWICK → LAMPENT → CHANDELURE

001-100
101-200
201-300
401-442
443-500
501-600
601-700
701-800
801-898

# LAMPENT

This Pokémon appears just before someone passes away, so it's feared as an emissary of death.

| Lamp Pokémon | |
|---|---|
| POKÉDEX NO. | **608** |
| TYPE | Ghost, Fire |
| ABILITY | Flash Fire, Flame Body |
| HEIGHT | 2'00" |
| WEIGHT | 28.7 lbs |

## Description

It lurks in cities, pretending to be a lamp. Once it finds someone whose death is near, it will trail quietly after them.

## Special Moves

Will-O-Wisp, Shadow Ball, Night Shade

Evolution

LITWICK → LAMPENT → CHANDELURE

# CHANDELURE

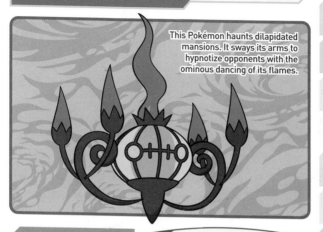

This Pokémon haunts dilapidated mansions. It sways its arms to hypnotize opponents with the ominous dancing of its flames.

| Luring Pokémon | |
|---|---|
| POKÉDEX NO. | **609** |
| TYPE | Ghost, Fire |
| ABILITY | Flash Fire, Flame Body |
| HEIGHT | 3'03" |
| WEIGHT | 75.6 lbs |

## Description

In homes illuminated by Chandelure instead of lights, funerals were a constant occurrence—or so it's said.

## Special Moves

Overheat, Inferno, Shadow Ball

001-100
101-200
201-300
401-442
443-500
501-600
601-700
701-800
801-898

**Evolution**

LITWICK          LAMPENT          CHANDELURE

# AXEW

| | |
|---|---|
| **Tusk Pokémon** | |
| **POKÉDEX NO.** | **610** |
| **TYPE** | Dragon |
| **ABILITY** | Rivalry, Mold Breaker |
| **HEIGHT** | 2'00" |
| **WEIGHT** | 39.7 lbs |

These Pokémon nest in the ground and use their tusks to crush hard berries. Crushing berries is also how they test each other's strength.

### Description

They play with each other by knocking their large tusks together. Their tusks break sometimes, but they grow back so quickly that it isn't a concern.

### Special Moves

Slash, Dragon Claw, Leer

**Evolution**

AXEW → FRAXURE → HAXORUS

# FRAXURE

Its skin is as hard as a suit of armor. Fraxure's favorite strategy is to tackle its opponents, stabbing them with its tusks at the same time.

## Axe Jaw Pokémon

| POKÉDEX NO. | 611 |
|---|---|
| TYPE | Dragon |
| ABILITY | Rivalry, Mold Breaker |
| HEIGHT | 3'03" |
| WEIGHT | 79.4 lbs |

### Description

After battle, this Pokémon carefully sharpens its tusks on river rocks. It needs to take care of its tusks—if one breaks, it will never grow back.

### Special Moves

Dragon Pulse, Crunch, Swords Dance

Evolution

AXEW → FRAXURE → HAXORUS

001-100
101-200
201-300
401-442
443-500
501-600
601-700
701-800
801-898

# HAXORUS

**Axe Jaw Pokémon**

**POKÉDEX NO.** 612

| TYPE | Dragon |
|---|---|
| ABILITY | Rivalry, Mold Breaker |
| HEIGHT | 5'11" |
| WEIGHT | 232.6 lbs |

Its resilient tusks are its pride and joy. It licks up dirt to take in the minerals it needs to keep its tusks in top condition.

### Description

While usually kindhearted, it can be terrifying if angered. Tusks that can slice through steel beams are how Haxorus deals with its adversaries.

### Special Moves

Dual Chop, Guillotine, Outrage

**Evolution**

AXEW → FRAXURE → HAXORUS

# CUBCHOO

| | |
|---|---|
| **Chill Pokémon** | |
| **POKÉDEX NO.** | **613** |
| **TYPE** | Ice |
| **ABILITY** | Snow Cloak, Slush Rush |
| **HEIGHT** | 1'08" |
| **WEIGHT** | 18.7 lbs |

It sniffles before performing a move, using its frosty snot to provide an icy element to any move that needs it.

## Description

When this Pokémon is in good health, its snot becomes thicker and stickier. It will smear its snot on anyone it doesn't like.

## Special Moves

Powder Snow, Icy Wind, Fury Swipes

**Evolution**

CUBCHOO → BEARTIC

001-100
101-200
201-300
401-442
443-500
501-600
601-700
701-800
801-898

# BEARTIC

It swims energetically through frigid seas. When it gets tired, it freezes the seawater with its breath so it can rest on the ice.

## Freezing Pokémon

| POKÉDEX NO. | 614 |
|---|---|
| TYPE | Ice |
| ABILITY | Snow Cloak, Slush Rush |
| HEIGHT | 8'06" |
| WEIGHT | 573.2 lbs |

### Description

It swims through frigid seas, searching for prey. From its frozen breath, it forms icy fangs that are harder than steel.

### Special Moves

Icicle Crash, Sheer Cold, Superpower

Evolution

CUBCHOO

→

BEARTIC

# CRYOGONAL

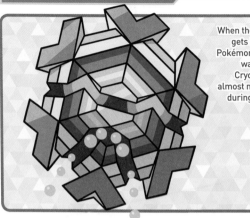

When the weather gets hot, these Pokémon turn into water vapor. Cryogonal are almost never seen during summer.

001-100
101-200
201-300
401-442
443-500
501-600
601-700
701-800
801-898

| Crystalizing Pokémon | |
|---|---|
| **POKÉDEX NO.** | **615** |
| TYPE | Ice |
| ABILITY | Levitate |
| HEIGHT | 3'07" |
| WEIGHT | 326.3 lbs |

### Description

With its icy chains, Cryogonal freezes those it encounters. It then takes its victims away to somewhere unknown.

### Special Moves

Freeze-Dry, Icy Shard, Night Slash

**Evolution**

CRYOGONAL

Does not evolve

203

# SHELMET

It has a strange physiology that responds to electricity. When it's together with Karrablast, * Shelmet evolves for some reason.

## Snail Pokémon

| | |
|---|---|
| POKÉDEX NO. | 616 |
| TYPE | Bug |
| ABILITY | Hydration, Shell Armor |
| HEIGHT | 1'04" |
| WEIGHT | 17.0 lbs |

### Description

When attacked, it tightly shuts the lid of its shell. This reaction fails to protect it from Karrablast, however, because they can still get into the shell.

### Special Moves

Absorb, Bug Buzz, Mega Drain

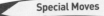

Evolution

SHELMET → ACCELGOR

 *Karrablast: A Pokémon you'll find on page 176.

# ACCELGOR

Discarding its shell made it nimble. To keep itself from dehydration, it wraps its body in bands of membrane.

| Shell Out Pokémon | |
|---|---|
| POKÉDEX NO. | **617** |
| TYPE | Bug |
| ABILITY | Hydration, Sticky Hold |
| HEIGHT | 2'07" |
| WEIGHT | 55.8 lbs |

## Description

It moves with blinding speed and lobs poison at foes. Featuring Accelgor as a main character is a surefire way to make a movie or comic popular.

## Special Moves

Water Shuriken, Double Team, Toxic

001-100
101-200
201-300
401-442
443-500
501-600
601-700
701-800
801-898

**Evolution**

SHELMET

ACCELGOR

# STUNFISK

| Trap Pokémon | |
|---|---|
| **POKÉDEX NO.** | **618** |
| **TYPE** | Ground, Electric |
| **ABILITY** | Static, Limber |
| **HEIGHT** | 2'04" |
| **WEIGHT** | 24.3 lbs |

For some reason, this Pokémon smiles slightly when it emits a strong electric current from the yellow markings on its body.

### Description

Thanks to bacteria that lived in the mud flats* with it, this Pokémon developed the organs it uses to generate electricity.

### Special Moves

Thunder Shock, Fissure, Mud Shot

**Evolution**  Does not evolve

STUNFISK

*Mud flat: A coastal wetland that is revealed at low tide.

# STUNFISK
## GALARIAN FORM

| Trap Pokémon | |
| --- | --- |
| POKÉDEX NO. | 618 |
| TYPE | Ground, Steel |
| ABILITY | Mimicry |
| HEIGHT | 2'04" |
| WEIGHT | 45.2 lbs |

Living in mud with a high iron content has given it a strong steel body.

### Description

Its conspicuous lips lure prey in as it lies in wait in the mud. When prey gets close, Stunfisk clamps its jagged steel fins down on it.

### Special Moves

Snap Trap, Metal Claw, Mud Shot

**Evolution**

STUNFISK
(GALARIAN FORM)

Does not evolve

001-100
101-200
201-300
401-442
443-500
501-600
601-700
701-800
801-898

# MIENFOO

Though small, Mienfoo's temperament is fierce. Any creature that approaches Mienfoo carelessly will be met with a flurry of attacks.

## Martial Arts Pokémon

| POKÉDEX NO. | 619 |
|---|---|
| TYPE | Fighting |
| ABILITY | Inner Focus, Regenerator |
| HEIGHT | 2'11" |
| WEIGHT | 44.1 lbs |

### Description

In one minute, a well-trained Mienfoo can chop with its arms more than 100 times.

### Special Moves

U-turn, Drain Punch, Hone Claws

**Evolution**

MIENFOO → MIENSHAO

# MIENSHAO

Delivered at blinding speeds, kicks from this Pokémon can shatter massive boulders into tiny pieces.

| Martial Arts Pokémon | |
|---|---|
| **POKÉDEX NO.** | **620** |
| TYPE | Fighting |
| ABILITY | Inner Focus, Regenerator |
| HEIGHT | 4'07" |
| WEIGHT | 78.3 lbs |

## Description

When Mienshao comes across a truly challenging opponent, it will lighten itself by biting off the fur on its arms.

## Special Moves

Force Palm, Aura Sphere, Fury Swipes

**Evolution**

 ➡

MIENFOO          MIENSHAO

001-100
101-200
201-300
401-442
501-600
601-700
801-898

# DRUDDIGON

Druddigon lives in caves, but it never skips sunbathing—it won't be able to move if its body gets too cold.

| Cave Pokémon | |
|---|---|
| POKÉDEX NO. | **621** |
| TYPE | Dragon |
| ABILITY | Rough Skin, Sheer Force |
| HEIGHT | 5'03" |
| WEIGHT | 306.4 lbs |

### Description

Druddigon are vicious and cunning. They take up residence in nests dug out by other Pokémon, treating the stolen nests as their own lairs.

### Special Moves

Dragon Tail, Superpower, Metal Claw

**Evolution**

DRUDDIGON

Does not evolve

# GOLETT

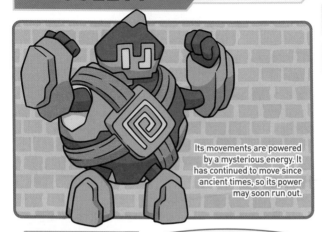

Its movements are powered by a mysterious energy. It has continued to move since ancient times, so its power may soon run out.

## Automaton Pokémon

| POKÉDEX NO. | 622 |
|---|---|
| TYPE | Ground, Ghost |
| ABILITY | Iron Fist, Klutz |
| HEIGHT | 3'03" |
| WEIGHT | 202.8 lbs |

### Description

They were sculpted from clay in ancient times. No one knows why, but some of them are driven to continually line up boulders.

### Special Moves

Mega Punch, Night Shade, Stomping Tantrum

Evolution

GOLETT

GOLURK

# GOLURK

**Automaton Pokémon**

| POKÉDEX NO. | **623** |
| --- | --- |
| TYPE | Ground, Ghost |
| ABILITY | Iron Fist, Klutz |
| HEIGHT | 9'02" |
| WEIGHT | 727.5 lbs |

Artillery platforms built into the walls of ancient castles served as perches from which Golurk could fire energy beams.

### Description

There's a theory that inside Golurk is a perpetual motion machine* that produces limitless energy, but this belief hasn't been proven.

### Special Moves

Phantom Force, High Horsepower, Earthquake

**Evolution**

GOLETT → GOLURK

*Perpetual motion machine: A device or machine that continues to move forever.

# PAWNIARD

## Sharp Blade Pokémon

| | |
|---|---|
| **POKÉDEX NO.** | **624** |
| **TYPE** | Dark, Steel |
| **ABILITY** | Inner Focus, Defiant |
| **HEIGHT** | 1'08" |
| **WEIGHT** | 22.5 lbs |

### Description

A pack of these Pokémon forms to serve a Bisharp boss. Each Pawniard trains diligently, dreaming of one day taking the lead.

It uses river stones to maintain the cutting edges of the blades covering its body. These sharpened blades allow it to bring down opponents.

### Special Moves

Slash, Fury Cutter, Metal Claw

**Evolution**

PAWNIARD → BISHARP

001-100
101-200
201-300
401-442
443-500
501-600
601-700
701-800
801-898

# BISHARP

### Sword Blade Pokémon

| POKÉDEX NO. | 625 |
|---|---|
| **TYPE** | Dark, Steel |
| **ABILITY** | Inner Focus, Defiant |
| **HEIGHT** | 5'03" |
| **WEIGHT** | 154.3 lbs |

Violent conflicts erupt between Bisharp and Fraxure* over places where sharpening stones can be found.

### Description

It's accompanied by a large retinue of Pawniard.** Bisharp keeps a keen eye on its minions, ensuring none of them even think of double-crossing it.

### Special Moves

Metal Burst, Night Slash, Guillotine

**Evolution**

PAWNIARD → BISHARP

*Fraxure: A Pokémon you'll find on page 199. **Pawniard: A Pokémon you'll find on page 213.

# BOUFFALANT

These Pokémon live in herds of about 20 individuals. Bouffalant that betray the herd will lose the hair on their heads for some reason.

## Bash Buffalo Pokémon

| | |
|---|---|
| POKÉDEX NO. | **626** |
| TYPE | Normal |
| ABILITY | Reckless, Sap Sipper |
| HEIGHT | 5'03" |
| WEIGHT | 208.6 lbs |

### Description

These Pokémon can crush a car with no more than a headbutt. Bouffalant with more hair on their heads hold higher positions within the herd.

### Special Moves

Head Charge, Giga Impact, Revenge

Evolution

BOUFFALANT

Does not evolve

001-100
101-200
201-300
401-442
443-500
501-600
601-700
701-800
801-898

# RUFFLET

A combative Pokémon, it's ready to pick a fight with anyone. It has talons that can crush hard berries.

| Eaglet Pokémon | |
|---|---|
| POKÉDEX NO. | **627** |
| TYPE | Normal, Flying |
| ABILITY | Keen Eye, Sheer Force |
| HEIGHT | 1'08" |
| WEIGHT | 23.1 lbs |

## Description

If it spies a strong Pokémon, Rufflet can't resist challenging it to a battle. But if Rufflet loses, it starts bawling.

## Special Moves

Whirlwind, Aerial Ace, Wing Attack

**Evolution**

RUFFLET

BRAVIARY

# BRAVIARY

| | |
|---|---|
| **Valiant Pokémon** | |
| **POKÉDEX NO.** | **628** |
| **TYPE** | Normal, Flying |
| **ABILITY** | Keen Eye, Sheer Force |
| **HEIGHT** | 4'11" |
| **WEIGHT** | 90.4 lbs |

001-100
101-200
201-300
401-442
443-500
501-600
601-700
701-800
801-898

### Description

Known for its bravery and pride, this majestic Pokémon is often seen as a motif for various kinds of emblems.

Because this Pokémon is hotheaded and belligerent, it's Corviknight* that's taken the role of transportation in Galar.

### Special Moves

Crush Claw, Brave Bird, Thrash

**Evolution**

  →

RUFFLET        BRAVIARY

*Corviknight: A Pokémon you'll find on page 443.

217

# VULLABY

Vullaby grow quickly. Bones that have gotten too small for older Vullaby to wear often get passed down to younger ones in the nest.

## Diapered Pokémon

| | |
|---|---|
| **POKÉDEX NO.** | **629** |
| TYPE | Dark, Flying |
| ABILITY | Big Pecks, Overcoat |
| HEIGHT | 1'08" |
| WEIGHT | 19.8 lbs |

### Description

It wears a bone to protect its rear. It often squabbles with others of its kind over particularly comfy bones.

### Special Moves

Gust, Nasty Plot, Knock Off

**Evolution**

VULLABY

MANDIBUZZ

# MANDIBUZZ

They adorn themselves with bones. There seem to be fashion trends among them, as different bones come into and fall out of popularity.

## Bone Vulture Pokémon

| POKÉDEX NO. | **630** |
|---|---|
| TYPE | Dark, Flying |
| ABILITY | Big Pecks, Overcoat |
| HEIGHT | 3'11" |
| WEIGHT | 87.1 lbs |

### Description

Although it's a bit of a ruffian, this Pokémon will take lost Vullaby under its wing and care for them till they're ready to leave the nest.

### Special Moves

Bone Rush, Sky Attack, Defog

Evolution

VULLABY

MANDIBUZZ

001-100
101-200
201-300
401-442
443-500
501-600
601-700
701-800
801-898

# HEATMOR

There's a hole in its tail that allows it to draw in the air it needs to keep its fire burning. If the hole gets blocked, this Pokémon will fall ill.

## Anteater Pokémon

| POKÉDEX NO. | 631 |
|---|---|
| TYPE | Fire |
| ABILITY | Flash Fire, Gluttony |
| HEIGHT | 4'07" |
| WEIGHT | 127.9 lbs |

### Description

It breathes through a hole in its tail while it burns with an internal fire. Durant* is its prey.

### Special Moves

Fire Lash, Fury Swipes, Swallow

**Evolution**

HEATMOR

Does not evolve

*Durant: A Pokémon you'll find on page 221.

# DURANT

With their large mandibles, these Pokémon can crunch their way through rock. They work together to protect their eggs from Sandaconda.*

| Iron Ant Pokémon | |
|---|---|
| **POKÉDEX NO.** | **632** |
| **TYPE** | Bug, Steel |
| **ABILITY** | Swarm, Hustle |
| **HEIGHT** | 1'00" |
| **WEIGHT** | 72.8 lbs |

### Description

They lay their eggs deep inside their nests. When attacked by Heatmor,** they retaliate using their massive mandibles.

### Special Moves

X-Scissor, Guillotine, Iron Defense

**Evolution**

DURANT

Does not evolve

---

*Sandaconda: A Pokémon you'll find on page 470. **Heatmor: A Pokémon you'll find on page 220.

# DEINO

Because it can't see, this Pokémon is constantly biting at everything it touches, trying to keep track of its surroundings.

## Irate Pokémon

| | |
|---|---|
| POKÉDEX NO. | **633** |
| TYPE | Dark, Dragon |
| ABILITY | Hustle |
| HEIGHT | 2'07" |
| WEIGHT | 38.1 lbs |

## Description

When it encounters something, its first urge is usually to bite it. If it likes what it tastes, it will commit the associated scent to memory.

## Special Moves

Bite, Dragon Breath, Focus Energy

Evolution

DEINO → ZWEILOUS → HYDREIGON

# ZWEILOUS

While hunting for prey, Zweilous wanders its territory, its two heads often bickering over which way to go.

## Hostile Pokémon

| POKÉDEX NO. | 634 |
|---|---|
| TYPE | Dark, Dragon |
| ABILITY | Hustle |
| HEIGHT | 4'07" |
| WEIGHT | 110.2 lbs |

### Description

Their two heads will fight each other over a single piece of food. Zweilous are covered in scars even without battling others.

### Special Moves

Double Hit, Body Slam, Crunch

001-100
101-200
201-300
401-442
443-500
501-600
601-700
701-800
801-898

Evolution

DEINO → ZWEILOUS → HYDREIGON

# HYDREIGON

### Brutal Pokémon

| | |
|---|---|
| **POKÉDEX NO.** | **635** |
| **TYPE** | Dark, Dragon |
| **ABILITY** | Levitate |
| **HEIGHT** | 5'11" |
| **WEIGHT** | 352.7 lbs |

The three heads take turns sinking their teeth into the opponent. Their attacks won't slow until their target goes down.

### Description

There are a slew of stories about villages that were destroyed by Hydreigon. It bites anything that moves.

### Special Moves

Dragon Rush, Hyper Beam, Outrage

**Evolution**

**DEINO**

→

**ZWEILOUS**

→

**HYDREIGON**

# LARVESTA

Larvesta's body is warm all over. It spouts fire from the tips of its horns to intimidate predators and scare prey.

## Torch Pokémon

| | |
|---|---|
| POKÉDEX NO. | **636** |
| TYPE | Bug, Fire |
| ABILITY | Flame Body |
| HEIGHT | 3'07" |
| WEIGHT | 63.5 lbs |

### Description

The people of ancient times believed that Larvesta fell from the sun.

### Special Moves

Ember, Flame Charge, Struggle Bug

**Evolution**

LARVESTA → VOLCARONA

001-100
101-200
201-300
401-442
443-500
501-600
601-700
701-800
801-898

# VOLCARONA

This Pokémon emerges from a cocoon formed of raging flames. Ancient murals depict Volcarona as a deity of fire.

## Sun Pokémon

| POKÉDEX NO. | **637** |
|---|---|
| TYPE | Bug, Fire |
| ABILITY | Flame Body |
| HEIGHT | 5'03" |
| WEIGHT | 101.4 lbs |

## Description

Volcarona scatters burning scales. Some say it does this to start fires. Others say it's trying to rescue those that suffer in the cold.

## Special Moves

Quiver Dance, Flare Blitz, Fire Blast

**Evolution**

  →

LARVESTA          VOLCARONA

# COBALION

**Iron Will Pokémon**

| POKÉDEX NO. | **638** | |
|---|---|---|
| **TYPE** | Steel, Fighting | |
| **ABILITY** | Justified | |
| **HEIGHT** | 6'11" | |
| **WEIGHT** | 551.2 lbs | |

This Pokémon appears in a legend alongside Terrakion* and Virizion,** fighting against humans in defense of the Unova region's Pokémon.

001-100
101-200
201-300
401-442
443-500
501-600
601-700
701-800
801-898

## Description

From the moment it's born, this Pokémon radiates the air of a leader. Its presence will calm even vicious foes.

## Special Moves

Sacred Sword, Metal Burst, Double Kick

**Evolution**

COBALION

 Does not evolve

*Terrakion: A Pokémon you'll find on page 228. **Virizion: A Pokémon you'll find on page 229.

# TERRAKION

| Cavern Pokémon | |
|---|---|
| POKÉDEX NO. | **639** |
| TYPE | Rock, Fighting |
| ABILITY | Justified |
| HEIGHT | 6'03" |
| WEIGHT | 573.2 lbs |

In Unovan legend, Terrakion battled against humans in an effort to protect other Pokémon.

### Description

It has phenomenal power. It will mercilessly crush anyone or anything that bullies small Pokémon.

### Special Moves

Sacred Sword, Take Down, Stone Edge

**Evolution**

TERRAKION

Does not evolve

# VIRIZION

**Grassland Pokémon**

| POKÉDEX NO. | 640 |
| --- | --- |
| **TYPE** | Grass, Fighting |
| **ABILITY** | Justified |
| **HEIGHT** | 6'07" |
| **WEIGHT** | 440.9 lbs |

A legend tells of this Pokémon working with Cobalion* and Terrakion** to protect the Pokémon of the Unova region.

## Description

It darts around opponents with a flurry of quick movements, slicing them up with its horns.

## Special Moves

Sacred Sword, Leaf Blade, Double Kick

001-100

101-200

201-300

401-442

443-500

501-600

601-700

701-800

801-898

**Evolution**

VIRIZION

Does not evolve

*Cobalion: A Pokémon you'll find on page 227. **Terrakion: A Pokémon you'll find on page 228.

229

# TORNADUS

**INCARNATE FORME**

| | |
|---|---|
| **Cyclone Pokémon** | |
| **POKÉDEX NO.** | **641** |
| **TYPE** | Flying |
| **ABILITY** | Prankster |
| **HEIGHT** | 4'11" |
| **WEIGHT** | 138.9 lbs |

Tornadus expels massive energy from its tail, causing severe storms. Its power is great enough to blow houses away.

### Description

The lower half of its body is wrapped in a cloud of energy. It zooms through the sky at 200 mph.

### Special Moves

Air Slash, Hammer Arm, Hurricane

**Evolution**

TORNADUS
(INCARNATE FORME)

Does not evolve

# TORNADUS

## THERIAN FORME

Tornadus expels massive energy from its tail, causing severe storms. Its power is great enough to blow houses away.

| Cyclone Pokémon | |
|---|---|
| POKÉDEX NO. | **641** |
| TYPE | Flying |
| ABILITY | Regenerator |
| HEIGHT | 4'07" |
| WEIGHT | 138.9 lbs |

### Description

In every direction it flies, creating winds so powerful, they blow everything away.

### Special Moves

Air Slash, Tailwind, Agility

**Evolution**

TORNADUS
(THERIAN FORME)

Does not evolve

001-100
101-200
201-300
401-442
443-500
501-600
601-700
701-800
801-898

# THUNDURUS

## INCARNATE FORME

| | |
|---|---|
| **Bolt Strike Pokémon** | |
| **POKÉDEX NO.** | **642** |
| TYPE | Electric, Flying |
| ABILITY | Prankster |
| HEIGHT | 4'11" |
| WEIGHT | 134.5 lbs |

The spikes on its tail discharge immense bolts of lightning. It flies around the Unova region firing off lightning bolts.

### Description

As it flies around, it shoots lightning all over the place and causes forest fires. It is therefore disliked.

### Special Moves

Volt Switch, Hammer Arm, Thunder

**Evolution**

Does not evolve

**THUNDURUS**
**(INCARNATE FORME)**

# THUNDURUS

THERIAN FORME

The spikes on its tail discharge immense bolts of lightning. It flies around the Unova region firing off lightning bolts.

| Bolt Strike Pokémon | |
|---|---|
| POKÉDEX NO. | 642 |
| TYPE | Electric, Flying |
| ABILITY | Volt Absorb |
| HEIGHT | 9'10" |
| WEIGHT | 134.5 lbs |

## Description

Countless charred remains mar the landscape of places through which Thundurus has passed.

## Special Moves

Shock Wave, Charge, Volt Switch

Evolution

THUNDURUS
[THERIAN FORME]

Does not evolve

# RESHIRAM

### Vast White Pokémon

| | |
|---|---|
| **POKÉDEX NO.** | **643** |
| **TYPE** | Dragon, Fire |
| **ABILITY** | Turboblaze |
| **HEIGHT** | 10'06" |
| **WEIGHT** | 727.5 lbs |

Reshiram
Overdrive Mode

According to myth, if people ignore truth and let themselves become consumed by greed, Reshiram will arrive to burn their kingdoms down.

### Description

Flames spew from its tail as it flies through the sky like a jet airplane. It's said that this Pokémon will scorch the world.

### Special Moves

Blue Flare,
Fusion Flame, Fire Blast

**Evolution**

RESHIRAM

Does not evolve

# ZEKROM

### Deep Black Pokémon

| POKÉDEX NO. | **644** |
| --- | --- |
| **TYPE** | Dragon, Electric |
| **ABILITY** | Teravolt |
| **HEIGHT** | 9'06" |
| **WEIGHT** | 760.6 lbs |

**Zekrom Overdrive Mode**

Mythology tells us that if people lose the righteousness in their hearts, their kingdoms will be razed by Zekrom's lightning.

### Description

When the interior part of its tail spins like a motor, Zekrom can generate many bolts of lightning to blast its surroundings.

### Special Moves

Bolt Strike, Fusion Bolt, Thunderbolt

**Evolution**

**ZEKROM**

Does not evolve

001-100
101-200
201-300
401-442
443-500
501-600
601-700
701-800
801-898

# LANDORUS

### INCARNATE FORME

| Abundance Pokémon | |
|---|---|
| POKÉDEX NO. | **645** |
| TYPE | Ground, Flying |
| ABILITY | Sand Force |
| HEIGHT | 4'11" |
| WEIGHT | 149.9 lbs |

Lands visited by Landorus grant such bountiful crops that it has been hailed as the Guardian of the Fields.

### Description

From the forces of lightning and wind, it creates energy to give nutrients to the soil and make the land abundant.

### Special Moves

Hammer Arm, Stone Edge, Fissure

**Evolution**  Does not evolve

LANDORUS
(INCARNATE FORME)

# LANDORUS

### THERIAN FORME

Lands visited by Landorus grant such bountiful crops that it has been hailed as the Guardian of the Fields.

| Abundance Pokémon | |
|---|---|
| **POKÉDEX NO.** | **645** |
| **TYPE** | Ground, Flying |
| **ABILITY** | Intimidate |
| **HEIGHT** | 4'03" |
| **WEIGHT** | 149.9 lbs |

### Description

The energy that comes pouring from its tail increases the nutrition in the soil, making crops grow to great size.

### Special Moves

Hammer Arm, Earth Power, Outrage

**Evolution**

LANDORUS
(THERIAN FORME)

Does not evolve

001-100
101-200
201-300
401-442
443-500
501-600
601-700
701-800
801-898

# KYUREM

**Boundary Pokémon**

| POKÉDEX NO. | 646 |
|---|---|
| TYPE | Dragon, Ice |
| ABILITY | Pressure |
| HEIGHT | 9'10" |
| WEIGHT | 716.5 lbs |

### Description

Dwelling within it is a power even greater than that of Reshiram* and Zekrom,** but the extreme cold keeps that power bound.

### Special Moves

Glaciate, Sheer Cold, Blizzard

It appears that this Pokémon uses its powers over ice to freeze its own body in order to stabilize its cellular structure.

**Evolution**

**KYUREM**

 Does not evolve

*Reshiram: A Pokémon you'll find on page 234. **Zekrom: A Pokémon you'll find on page 235.

# KYUREM

WHITE KYUREM

## Boundary Pokémon

| POKÉDEX NO. | 646 |
|---|---|

| TYPE | Dragon, Ice |
|---|---|
| ABILITY | Turboblaze |
| HEIGHT | 11'10" |
| WEIGHT | 716.5 lbs |

001-100
101-200
201-300
401-442
443-500
501-600
601-700
701-800
801-898

White Kyurem
Overdrive Mode

It has foreseen that a world of truth will arrive for people and Pokémon. It strives to protect that future.

### Description

The sameness of Reshiram's* and Kyurem's genes allowed Kyurem to absorb Reshiram. Kyurem can now use the power of both fire and ice.

### Special Moves

Ice Burn, Fusion Flare, Blizzard

**Evolution**

KYUREM
[WHITE KYUREM]

Does not evolve

*Reshiram: A Pokémon you'll find on page 234.

# KYUREM

## BLACK KYUREM

### Boundary Pokémon

| POKÉDEX NO. | 646 |
|---|---|
| TYPE | Dragon, Ice |
| ABILITY | Teravolt |
| HEIGHT | 10'10" |
| WEIGHT | 716.5 lbs |

**Black Kyurem Overdrive Mode**

It's said that this Pokémon battles in order to protect the ideal world that will exist in the future for people and Pokémon.

### Description

The sameness of Zekrom's* and Kyurem's genes allowed Kyurem to absorb Zekrom. Kyurem can now use the power of both electricity and ice.

### Special Moves

Freeze Shock, Fusion Bolt, Blizzard

### Evolution

**KYUREM**
**(BLACK KYUREM)**

Does not evolve

*Zekrom: A Pokémon you'll find on page 231.

# KELDEO

## ORDINARY FORM

### Colt Pokémon

| POKÉDEX NO. | **647** |
|---|---|
| **TYPE** | Water, Fighting |
| **ABILITY** | Justified |
| **HEIGHT** | 4'07" |
| **WEIGHT** | 106.9 lbs |

001-100
101-200
201-300
401-442
443-500
501-600
601-700
701-800
801-898

They say that Keldeo must survive harsh battles and fully develop the horn on its forehead before this Pokémon's true power will awaken.

### Description

Cobalion,* Terrakion,** and Virizion*** taught this Pokémon how to fight. It dashes across the world, seeking more opportunities to further its training.

### Special Moves

Sacred Sword, Aqua Tail, Double Kick

### Evolution

**KELDEO**
(ORDINARY FORM)

Does not evolve

*Cobalion: A Pokémon you'll find on page 227. **Terrakion: A Pokémon you'll find on page 228. ***Virizion: A Pokémon you'll find on page 229.

# KELDEO

## RESOLUTE FORM

| | |
|---|---|
| **Colt Pokémon** | |
| **POKÉDEX NO.** | **647** |
| **TYPE** | Water, Fighting |
| **ABILITY** | Justified |
| **HEIGHT** | 4'07" |
| **WEIGHT** | 106.9 lbs |

## Description

Keldeo has strengthened its resolve for battle, filling its body with power and changing its form.

The power that lay hidden in its body now covers its horn, turning it into a sword that can slice though anything.

## Special Moves

Secret Sword, Sacred Sword, Double Kick

**Evolution**   Does not evolve

**KELDEO**
(RESOLUTE FORM)

# MELOETTA

## ARIA FORME

Melody Pokémon

| POKÉDEX NO. | **648** |
|---|---|
| TYPE | Normal, Psychic |
| ABILITY | Serene Grace |
| HEIGHT | 2'00" |
| WEIGHT | 14.3 lbs |

001-100
101-200
201-300
401-442
443-500
501-600
601-700
701-800
801-898

### Description

The melodies sung by Meloetta have the power to make Pokémon that hear them happy or sad.

Its melodies are sung with a special vocalization method that can control the feelings of those who hear it.

### Special Moves

Relic Song, Psychic, Sing

Evolution  Does not evolve

MELOETTA
(ARIA FORME)

# MELOETTA

## PIROUETTE FORME

### Melody Pokémon

| POKÉDEX NO. | **648** |
|---|---|
| **TYPE** | Normal, Fighting |
| **ABILITY** | Serene Grace |
| **HEIGHT** | 2'00" |
| **WEIGHT** | 14.3 lbs |

Many famous songs have been inspired by the melodies that Meloetta plays.

### Description

The melodies sung by Meloetta have the power to make Pokémon that hear them happy or sad.

### Special Moves

Relic Song, Wake-Up Slap, Sing

**Evolution**

MELOETTA
(PIROUETTE FORME)

Does not evolve

# GENESECT

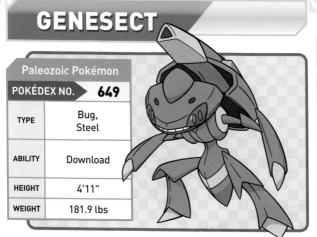

| Paleozoic Pokémon | |
|---|---|
| **POKÉDEX NO.** | **649** |
| **TYPE** | Bug, Steel |
| **ABILITY** | Download |
| **HEIGHT** | 4'11" |
| **WEIGHT** | 181.9 lbs |

This Pokémon existed 300 million years ago. Team Plasma* altered it and attached a cannon to its back.

## Description

This ancient bug Pokémon was altered by Team Plasma. They upgraded the cannon on its back.

## Special Moves

Techno Blast,
Zap Cannon, X-Scissor

**Evolution**  Does not evolve

GENESECT

---

*Team Plasma: An organization in the Unova region.

001-100
101-200
201-300
401-442
443-500
501-600
601-700
701-800
801-898

# CHESPIN

**Spiny Nut Pokémon**

| POKÉDEX NO. | 650 |
|---|---|
| TYPE | Grass |
| ABILITY | Overgrow |
| HEIGHT | 1'04" |
| WEIGHT | 19.8 lbs |

### Description

The quills on its head are usually soft. When it flexes them, the points become so hard and sharp that they can pierce rock.

Such a thick shell of wood covers its head and back that even a direct hit from a truck wouldn't faze it.

### Special Moves

Vine Whip, Body Slam, Leech Seed

Evolution

CHESPIN → QUILLADIN → CHESNAUGHT

# QUILLADIN

It relies on its sturdy shell to deflect predators' attacks. It counterattacks with its sharp quills.

001-100

101-200

201-300

401-442

443-500

501-600

601-700

701-800

801-898

## Spiny Armor Pokémon

| POKÉDEX NO. | 651 |
|---|---|
| TYPE | Grass |
| ABILITY | Overgrow |
| HEIGHT | 2'04" |
| WEIGHT | 63.9 lbs |

### Description

They strengthen their lower bodies by running into one another. They are very kind and won't start fights.

### Special Moves

Needle Arm, Pin Missile, Take Down

**Evolution**

CHESPIN → QUILLADIN → CHESNAUGHT

# CHESNAUGHT

**Spiny Armor Pokémon**

| | |
|---|---|
| **POKÉDEX NO.** | **652** |
| **TYPE** | Grass, Fighting |
| **ABILITY** | Overgrow |
| **HEIGHT** | 5'03" |
| **WEIGHT** | 198.4 lbs |

When it takes a defensive posture with its fists guarding its face, it can withstand a bomb blast.

### Description

Its Tackle is forceful enough to flip a 50-ton tank. It shields its allies from danger with its own body.

### Special Moves

Spiky Shield, Wood Hammer, Rollout

**Evolution**

CHESPIN ➡ QUILLADIN ➡ CHESNAUGHT

# FENNEKIN

## Fox Pokémon

| | |
|---|---|
| **POKÉDEX NO.** | **653** |
| **TYPE** | Fire |
| **ABILITY** | Blaze |
| **HEIGHT** | 1'04" |
| **WEIGHT** | 20.7 lbs |

Eating a twig fills it with energy, and its roomy ears give vent to air hotter than 390 degrees Fahrenheit.

### Description

As it walks, it munches on a twig in place of a snack. It intimidates opponents by puffing hot air out of its ears.

### Special Moves

Scratch, Fire Spin, Tail Whip

**Evolution**

FENNEKIN → BRAIXEN → DELPHOX

001-100
101-200
201-300
401-442
443-500
501-600
601-700
701-800
801-898

# BRAIXEN

It has a twig stuck in its tail. With friction from its tail fur, it sets the twig on fire and launches into battle.

## Fox Pokémon

| POKÉDEX NO. | **654** |
|---|---|
| TYPE | Fire |
| ABILITY | Blaze |
| HEIGHT | 3'03" |
| WEIGHT | 32.0 lbs |

### Description

When the twig is plucked from its tail, friction sets the twig alight. The flame is used to send signals to its allies.

### Special Moves

Flame Charge, Psybeam, Will-O-Wisp

Evolution

FENNEKIN → BRAIXEN → DELPHOX

# DELPHOX

**Fox Pokémon**

| POKÉDEX NO. | 655 |
|---|---|
| TYPE | Fire, Psychic |
| ABILITY | Blaze |
| HEIGHT | 4'11" |
| WEIGHT | 86.0 lbs |

Using psychic power, it generates a fiery vortex of 5,400 degrees Fahrenheit, incinerating foes swept into this whirl of flame.

### Description

It gazes into the flame at the tip of its branch to achieve a focused state, which allows it to see into the future.

### Special Moves

Mystical Fire, Fire Blast, Lucky Chant

**Evolution**

FENNEKIN

BRAIXEN

DELPHOX

001-100
101-200
201-300
401-442
663-500
501-600
601-700
701-800
801-898

# FROAKIE

| Bubble Frog Pokémon | |
|---|---|
| **POKÉDEX NO.** | **656** |
| **TYPE** | Water |
| **ABILITY** | Torrent |
| **HEIGHT** | 1'00" |
| **WEIGHT** | 15.4 lbs |

### Description

It protects its skin by covering its body in delicate bubbles. Beneath its happy-go-lucky air, it keeps a watchful eye on its surroundings.

### Special Moves

Pound, Water Pulse, Quick Attack

It secretes flexible bubbles from its chest and back. The bubbles reduce the damage it would otherwise take when attacked.

**Evolution**

FROAKIE → FROGADIER → GRENINJA

# FROGADIER

It can throw bubble-covered pebbles with precise control, hitting empty cans up to 100 feet away.

## Bubble Frog Pokémon

| POKÉDEX NO. | 657 |
| --- | --- |
| TYPE | Water |
| ABILITY | Torrent |
| HEIGHT | 2'00" |
| WEIGHT | 24.0 lbs |

### Description

Its swiftness is unparalleled. It can scale a tower of more than 2,000 feet in a minute's time.

### Special Moves

Water Pulse, Round, Fling

**Evolution**

 FROAKIE →  FROGADIER →  GRENINJA

001-100
101-200
201-300
401-442
443-500
501-600
601-700
701-800
801-898

# GRENINJA

### Ninja Pokémon

| | |
|---|---|
| **POKÉDEX NO.** | **658** |
| **TYPE** | Water, Dark |
| **ABILITY** | Torrent |
| **HEIGHT** | 4'11" |
| **WEIGHT** | 88.2 lbs |

It appears and vanishes with a ninja's grace. It toys with its enemies using swift movements, while slicing them with throwing stars of the sharpest water.

### Description

It creates throwing stars out of compressed water. When it spins them and throws them at high speed, these stars can split metal in two.

### Special Moves

Water Shuriken, Hydro Pump, Spikes

**Evolution**

FROAKIE

FROGADIER

GRENINJA

# BUNNELBY

It excels at digging holes. Using its ears, it can dig a nest 33 feet deep in one night.

| Digging Pokémon | |
|---|---|
| **POKÉDEX NO.** | **659** |
| TYPE | Normal |
| ABILITY | Pickup, Cheek Pouch |
| HEIGHT | 1'04" |
| WEIGHT | 11.0 lbs |

### Description

It's very sensitive to danger. The sound of Corviknight's* flapping will have Bunnelby digging a hole to hide underground in moments.

### Special Moves

Mud-Slap, Dig, Quick Attack

**Evolution**

BUNNELBY

DIGGERSBY

*Corviknight: A Pokémon you'll find on page 443.

# DIGGERSBY

The fur on its belly retains heat exceptionally well. People used to make heavy winter clothing from fur shed by this Pokémon.

| Digging Pokémon | |
|---|---|
| POKÉDEX NO. | **660** |
| TYPE | Normal, Ground |
| ABILITY | Pickup, Cheek Pouch |
| HEIGHT | 3'03" |
| WEIGHT | 93.5 lbs |

### Description

With power equal to an excavator, it can dig through dense bedrock. It's a huge help during tunnel construction.

### Special Moves

Super Fang, Hammer Arm, Bulldoze

Evolution

BUNNELBY

DIGGERSBY

# FLETCHLING

001-100
101-200
201-300
401-442
443-500
501-600
601-700
701-800
801-898

## Tiny Robin Pokémon

| POKÉDEX NO. | **661** |
|---|---|
| TYPE | Normal, Flying |
| ABILITY | Big Pecks |
| HEIGHT | 1'00" |
| WEIGHT | 3.7 lbs |

### Description

When this Pokémon gets excited, its body temperature increases sharply. If you touch a Fletchling with bare hands, you might get burned.

### Special Moves

Ember, Acrobatics, Agility

Its melodious cries are actually warnings. Fletchling will mercilessly peck at anything that enters its territory.

**Evolution**

FLETCHLING → FLETCHINDER → TALONFLAME

257

# FLETCHINDER

Fletchinder are exceedingly territorial and aggressive. These Pokémon fight among themselves over feeding grounds.

## Ember Pokémon

| POKÉDEX NO. | 662 |
| --- | --- |
| TYPE | Fire, Flying |
| ABILITY | Flame Body |
| HEIGHT | 2'04" |
| WEIGHT | 35.3 lbs |

### Description

Fletchinder launches ember into the den of its prey. When the prey comes leaping out, Fletchinder's sharp talons finish it off.

### Special Moves

Flame Charge, Fly, Roost

Evolution

FLETCHLING

FLETCHINDER

TALONFLAME

# TALONFLAME

Scorching Pokémon

| | |
|---|---|
| **POKÉDEX NO.** | **663** |
| **TYPE** | Fire, Flying |
| **ABILITY** | Flame Body |
| **HEIGHT** | 3'11" |
| **WEIGHT** | 54.0 lbs |

## Description

Talonflame mainly preys upon other bird Pokémon. To intimidate opponents, it sends embers spewing from gaps between its feathers.

Talonflame dives toward prey at speeds of up to 310 mph and assaults them with powerful kicks, giving the prey no chance to escape.

## Special Moves

Flare Blitz, Brave Bird, Tailwind

**Evolution**

FLETCHLING → FLETCHINDER → TALONFLAME

101-200
201-300
401-442
443-500
501-600
601-700
701-800
801-898

# SCATTERBUG

The powder that covers its body regulates its temperature, so it can live in any region or climate.

| Scatterbug Pokémon | |
|---|---|
| POKÉDEX NO. | **664** |
| TYPE | Bug |
| ABILITY | Shield Dust, Compound Eyes |
| HEIGHT | 1'00" |
| WEIGHT | 5.5 lbs |

## Description

When under attack from bird Pokémon, it spews a poisonous black powder that causes paralysis on contact.

## Special Moves

Tackle, String Shot, Stun Spore

**Evolution**

 SCATTERBUG →  SPEWPA →  VIVILLON

# SPEWPA

The beaks of birds can't begin to scratch its stalwart body. To defend itself, it spews powder.

## Scatterdust Pokémon

| | |
|---|---|
| POKÉDEX NO. | **665** |
| TYPE | Bug |
| ABILITY | Shed Skin |
| HEIGHT | 1'00" |
| WEIGHT | 18.5 lbs |

### Description

It lives hidden within thicket shadows. When predators attack, it quickly bristles the fur covering its body in an effort to threaten them.

### Special Moves

Protect,
Harden

**Evolution**

SCATTERBUG →
SPEWPA →
VIVILLON

# VIVILLON

The patterns on this Pokémon's wings depend on the climate and topography of its habitat. It scatters colorful scales.

## Scale Pokémon

| POKÉDEX NO. | **666** |
| --- | --- |
| TYPE | Bug, Flying |
| ABILITY | Shield Dust, Compound Eyes |
| HEIGHT | 3'11" |
| WEIGHT | 37.5 lbs |

### Description

Vivillon with many different patterns are found all over the world. These patterns are affected by the climate of their habitat.

### Special Moves

Gust, Draining Kiss, Quiver Dance

Evolution

SCATTERBUG    SPEWPA    VIVILLON

# VIVILLON WING PATTERNS

Ocean

Archipelago

High Plains

Sandstorm

Savanna

Jungle

Monsoon

Tundra

River

Sun

Continental

Garden

Meadow

Icy Snow

Fancy

Poké Ball

Marine

Elegant

Modern

Polar

001-100
101-200
201-300
401-442
443-500
501-600
601-700
701-800
801-898

# LITLEO

This hot-blooded Pokémon is filled with curiosity. When it gets angry or starts fighting, its short mane gets hot.

## Lion Cub Pokémon

| POKÉDEX NO. | 667 |
|---|---|
| TYPE | Fire, Normal |
| ABILITY | Rivalry, Unnerve |
| HEIGHT | 2'00" |
| WEIGHT | 29.8 lbs |

### Description

When they're young, they live with a pride. Once they're able to hunt prey on their own, they're kicked out and have to make their own way.

### Special Moves

Tackle, Fire Fang, Crunch

Evolution

LITLEO → PYROAR

# PYROAR

Male

## Royal Pokémon

| POKÉDEX NO. | 668 |
|---|---|
| TYPE | Fire, Normal |
| ABILITY | Rivalry, Unnerve |
| HEIGHT | 4'11" |
| WEIGHT | 179.7 lbs |

Female

### Description

The males are usually lazy, but when attacked by a strong foe, a male will protect its friends with no regard for its own safety.

The temperature of its breath is over 10,000 degrees Fahrenheit, but Pyroar doesn't use it on its prey. This Pokémon prefers to eat raw meat.

### Special Moves

Flamethrower, Overheat, Take Down

Evolution

LITLEO → PYROAR

001-100
101-200
201-300
401-442
443-500
501-600
601-700
701-800
801-898

265

# FLABÉBÉ

**Single Bloom Pokémon**

| | |
|---|---|
| **POKÉDEX NO.** | **669** |
| **TYPE** | Fairy |
| **ABILITY** | Flower Veil |
| **HEIGHT** | 0'04" |
| **WEIGHT** | 0.2 lbs |

Red Flower

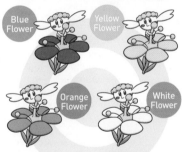

Blue Flower

Yellow Flower

Orange Flower

White Flower

Flabébé wears a crown made from pollen it's collected from its flower. The crown has hidden healing properties.

## Description

It's not safe without the power of a flower, but it will keep traveling around until it finds one with the color and shape it wants.

## Special Moves

Tackle, Vine Whip, Razor Leaf

**Evolution**

FLABÉBÉ → FLOETTE → FLORGES

# FLOETTE

**Single Bloom Pokémon**

| POKÉDEX NO. | 670 |
| --- | --- |
| **TYPE** | Fairy |
| **ABILITY** | Flower Veil |
| **HEIGHT** | 0'08" |
| **WEIGHT** | 2.0 lbs |

Red Flower

Blue Flower
Yellow Flower
Orange Flower
White Flower

It gives its own power to flowers, pouring its heart into caring for them. Floette never forgives anyone who messes up a flower bed.

## Description

It raises flowers and uses them as weapons. The more gorgeous the bloom, the more power it contains.

## Special Moves

Magical Leaf, Vine Whip, Wish

**Evolution**

FLABÉBÉ → FLOETTE → FLORGES

001-100
101-200
201-300
401-442
443-500
501-600
601-700
701-800
801-898

# FLORGES

**Garden Pokémon**

| POKÉDEX NO. | 671 |
|---|---|
| **TYPE** | Fairy |
| **ABILITY** | Flower Veil |
| **HEIGHT** | 3'07" |
| **WEIGHT** | 22.0 lbs |

Red Flower

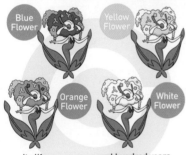

Blue Flower

Yellow Flower

Orange Flower

White Flower

Its life can span several hundred years. It's said to devote its entire life to protecting gardens.

### Description

It controls the flowers it grows. The petal blizzards that Florges triggers are overwhelming in their beauty and power.

### Special Moves

Moonblast, Petal Blizzard, Lucky Chant

**Evolution**

FLABÉBÉ → FLOETTE → FLORGES

# SKIDDO

Thought to be one of the first Pokémon to live in harmony with humans, it has a placid disposition.

| Mount Pokémon | |
|---|---|
| POKÉDEX NO. | 672 |
| TYPE | Grass |
| ABILITY | Sap Sipper |
| HEIGHT | 2'11" |
| WEIGHT | 68.3 lbs |

### Description

If it has sunshine and water, it doesn't need to eat, because it can generate energy from the leaves on its back.

### Special Moves

Tackle, Razor Leaf, Seed Bomb

Evolution

SKIDDO

GOGOAT

# GOGOAT

**Mount Pokémon**

| POKÉDEX NO. | 673 |
|---|---|

| TYPE | Grass |
|---|---|
| ABILITY | Sap Sipper |
| HEIGHT | 5'07" |
| WEIGHT | 200.6 lbs |

They inhabit mountainous regions.
The leader of the herd is decided by
a battle of clashing horns.

### Description

It can tell how its
Trainer is feeling by
subtle shifts in the
grip on its horns.This
empathetic sense
lets them run as if
one being.

### Special Moves

Horn Leech,
Leaf Blade, Take Down

**Evolution**

SKIDDO

GOGOAT

# PANCHAM

## Playful Pokémon

| POKÉDEX NO. | **674** |
|---|---|
| TYPE | Fighting |
| ABILITY | Iron Fist, Mold Breaker |
| HEIGHT | 2'00" |
| WEIGHT | 17.6 lbs |

It chooses a Pangoro as its master and then imitates its master's actions. This is how it learns to battle and hunt for prey.

### Description

Wanting to make sure it's taken seriously, Pancham's always giving others a glare. But if it's not focusing, it ends up smiling.

### Special Moves

Leer, Taunt, Low Sweep

**Evolution**

PANCHAM
→

PANGORO

001-100
101-200
201-300
401-442
443-500
501-600
601-700
701-800
801-898

# PANGORO

This Pokémon is quick to anger, and it has no problem using its prodigious strength to get its way. It lives for duels against Obstagoon.*

| Daunting Pokémon | |
|---|---|
| POKÉDEX NO. | **675** |
| TYPE | Fighting, Dark |
| ABILITY | Iron Fist, Mold Breaker |
| HEIGHT | 6'11" |
| WEIGHT | 299.8 lbs |

## Description

Using its leaf, Pangoro can predict the moves of its opponents. It strikes with punches that can turn a dump truck into scrap with just one hit.

## Special Moves

Night Slash, Bullet Punch, Parting Shot

**Evolution**

PANCHAM

PANGORO

*Obstagoon: A Pokémon you'll find on page 498.

# FURFROU

There was an era when aristocrats would compete to see who could trim their Furfrou's fur into the most exquisite style.

## Poodle Pokémon

| POKÉDEX NO. | 676 |
|---|---|
| TYPE | Normal |
| ABILITY | Fur Coat |
| HEIGHT | 3'11" |
| WEIGHT | 61.7 lbs |

### Description

Left alone, its fur will grow longer and longer, but it will only allow someone it trusts to cut it.

### Special Moves

Cotton Guard, Take Down, Odor Sleuth

Evolution

FURFROU

Does not evolve

001-100
101-200
201-300
401-442
443-500
501-600
601-700
701-800
801-898

273

# FURFROU TRIMS

**Furfrou's appearance can be changed by being groomed.
There are nine appearances in all.**

Kabuki Trim

Pharaoh Trim

La Reine Trim

Dandy Trim

Star Trim

Diamond Trim

Heart Trim

Matron Trim

Debutante Trim

# ESPURR

## Restraint Pokémon

| POKÉDEX NO. | **677** |
| --- | --- |
| TYPE | Psychic |
| ABILITY | Keen Eye, Infiltrator |
| HEIGHT | 1'00" |
| WEIGHT | 7.7 lbs |

Though Espurr's expression never changes, behind that blank stare is an intense struggle to contain its devastating psychic power.

001-100
101-200
201-300
401-442
443-500
501-600
601-700
701-800
801-898

### Description

There's enough psychic power in Espurr to send a wrestler flying, but because this power can't be controlled, Espurr finds it troublesome.

### Special Moves

Confusion, Light Screen, Disarming Voice

**Evolution**

ESPURR → MEOWSTIC (MALE)  MEOWSTIC (FEMALE)

# MEOWSTIC

## MALE

The defensive instinct of the males is strong. It's when they're protecting themselves or their partners that they unleash their full power.

## Constraint Pokémon

| POKÉDEX NO. | **678** |
|---|---|
| **TYPE** | Psychic |
| **ABILITY** | Keen Eye, Infiltrator |
| **HEIGHT** | 2'00" |
| **WEIGHT** | 18.7 lbs |

### Description

Revealing the eyelike patterns on the insides of its ears will unleash its psychic powers. It normally keeps the patterns hidden, however.

### Special Moves

Psyshock, Quick Guard, Helping Hand

### Evolution

 →

ESPURR    MEOWSTIC
[MALE]

# MEOWSTIC

FEMALE

If it doesn't hold back when it unleashes its psychic power, it can tear apart a tanker. Its unfriendliness is part of its charm.

| Constraint Pokémon | |
|---|---|
| **POKÉDEX NO.** | **678** |
| TYPE | Psychic |
| ABILITY | Keen Eye, Infiltrator |
| HEIGHT | 2'00" |
| WEIGHT | 18.7 lbs |

### Description

The females are a bit more selfish and aggressive than males. If they don't get what they want, they will torment you with their psychic abilities.

### Special Moves

Psyshock, Quick Guard, Helping Hand

**Evolution**

ESPURR

MEOWSTIC
(FEMALE)

001-100
101-200
201-300
401-442
443-500
501-600
601-700
701-800
801-898

# HONEDGE

The blue eye on the sword's handguard is the true body of Honedge. With its old cloth, it drains people's lives away.

## Sword Pokémon

| POKÉDEX NO. | 679 |
| --- | --- |
| TYPE | Steel, Ghost |
| ABILITY | No Guard |
| HEIGHT | 2'07" |
| WEIGHT | 4.4 lbs |

### Description

Honedge's soul once belonged to a person who was killed a long time ago by the sword that makes up Honedge's body.

### Special Moves

Slash, Retaliate, Iron Head

**Evolution**

HONEDGE → DOUBLADE → AEGISLASH (SHIELD FORME)

# DOUBLADE

The two swords employ a strategy of rapidly alternating between offense and defense to bring down their prey.

| Sword Pokémon | |
|---|---|
| **POKÉDEX NO.** | **680** |
| TYPE | Steel, Ghost |
| ABILITY | No Guard |
| HEIGHT | 2'07" |
| WEIGHT | 9.9 lbs |

### Description

Honedge evolves into twins. The two blades rub together to emit a metallic sound that unnerves opponents.

### Special Moves

Fury Cutter, Aerial Ace, Swords Dance

**Evolution**

HONEDGE

DOUBLADE

AEGISLASH
(SHIELD FORME)

# AEGISLASH

## SHIELD FORME

In this defensive stance, Aegislash uses its steel body and a force field of spectral power to reduce the damage of any attack.

| Royal Sword Pokémon | |
|---|---|
| **POKÉDEX NO.** | **681** |
| **TYPE** | Steel, Ghost |
| **ABILITY** | Stance Change |
| **HEIGHT** | 5'07" |
| **WEIGHT** | 116.8 lbs |

### Description

Its potent spectral powers allow it to manipulate others. It once used its powers to force people and Pokémon to build a kingdom to its liking.

### Special Moves

Sacred Sword, Iron Defense, King's Shield

**Evolution**

HONEDGE → DOUBLADE → AEGISLASH [SHIELD FORME]

# AEGISLASH

## BLADE FORME*

This stance is dedicated to offense. It can cleave any opponent with the strength and weight of its steel blade.

| Royal Sword Pokémon | |
|---|---|
| **POKÉDEX NO.** | **681** |
| **TYPE** | Steel, Ghost |
| **ABILITY** | Stance Change |
| **HEIGHT** | 5'07" |
| **WEIGHT** | 116.8 lbs |

### Description

Once upon a time, a king with an Aegislash reigned over the land. His Pokémon eventually drained him of life, and his kingdom fell with him.

### Special Moves

Sacred Sword, Shadow Sneak, King's Shield

**Evolution**

HONEDGE → DOUBLADE → AEGISLASH (SHIELD FORME)

*Blade Forme: Aegislash is usually in its Shield Forme and will change to Blade Forme when attacking.

001-100
101-200
201-300
401-442
443-500
501-600
601-700
701-800
801-898

# SPRITZEE

The scent its body gives off enraptures those who smell it. Noble ladies had no shortage of love for Spritzee.

## Perfume Pokémon

| POKÉDEX NO. | 682 |
|---|---|
| TYPE | Fairy |
| ABILITY | Healer |
| HEIGHT | 0'08" |
| WEIGHT | 1.1 lbs |

### Description

A scent pouch within this Pokémon's body allows it to create various scents. A change in its diet will alter the fragrance it produces.

### Special Moves

Sweet Scent, Sweet Kiss, Attract

Evolution

SPRITZEE → AROMATISSE

# AROMATISSE

The scents Aromatisse can produce range from sweet smells that bolster allies to foul smells that sap an opponent's will to fight.

## Fragrance Pokémon

| POKÉDEX NO. | 683 |
|---|---|
| TYPE | Fairy |
| ABILITY | Healer |
| HEIGHT | 2'07" |
| WEIGHT | 34.2 lbs |

### Description

The scent that it constantly emits from its fur is so powerful that this Pokémon's companions will eventually lose their sense of smell.

### Special Moves

Fairy Wind, Heal Pulse, Calm Mind

Evolution

SPRITZEE

AROMATISSE

001-100
101-200
201-300
401-442
443-500
501-600
601-700
701-800
801-898

# SWIRLIX

**Cotton Candy Pokémon**

| POKÉDEX NO. | **684** |
| --- | --- |
| TYPE | Fairy |
| ABILITY | Sweet Veil |
| HEIGHT | 1'04" |
| WEIGHT | 7.7 lbs |

The sweet smell of cotton candy perfumes Swirlix's fluffy fur. This Pokémon spits out sticky string to tangle up its enemies.

## Description

It eats its own weight in sugar every day. If it doesn't get enough sugar, it becomes incredibly grumpy.

## Special Moves

Sweet Scent, Draining Kiss, Play Rough

**Evolution**

SWIRLIX → SLURPUFF

# SLURPUFF

Slurpuff's fur contains a lot of air, making it soft to the touch and lighter than it looks.

001-100
101-200
201-300
401-442
443-500
501-600
601-700
701-800
801-898

## Meringue Pokémon

| POKÉDEX NO. | 685 |
| --- | --- |
| TYPE | Fairy |
| ABILITY | Sweet Veil |
| HEIGHT | 2'07" |
| WEIGHT | 11.0 lbs |

### Description

By taking in a person's scent, it can sniff out their mental and physical condition. It's hoped that this skill will have many medical applications.

### Special Moves

Cotton Guard, Energy Ball, Fake Tears

### Evolution

SWIRLIX

SLURPUFF

# INKAY

**Revolving Pokémon**

| | |
|---|---|
| **POKÉDEX NO.** | **686** |
| **TYPE** | Dark, Psychic |
| **ABILITY** | Suction Cups, Contrary |
| **HEIGHT** | 1'04" |
| **WEIGHT** | 7.7 lbs |

By exposing foes to the blinking of its luminescent spots, Inkay demoralizes them, and then it seizes the chance to flee.

## Description

It spins while making its luminescent spots flash. These spots allow it to communicate with others by using different patterns of light.

## Special Moves

Topsy-Turvy, Psybeam, Foul Play

**Evolution**

INKAY → MALAMAR

# MALAMAR

Gazing at its luminescent spots will quickly induce a hypnotic state, putting the observer under Malamar's control.

## Overturning Pokémon

| POKÉDEX NO. | **687** |
|---|---|
| TYPE | Dark, Psychic |
| ABILITY | Suction Cups, Contrary |
| HEIGHT | 4'11" |
| WEIGHT | 103.6 lbs |

### Description

It's said that Malamar's hypnotic powers played a role in certain history-changing events.

### Special Moves

Topsy-Turvy, Psycho Cut, Night Slash

### Evolution

 ➡

INKAY     MALAMAR

001-100
101-200
201-300
401-442
443-500
501-600
601-700
701-800
801-898

# BINACLE

| | |
|---|---|
| **Two-Handed Pokémon** | |
| **POKÉDEX NO.** | **688** |
| **TYPE** | Rock, Water |
| **ABILITY** | Sniper, Tough Claws |
| **HEIGHT** | 1'08" |
| **WEIGHT** | 68.3 lbs |

If the two Binacle don't work well together, both their offense and defense fall apart. Without good teamwork, they won't survive.

## Description

After two Binacle find a suitably sized rock, they adhere themselves to it and live together. They cooperate to gather food during high tide.

## Special Moves

Mud-Slap, Ancient Power, Fury Swipes

Evolution

 →

**BINACLE** → **BARBARACLE**

# BARBARACLE

Seven Binacle come together to form one Barbaracle. The Binacle that serves as the head gives orders to those serving as the limbs.

| Collective Pokémon | |
|---|---|
| **POKÉDEX NO.** | **689** |
| **TYPE** | Rock, Water |
| **ABILITY** | Sniper, Tough Claws |
| **HEIGHT** | 4'03" |
| **WEIGHT** | 211.6 lbs |

### Description

Having an eye on each palm allows it to keep watch in all directions. In a pinch, its limbs start to act on their own to ensure the enemy's defeat.

### Special Moves

Stone Edge, Cross Chop, Hone Claws

**Evolution**

BINACLE → BARBARACLE

001-100
101-200
201-300
401-442
443-500
501-600
601-700
701-800
801-898

# SKRELP

Skrelp looks like a piece of rotten seaweed, so it can blend in with seaweed drifting in the ocean and avoid being detected by enemies.

## Mock Kelp Pokémon

| POKÉDEX NO. | 690 |
| --- | --- |
| TYPE | Poison, Water |
| ABILITY | Poison Point, Poison Touch |
| HEIGHT | 1'08" |
| WEIGHT | 16.1 lbs |

### Description

It drifts in the ocean, blending in with floating seaweed. When other Pokémon come to feast on the seaweed, Skrelp feasts on them instead.

### Special Moves

Smokescreen, Acid, Water Gun

### Evolution

  SKRELP →  DRAGALGE

# DRAGALGE

Dragalge generates dragon energy by sticking the plume on its head out above the ocean's surface and bathing it in sunlight.

## Mock Kelp Pokémon

| POKÉDEX NO. | 691 |
|---|---|
| TYPE | Poison, Dragon |
| ABILITY | Poison Point, Poison Touch |
| HEIGHT | 5'11" |
| WEIGHT | 179.7 lbs |

### Description

Dragalge uses a poisonous liquid capable of corroding metal to send tankers that enter its territory to the bottom of the sea.

### Special Moves

Poison Tail, Toxic, Hydro Pump

Evolution

SKRELP

DRAGALGE

001-100
101-200
201-300
401-442
443-500
501-600
601-700
701-800
801-898

# CLAUNCHER

By detonating gas that accumulates in its right claw, this Pokémon launches water like a bullet. This is how Clauncher defeats its enemies.

## Water Gun Pokémon

| POKÉDEX NO. | 692 |
| --- | --- |
| TYPE | Water |
| ABILITY | Mega Launcher |
| HEIGHT | 1'08" |
| WEIGHT | 18.3 lbs |

### Description

Clauncher's claws can fall off during a battle, but they'll regenerate. The meat inside the claws is popular as a delicacy in Galar.

### Special Moves

Water Gun, Water Pulse, Muddy Water

Evolution

CLAUNCHER

CLAWITZER

# CLAWITZER

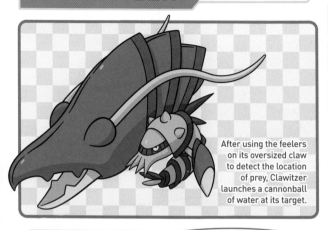

After using the feelers on its oversized claw to detect the location of prey, Clawitzer launches a cannonball of water at its target.

| Howitzer Pokémon | |
|---|---|
| POKÉDEX NO. | 693 |
| TYPE | Water |
| ABILITY | Mega Launcher |
| HEIGHT | 4'03" |
| WEIGHT | 77.8 lbs |

## Description

Clawitzer's right arm is a cannon that launches projectiles made of seawater. Shots from a Clawitzer's cannon arm can sink a tanker.

## Special Moves

Aqua Jet, Muddy Water, Aura Sphere

Evolution

 ➡️

CLAUNCHER      CLAWITZER

001-100
101-200
201-300
401-442
443-500
501-600
601-700
701-800
801-898

# HELIOPTILE

The sun powers this Pokémon's electricity generation. Interruption of that process stresses Helioptile to the point of weakness.

## Generator Pokémon

| POKÉDEX NO. | 694 |
|---|---|
| TYPE | Electric, Normal |
| ABILITY | Sand Veil, Dry Skin |
| HEIGHT | 1'08" |
| WEIGHT | 13.2 lbs |

### Description

When spread, the frills on its head act like solar panels, generating the power behind this Pokémon's electric moves.

### Special Moves

Mud Slap, Thunder Shock, Quick Attack

**Evolution**

 →

HELIOPTILE      HELIOLISK

# HELIOLISK

One Heliolisk basking in the sun with its frill outspread is all it would take to produce enough electricity to power a city.

| Generator Pokémon | |
|---|---|
| **POKÉDEX NO.** | **695** |
| TYPE | Electric, Normal |
| ABILITY | Sand Veil, Dry Skin |
| HEIGHT | 3'03" |
| WEIGHT | 46.3 lbs |

## Description

It stimulates its muscles with electricity, boosting the strength in its legs and enabling it to run 100 yards in five seconds.

## Special Moves

Parabolic Charge, Electrify, Eerie Impulse

**Evolution**

HELIOPTILE

HELIOLISK

001-100
101-200
201-300
401-442
443-500
501-600
601-700
701-800
801-898

# TYRUNT

This is an ancient Pokémon that was revived in modern times. It has a violent disposition, and it'll tear apart anything it gets between its hefty jaws.

## Royal Heir Pokémon

| POKÉDEX NO. | 696 |
| --- | --- |
| TYPE | Rock, Dragon |
| ABILITY | Strong Jaw |
| HEIGHT | 2'07" |
| WEIGHT | 57.3 lbs |

### Description

This Pokémon is selfish and likes to be pampered. It can also inflict grievous wounds on its Trainer just by playing around.

### Special Moves

Rock Slide, Crunch, Dragon Tail

Evolution

TYRUNT → TYRANTRUM

# TYRANTRUM

A single bite from Tyrantrum's massive jaws will demolish a car. This Pokémon was the king of the ancient world.

| Despot Pokémon | |
|---|---|
| **POKÉDEX NO.** | **697** |
| TYPE | Rock, Dragon |
| ABILITY | Strong Jaw |
| HEIGHT | 8'02" |
| WEIGHT | 595.2 lbs |

### Description

This Pokémon is from about 100 million years ago. It has the presence of a king, vicious but magnificent.

### Special Moves

Giga Impact, Horn Drill, Stomp

**Evolution**

TYRUNT

TYRANTRUM

# AMAURA

Amaura is an ancient Pokémon that has gone extinct. Specimens of this species can sometimes be found frozen in ice.

## Tundra Pokémon

| POKÉDEX NO. | 698 |
|---|---|
| TYPE | Rock, Ice |
| ABILITY | Refrigerate |
| HEIGHT | 4'03" |
| WEIGHT | 55.6 lbs |

### Description

This Pokémon was successfully restored from a fossil. In the past, it lived with others of its kind in cold lands where there were fewer predators.

### Special Moves

Powder Snow, Ancient Power, Aurora Beam

### Evolution

AMAURA → AURORUS

# AURORUS

When gripped by rage, Aurorus will emanate freezing air, covering everything around it in ice.

## Tundra Pokémon

| POKÉDEX NO. | 699 |
|---|---|
| TYPE | Rock, Ice |
| ABILITY | Refrigerate |
| HEIGHT | 8'10" |
| WEIGHT | 496.0 lbs |

### Description

Aurorus was restored from a fossil. It's said that when this Pokémon howls, auroras appear in the night sky.

### Special Moves

Freeze-Dry, Ice Beam, Blizzard

### Evolution

  →

AMAURA → AURORUS

001-100
101-200
201-300
481-442
443-500
501-600
601-700
701-800
801-898

# SYLVEON

Intertwining Pokémon

| POKÉDEX NO. | 700 |
|---|---|
| **TYPE** | Fairy |
| **ABILITY** | Cute Charm |
| **HEIGHT** | 3'03" |
| **WEIGHT** | 51.8 lbs |

By releasing enmity-erasing waves from its ribbonlike feelers, Sylveon stops any conflict.

### Description

Sylveon wraps its ribbonlike feelers around its Trainer's arm because this touch enables it to read its Trainer's feelings.

### Special Moves

Disarming Voice, Moonblast, Charm

**Evolution**

EEVEE → SYLVEON

# HAWLUCHA

## Wrestling Pokémon

| POKÉDEX NO. | **701** |
|---|---|
| TYPE | Flying, Fighting |
| ABILITY | Limber, Unburden |
| HEIGHT | 2'07" |
| WEIGHT | 47.4 lbs |

001-100

101-200

201-300

401-442

443-500

501-600

701-800

801-898

It drives its opponents to exhaustion with its agile maneuvers, then ends the fight with a flashy finishing move.

### Description

It always strikes a pose before going for its finishing move. Sometimes opponents take advantage of that time to counterattack.

### Special Moves

Flying Press, Aerial Ace, Hone Claws

Evolution    Does not evolve

HAWLUCHA

# DEDENNE

**Antenna Pokémon**

| POKÉDEX NO. | **702** |
| --- | --- |
| **TYPE** | Electric, Fairy |
| **ABILITY** | Pickup, Cheek Pouch |
| **HEIGHT** | 0'08" |
| **WEIGHT** | 4.9 lbs |

### Description

A Dedenne's whiskers pick up electrical waves other Dedenne send out. These Pokémon share locations of food and electricity with one other.

Since Dedenne can't generate as much electricity on its own, it steals electricity from outlets or other electric Pokémon.

### Special Moves

Nuzzle,
Thunder Shock, Charm

**Evolution**  Does not evolve

DEDENNE

# CARBINK

It's said that somewhere in the world, there's a mineral vein housing a large pack of slumbering Carbink. It's also said that this pack has a queen.

| Jewel Pokémon | |
|---|---|
| **POKÉDEX NO.** | **703** |
| TYPE | Rock, Fairy |
| ABILITY | Clear Body |
| HEIGHT | 1'00" |
| WEIGHT | 12.6 lbs |

### Description

When beset by attackers, Carbink wipes them all out by firing high-energy beams from the gems embedded in its body.

### Special Moves

Harden, Power Gem, Light Screen

**Evolution**

CARBINK

Does not evolve

001-100
101-200
201-300
401-442
443-500
501-600
701-800
801-898

# GOOMY

**Soft Tissue Pokémon**

| POKÉDEX NO. | 704 |
| --- | --- |
| TYPE | Dragon |
| ABILITY | Hydration, Sap Sipper |
| HEIGHT | 1'00" |
| WEIGHT | 6.2 lbs |

Their horns are powerful sensors. As soon as Goomy pick up any sign of enemies, they go into hiding. This is how they've survived.

## Description

Because most of its body is water, it will dry up if the weather becomes too arid. It's considered the weakest dragon Pokémon.

## Special Moves

Absorb, Water Gun, Dragon Breath

**Evolution**

GOOMY → SLIGGOO → GOODRA

# SLIGGOO

The lump on its back contains its tiny brain. It thinks only of food and escaping its enemies.

| Soft Tissue Pokémon | |
| --- | --- |
| POKÉDEX NO. | **705** |
| TYPE | Dragon |
| ABILITY | Hydration, Sap Sipper |
| HEIGHT | 2'07" |
| WEIGHT | 38.6 lbs |

## Description

Although this Pokémon isn't very strong, its body is coated in a caustic slime that can melt through anything, so predators steer clear of it.

## Special Moves

Acid Spray, Water Pulse, Muddy Water

Evolution

GOOMY → SLIGGOO → GOODRA

001-100
101-200
201-300
401-442
443-500
501-600
601-700
701-800
801-898

# GOODRA

Its form of offense is forcefully stretching out its horns. The strikes land 100 times harder than any blow from a heavyweight boxer.

| Dragon Pokémon | |
|---|---|
| **POKÉDEX NO.** | **706** |
| TYPE | Dragon |
| ABILITY | Hydration, Sap Sipper |
| HEIGHT | 6'07" |
| WEIGHT | 331.8 lbs |

## Description

Sometimes it misunderstands instructions and appears dazed or bewildered. Many Trainers don't mind, finding this behavior to be adorable.

## Special Moves

Aqua Tail, Dragon Pulse, Rain Dance

**Evolution**

GOOMY → SLIGGOO → GOODRA

# KLEFKI

Klefki sucks in metal ions with the horn topping its head. It seems this Pokémon loves keys so much that its head needed to look like one, too.

001-100
101-200
201-300
401-442
443-500
501-600
701-800
801-898

| Key Ring Pokémon | |
|---|---|
| **POKÉDEX NO.** | **707** |
| TYPE | Steel, Fairy |
| ABILITY | Prankster |
| HEIGHT | 0'08" |
| WEIGHT | 6.6 lbs |

### Description

This Pokémon is constantly collecting keys. Entrust a Klefki with important keys, and the Pokémon will protect them no matter what.

### Special Moves

Fairy Lock, Metal Sound, Imprison

**Evolution**

KLEFKI

Does not evolve

# PHANTUMP

With a voice like a human child's, it cries out to lure adults deep into the forest, getting them lost among the trees.

## Stump Pokémon

| POKÉDEX NO. | 708 |
|---|---|
| TYPE | Ghost, Grass |
| ABILITY | Natural Cure, Frisk |
| HEIGHT | 1'04" |
| WEIGHT | 15.4 lbs |

### Description

After a lost child perished in the forest, their spirit possessed a tree stump, causing the spirit's rebirth as this Pokémon.

### Special Moves

Will-O-Wisp, Leech Seed, Forest's Curse

**Evolution**

PHANTUMP

TREVENANT

# TREVENANT

Small roots that extend from the tips of this Pokémon's feet can tie into the trees of the forest and give Trevenant control over them.

## Elder Tree Pokémon

| POKÉDEX NO. | 709 |
|---|---|
| TYPE | Ghost, Grass |
| ABILITY | Natural Cure, Frisk |
| HEIGHT | 4'11" |
| WEIGHT | 156.5 lbs |

### Description

People fear it due to a belief that it devours any who try to cut down trees in its forest, but to the Pokémon it shares its wood with, it's kind.

### Special Moves

Shadow Claw, Growth, Forest's Curse

**Evolution**

PHANTUMP

TREVENANT

001-100
101-200
201-300
401-442
443-500
501-600
701-800
801-898

# PUMPKABOO

## Pumpkin Pokémon

| POKÉDEX NO. | **710** |
|---|---|

| TYPE | Ghost, Grass |
|---|---|
| ABILITY | Pickup, Frisk |

Pumpkaboo has four sizes. They look the same, but their height and weight are different.

The light that streams out of the holes in the pumpkin can hypnotize and control the people and Pokémon that see it.

| Small Size | |
|---|---|
| HEIGHT | 1'00" |
| WEIGHT | 7.7 lbs |
| Average Size | |
| HEIGHT | 1'04" |
| WEIGHT | 11.0 lbs |
| Large Size | |
| HEIGHT | 1'08" |
| WEIGHT | 16.5 lbs |
| Super Size | |
| HEIGHT | 2'07" |
| WEIGHT | 33.1 lbs |

### Description

Spirits that wander this world are placed into Pumpkaboo's body. They're then moved on to the afterlife.

### Special Moves

Trick-or-Treat, Trick, Razor Leaf

Evolution  →

PUMPKABOO    GOURGEIST

# GOURGEIST

## Pumpkin Pokémon

**POKÉDEX NO.** ▶ **711**

| TYPE | Ghost, Grass |
|---|---|
| ABILITY | Pickup, Frisk |

Gourgeist has four sizes. They look the same, but their height and weight are different.

| Small Size | |
|---|---|
| HEIGHT | 2'04" |
| WEIGHT | 20.9 lbs |
| Average Size | |
| HEIGHT | 2'11" |
| WEIGHT | 27.6 lbs |
| Large Size | |
| HEIGHT | 3'07" |
| WEIGHT | 30.9 lbs |
| Super Size | |
| HEIGHT | 5'07" |
| WEIGHT | 86.0 lbs |

Eerie cries emanate from its body in the dead of night. The sounds are said to be the wails of spirits who are suffering in the afterlife.

### Description

In the darkness of a new-moon night, Gourgeist will come knocking. Whoever answers the door will be swept off to the afterlife.

### Special Moves

Trick-or-Treat, Phantom Force, Explosion

**Evolution**

PUMPKABOO

GOURGEIST

001-100
101-200
201-300
401-442
443-500
501-600
701-800
801-898

# BERGMITE

They chill the air around them to -150 degrees Fahrenheit, freezing the water in the air into ice that they use as armor.

## Ice Chunk Pokémon

| | |
|---|---|
| POKÉDEX NO. | **712** |
| TYPE | Ice |
| ABILITY | Own Tempo, Ice Body |
| HEIGHT | 3'03" |
| WEIGHT | 219.4 lbs |

### Description

This Pokémon lives in areas of frigid cold. It secures itself to the back of an Avalugg by freezing its feet in place.

### Special Moves

Rapid Spin, Powder Snow, Double-Edge

**Evolution**

BERGMITE ➡ AVALUGG

# AVALUGG

As Avalugg moves about during the day, the cracks in its body deepen. The Pokémon's body returns to its pristine state overnight.

| Iceberg Pokémon | |
|---|---|
| **POKÉDEX NO.** | **713** |
| TYPE | Ice |
| ABILITY | Own Tempo, Ice Body |
| HEIGHT | 6'07" |
| WEIGHT | 1113.3 lbs |

## Description

Its ice-covered body is as hard as steel. Its cumbersome frame crushes anything that stands in its way.

## Special Moves

Icy Wind, Ice Fang, Avalanche

**Evolution**

 ➡

BERGMITE          AVALUGG

# NOIBAT

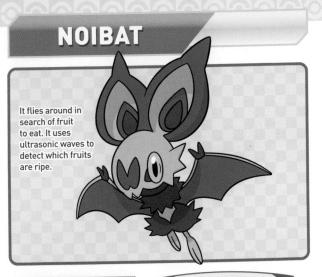

It flies around in search of fruit to eat. It uses ultrasonic waves to detect which fruits are ripe.

| Sound Wave Pokémon | |
|---|---|
| POKÉDEX NO. | **714** |
| TYPE | Flying, Dragon |
| ABILITY | Frisk, Infiltrator |
| HEIGHT | 1'08" |
| WEIGHT | 17.6 lbs |

### Description

After nightfall, they emerge from the caves they nest in during the day. Using their ultrasonic waves, they go on the hunt for ripened fruit.

### Special Moves

Absorb, Wing Attack, Supersonic

**Evolution**

NOIBAT → NOIVERN

# NOIVERN

Although it has a violent disposition, if you give it a nice, ripe fruit that it loves, Noivern will suddenly become tame.

## Sound Wave Pokémon

| POKÉDEX NO. | 715 |
| --- | --- |
| TYPE | Flying, Dragon |
| ABILITY | Frisk, Infiltrator |
| HEIGHT | 4'11" |
| WEIGHT | 187.4 lbs |

### Description

Aggressive and cruel, this Pokémon will ruthlessly torment enemies that are helpless in the dark.

### Special Moves

Dragon Pulse, Boomburst, Whirlwind

### Evolution

 ➡

NOIBAT          NOIVERN

001-100
101-200
201-300
401-442
443-500
501-600
701-800
801-898

# XERNEAS

| | |
|---|---|
| **Life Pokémon** | |
| **POKÉDEX NO.** | **716** |
| **TYPE** | Fairy |
| **ABILITY** | Fairy Aura |
| **HEIGHT** | 9'10" |
| **WEIGHT** | 474.0 lbs |

## Description

When the horns on its head shine in seven colors, it is said to be sharing everlasting life.

It slept for 1,000 years in the form of a tree before its revival.

## Special Moves

Geomancy, Horn Leech, Outrage

**Evolution**  Does not evolve

XERNEAS

# YVELTAL

**Destruction Pokémon**

| POKÉDEX NO. | 717 |
|---|---|
| TYPE | Dark, Flying |
| ABILITY | Dark Aura |
| HEIGHT | 19'00" |
| WEIGHT | 447.5 lbs |

### Description

When this Legendary Pokémon's wings and tail feathers spread wide and glow red, it absorbs the life force of living creatures.

When its life comes to an end, it absorbs the life energy of every living thing and turns into a cocoon once more.

### Special Moves

Oblivion Wing, Sky Attack, Dark Pulse

**Evolution**

YVELTAL

Does not evolve

001-100
101-200
201-300
401-442
443-500
501-600
601-700
701-800
801-898

# ZYGARDE

## 10% FORME

### Order Pokémon

| POKÉDEX NO. | **718** |
|---|---|
| **TYPE** | Dragon, Ground |
| **ABILITY** | Aura Break |
| **HEIGHT** | 3'11" |
| **WEIGHT** | 73.9 lbs |

The Zygarde Cores act as its brain, and by gathering the Zygarde Cells, you can create the various Zygarde Formes.

Zygarde Cell     Zygarde Core

Its sharp fangs make short work of finishing off its enemies, but it's unable to maintain this body indefinitely. After a period of time, it falls apart.

### Description

This is Zygarde's form when about 10% of its cells have beengathered. It runs across the land at speeds greater than 60 mph.

### Special Moves

Thousand Arrows, Thousand Waves, Earthquake

Evolution          Does not evolve

**ZYGARDE**
(10% FORME)

# ZYGARDE

## 50% FORME

### Order Pokémon

| POKÉDEX NO. | 718 |
| --- | --- |

| | |
| --- | --- |
| **TYPE** | Dragon, Ground |
| **ABILITY** | Aura Break |
| **HEIGHT** | 16'05" |
| **WEIGHT** | 672.4 lbs |

001-100

101-200

201-300

401-442

443-500

501-600

701-800

801-898

Some say it can change into an even more powerful form when battling those who threaten the ecosystem.

### Description

This is Zygarde's form when it has gathered 50% of its cells. It wipes out all those who oppose it, showing not a shred of mercy.

### Special Moves

Land's Wrath, Dragon Pulse, Earthquake

**Evolution**

ZYGARDE
(50% FORME)

Does not evolve

# ZYGARDE

**COMPLETE FORME**

## Order Pokémon

| POKÉDEX NO. | 718 |
|---|---|
| **TYPE** | Dragon, Ground |
| **ABILITY** | Power Construct |
| **HEIGHT** | 14'09" |
| **WEIGHT** | 1344.8 lbs |

### Description

This is Zygarde's perfected form. From the orifice on its chest, it radiates high-powered energy that eliminates everything.

Born when all of Zygarde's cells have been gathered together, it uses force to neutralize those who harm the ecosystem.

### Special Moves

Core Enforcer, Earthquake, Thousand Arrows

**Evolution**   Does not evolve

ZYGARDE
(COMPLETE FORME)

# DIANCIE

| Jewel Pokémon | |
|---|---|
| **POKÉDEX NO.** | **719** |
| TYPE | Rock, Fairy |
| ABILITY | Clear Body |
| HEIGHT | 2'04" |
| WEIGHT | 19.4 lbs |

001-100
101-200
201-300
401-442
443-500
501-600
701-800
801-898

### Description

It can instantly create many diamonds by compressing the carbon in the air between its hands.

A sudden transformation of Carbink,* its pink, glimmering body is said to be the loveliest sight in the whole world.

### Special Moves

Diamond Storm, Power Gem, Rock Slide

**Evolution**

DIANCIE

Does not evolve

*Carbink: A Pokémon you'll find on page 303.

# MEGA DIANCIE

A sudden transformation of Carbink,* its pink, glimmering body is said to be the loveliest sight in the whole world.

**DIANCIE**

## Jewel Pokémon

| POKÉDEX NO. | **719** |
|---|---|
| **TYPE** | Rock, Fairy |
| **ABILITY** | Magic Bounce |
| **HEIGHT** | 3'07" |
| **WEIGHT** | 61.3 lbs |

### Description

It can instantly create many diamonds by compressing the carbon in the air between its hands.

### Special Moves

Diamond Storm, Moonblast, Stone Edge

*Carbink: A Pokémon you'll find on page 303.

# HOOPA

HOOPA CONFINED

| Mischief Pokémon | |
|---|---|
| **POKÉDEX NO.** | **720** |
| TYPE | Psychic, Ghost |
| ABILITY | Magician |
| HEIGHT | 1'08" |
| WEIGHT | 19.8 lbs |

001-100
101-200
201-300
01-42
443-500
501-600
01-00
701-800
801-898

This troublemaker sends anything and everything to faraway places using its loop, which can warp space.

### Description

It gathers things it likes and passes them through its loop to teleport them to a secret place.

### Special Moves

Hyperspace Hole, Psychic, Trick

**Evolution**

HOOPA
(HOOPA CONFINED)

Does not evolve

# HOOPA

## HOOPA UNBOUND

It is said to be able to seize anything it desires with its six rings and six huge arms. With its powers sealed, it is transformed into a much smaller form.*

| Djinn Pokémonn | |
|---|---|
| **POKÉDEX NO.** | **720** |
| **TYPE** | Psychic, Dark |
| **ABILITY** | Magician |
| **HEIGHT** | 21'04" |
| **WEIGHT** | 1080.3 lbs |

### Description

In its true form, it possesses a huge amount of power. Legends of its avarice tell how it once carried off an entire castle to gain the treasure hidden within.

### Special Moves

Hyperspace Fury, Dark Pulse, Trick

**Evolution**

HOOPA
(HOOPA UNBOUND)

Does not evolve

*Smaller form: Hoopa Confined.

# VOLCANION

001-100
101-200
201-300
401-442
443-500
501-600
701-800
801-898

## Steam Pokémon

**POKÉDEX NO.** 721

| | |
|---|---|
| TYPE | Fire, Water |
| ABILITY | Water Absorb |
| HEIGHT | 5'07" |
| WEIGHT | 429.9 lbs |

### Description

It lets out billows of steam and disappears into the dense fog. It's said to live in mountains where humans do not tread.

It expels its internal steam from the arms on its back. It has enough power to blow away a mountain.

### Special Moves

Steam Eruption, Scald, Incinerate

Evolution   Does not evolve

VOLCANION

# ROWLET

| | |
|---|---|
| **POKÉDEX NO.** | **722** |
| **TYPE** | Grass, Flying |
| **ABILITY** | Overgrow |
| **HEIGHT** | 1'00" |
| **WEIGHT** | 3.3 lbs |

During the day, it builds up energy via photosynthesis. At night, it flies silently through the sky, on the prowl for prey.

## Description

At a distance, it launches its sharp feathers while flying about. If the enemy gets too close, Rowlet switches tactics and delivers vicious kicks.

## Special Moves

Leafage, Razor Leaf, Synthesis

**Evolution**

ROWLET → DARTRIX → DECIDUEYE

# DARTRIX

It never slacks when it comes to the task of cleaning its feathers. Thorough preening keeps it looking spiffy and its blade quills nice and sharp.

| Blade Quill Pokémon | |
|---|---|
| **POKÉDEX NO.** | **723** |
| TYPE | Grass, Flying |
| ABILITY | Overgrow |
| HEIGHT | 2'04" |
| WEIGHT | 35.3 lbs |

## Description

It throws one knifelike feather after another at its enemies, and each one precisely strikes a weak point. These feathers are known as blade quills.

## Special Moves

Leaf Blade, Pluck, Nasty Plot

**Evolution**

 ROWLET →  DARTRIX →  DECIDUEYE

001-100
101-200
201-300
401-442
443-500
501-600
701-800
801-898

# DECIDUEYE

## Arrow Quill Pokémon

| POKÉDEX NO. | 724 |
| --- | --- |
| TYPE | Grass, Ghost |
| ABILITY | Overgrow |
| HEIGHT | 5'03" |
| WEIGHT | 80.7 lbs |

In a tenth of a second, it can nock and fire an arrow quill, piercing an opponent's weak point before they notice what's happening.

### Description

As if wielding a bow, it launches the arrow quills hidden among the feathers of its wings. Decidueye's shots never miss.

### Special Moves

Spirit Shackle, Brave Bird, Leaf Storm

**Evolution**

ROWLET

DARTRIX

DECIDUEYE

# LITTEN

## Fire Cat Pokémon

| POKÉDEX NO. | 725 |
|---|---|
| TYPE | Fire |
| ABILITY | Blaze |
| HEIGHT | 1'04" |
| WEIGHT | 9.5 lbs |

Trying to pet Litten before it trusts you will result in a nasty scratch from its sharp claws. Be careful.

### Description

It spends even the smallest amount of downtime grooming its fur with its tongue. Loose fur gathers in its stomach and serves as fuel for fiery moves.

### Special Moves

Scratch, Fire Fang, Lick

001-100
101-200
201-300
401-442
443-500
501-600
701-800
801-898

Evolution

  LITTEN  TORRACAT   INCINEROAR

# TORRACAT

In the midst of battle, the fire pouch on Torracat's neck rings like a bell and produces stronger flames than usual.

## Fire Cat Pokémon

| POKÉDEX NO. | 726 |
|---|---|
| TYPE | Fire |
| ABILITY | Blaze |
| HEIGHT | 2'04" |
| WEIGHT | 55.1 lbs |

## Description

When its mane is standing on end, you can tell it's feeling good. When it isn't feeling well, its fur will lie down flat.

## Special Moves

Fire Fang, Fury Swipes, Thrash

**Evolution**

LITTEN → TORRACAT → INCINEROAR

# INCINEROAR

**Heel Pokémon**

| POKÉDEX NO. | 727 |
|---|---|

| TYPE | Fire, Dark |
|---|---|
| ABILITY | Blaze |
| HEIGHT | 5'11" |
| WEIGHT | 183.0 lbs |

001-100
101-200
201-300
401-442
443-500
501-600
601-700
701-800
801-898

Incineroar's rough and aggressive behavior is its most notable trait, but the way it helps out small Pokémon shows that it has a kind side as well.

### Description

It excels at violent, no-holds-barred battles. The temperature of the flames that issue from its navel exceeds 3,600 degrees Fahrenheit.

### Special Moves

Darkest Lariat, Flare Blitz, Swagger

**Evolution**

LITTEN → TORRACAT → INCINEROAR

331

# POPPLIO

| Sea Lion Pokémon | |
|---|---|
| POKÉDEX NO. | **728** |
| TYPE | Water |
| ABILITY | Torrent |
| HEIGHT | 1'04" |
| WEIGHT | 16.5 lbs |

### Description

The balloons it inflates with its nose grows larger and larger as it practices day by day.

Popplio gets on top of its bouncy water balloons to jump higher. It's quite the acrobatic fighter!

### Special Moves

Sing, Water Gun, Bubble Beam

**Evolution**

POPPLIO → BRIONNE → PRIMARINA

# BRIONNE

On nights when the sea is calm, Brionne dance with one another to the singing of the Primarina that's leading them.

| Pop Star Pokémon | |
|---|---|
| **POKÉDEX NO.** | **729** |
| TYPE | Water |
| ABILITY | Torrent |
| HEIGHT | 2'00" |
| WEIGHT | 38.6 lbs |

## Description

As if dancing, it artfully dodges the attacks of its enemies. All the while, it's busy forming a bunch of balloons to overwhelm its foes.

## Special Moves

Aqua Jet, Bubble Beam, Sing

**Evolution**

POPPLIO

BRIONNE

PRIMARINA

001-100
101-200
201-300
401-442
443-500
501-600
701-800
801-898

# PRIMARINA

## Soloist Pokémon

| POKÉDEX NO. | **730** |
| --- | --- |

| TYPE | Water, Fairy |
| --- | --- |
| ABILITY | Torrent |
| HEIGHT | 5'11" |
| WEIGHT | 97.0 lbs |

### Description

For Primarina, every battle is a stage. Its singing and the dancing of its balloons will mesmerize the audience.

### Special Moves

Sparkling Aria, Hydro Pump, Sing

With its mouth, it makes sonic waves that sound like beautiful singing. It uses the sonic waves to control its water balloons.

Evolution

POPPLIO → BRIONNE → PRIMARINA

# PIKIPEK

It may look spindly, but its neck muscles are heavy-duty. It can peck at a tree 16 times per second!

001-100
101-200
201-300
401-442
443-500
501-600
651-700
701-800
801-898

| Woodpecker Pokémon | |
|---|---|
| **POKÉDEX NO.** | **731** |
| TYPE | Normal, Flying |
| ABILITY | Keen Eye, Skill Link |
| HEIGHT | 1'00" |
| WEIGHT | 2.6 lbs |

### Description

It pecks at trees with its hard beak. You can get some idea of its mood or condition from the rhythm of its pecking.

### Special Moves

Peck, Supersonic, Bullet Seed

**Evolution**

PIKIPEK

TRUMBEAK

TOUCANNON

# TRUMBEAK

From its mouth, it fires the seeds of berries it has eaten. The scattered seeds give rise to new plants.

## Bugle Beak Pokémon

| POKÉDEX NO. | 732 |
| --- | --- |
| TYPE | Normal, Flying |
| ABILITY | Keen Eye, Skill Link |
| HEIGHT | 2'00" |
| WEIGHT | 32.6 lbs |

### Description

It can bend the tip of its beak to produce over a hundred different cries at will.

### Special Moves

Rock Blast, Rock Smash, Echoed Voice

Evolution

PIKIPEK → TRUMBEAK → TOUCANNON

# TOUCANNON

Known for forming harmonious couples, this Pokémon is brought to wedding ceremonies as a good luck charm.

001-100
101-200
201-300
401-442
443-500
501-600
601-700
701-800
801-898

| Cannon Pokémon | |
|---|---|
| POKÉDEX NO. | **733** |
| TYPE | Normal, Flying |
| ABILITY | Keen Eye, Skill Link |
| HEIGHT | 3'07" |
| WEIGHT | 57.3 lbs |

## Description

They smack beaks with others of their kind to communicate. The strength and number of hits tell each other how they feel.

## Special Moves

Beak Blast, Fury Attack, Roost

**Evolution**

PIKIPEK    TRUMBEAK    TOUCANNON

# YUNGOOS

Although it will eat anything, it prefers fresh, living things, so it marches down streets in search of prey.

## Loitering Pokémon

| POKÉDEX NO. | 734 |
| --- | --- |
| TYPE | Normal |
| ABILITY | Strong Jaw, Stakeout |
| HEIGHT | 1'04" |
| WEIGHT | 13.2 lbs |

### Description

Its stomach takes up most of its long torso. It's a big eater, so the amount Trainers have to spend on its food is no laughing matter.

### Special Moves

Tackle, Crunch, Super Fang

### Evolution

YUNGOOS

GUMSHOOS

338

# GUMSHOOS

Patient by nature, this Pokémon loses control of itself and pounces when it spots its favorite meal—Rattata!*

001-100
101-200
201-300
401-442
443-500
501-600
601-700
701-800
801-898

## Stakeout Pokémon

| POKÉDEX NO. | 735 |
|---|---|
| TYPE | Normal |
| ABILITY | Strong Jaw, Stakeout |
| HEIGHT | 2'04" |
| WEIGHT | 31.3 lbs |

### Description

Although it wasn't originally found in Alola, this Pokémon was brought over a long time ago when there was a huge Rattata outbreak.

### Special Moves

Hyper Fang, Crunch, Odor Sleuth

**Evolution**

YUNGOOS → GUMSHOOS

*Rattata: A Pokémon you'll find in volume 1.

# GRUBBIN

It uses its big jaws to dig nests into the forest floor, and it loves to feed on sweet tree sap.

| Larva Pokémon | |
|---|---|
| POKÉDEX NO. | **736** |
| TYPE | Bug |
| ABILITY | Swarm |
| HEIGHT | 1'04" |
| WEIGHT | 9.7 lbs |

### Description

Its natural enemies, like Rookidee,* may flee rather than risk getting caught in its large mandibles, that can snap thick tree branches.

### Special Moves

Mud-Slap, Dig, Sticky Web

**Evolution**

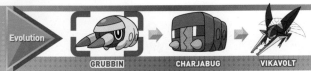

GRUBBIN → CHARJABUG → VIKAVOLT

*Rookidee: A Pokémon you'll find on page 441.

# CHARJABUG

While its durable shell protects it from attacks, Charjabug strikes at enemies with jolts of electricity discharged from the tips of its jaws.

## Battery Pokémon

| POKÉDEX NO. | **737** |
|---|---|
| TYPE | Bug, Electric |
| ABILITY | Battery |
| HEIGHT | 1'08" |
| WEIGHT | 23.1 lbs |

### Description

Its digestive processes convert the leaves it eats into electricity. An electric sac in its belly stores the electricity for later use.

### Special Moves

Charge, Spark, Sticky Web

**Evolution**

 GRUBBIN ⇒  CHARJABUG ⇒  VIKAVOLT

001-100
101-200
201-300
401-442
443-500
501-600
701-800
801-898

# VIKAVOLT

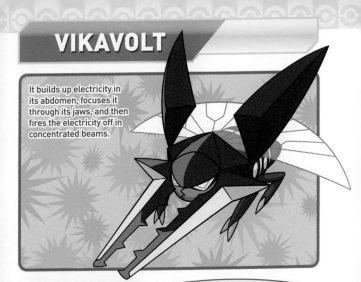

It builds up electricity in its abdomen, focuses it through its jaws, and then fires the electricity off in concentrated beams.

| Stag Beetle Pokémon | |
|---|---|
| **POKÉDEX NO.** | **738** |
| **TYPE** | Bug, Electric |
| **ABILITY** | Levitate |
| **HEIGHT** | 4'11" |
| **WEIGHT** | 99.2 lbs |

## Description

If it carries a Charjabug to use as a spare battery, a flying Vikavolt can rapidly fire high-powered beams of electricity.

## Special Moves

Thunderbolt, Zap Cannon, X-Scissor

**Evolution**

GRUBBIN → CHARJABUG → VIKAVOLT

# CRABRAWLER

Its hard pincers are well suited to both offense and defense. Fights between two Crabrawler are like boxing matches.

| Boxing Pokémon | |
|---|---|
| **POKÉDEX NO.** | **739** |
| TYPE | Fighting |
| ABILITY | Hyper Cutter, Iron Fist |
| HEIGHT | 2'00" |
| WEIGHT | 15.4 lbs |

### Description

Crabrawler has been known to mistake Exeggutor\* for a coconut tree and climb it. The enraged Exeggutor shakes it off and stomps on it.

### Special Moves

Bubble, Dizzy Punch, Bubble Beam

**Evolution**

  CRABRAWLER  CRABOMINABLE

\*Exeggutor: A Pokémon you'll find in volume 1.

001-100
101-200
201-300
401-442
443-500
501-600
701-800
801-898

# CRABOMINABLE

It stores coldness in its pincers and pummels its foes. It can even smash thick walls of ice to bits!

| Woolly Crab Pokémon | |
|---|---|
| **POKÉDEX NO.** | **740** |
| **TYPE** | Fighting, Ice |
| **ABILITY** | Hyper Cutter, Iron Fist |
| **HEIGHT** | 5'07" |
| **WEIGHT** | 396.8 lbs |

### Description

Before it stops to think, it starts pummeling. There are records of its turning back avalanches with a flurry of punches.

### Special Moves

Ice Punch, Ice Hammer, Iron Defense

**Evolution**

CRABRAWLER

CRABOMINABLE

# ORICORIO

## POM-POM STYLE

It lifts its opponents' spirits with its cheerful dance moves. When it lets its guard down, it electrocutes them with a jolt.

### Dancing Pokémon

| POKÉDEX NO. | 741 |
| --- | --- |
| TYPE | Electric, Flying |
| ABILITY | Dancer |
| HEIGHT | 2'00" |
| WEIGHT | 7.5 lbs |

### Description

This Oricorio has drunk bright yellow nectar. When it sees someone looking glum, it will try to cheer them up with a dance.

### Special Moves

Revelation Dance, Mirror Move, Hurricane

**Evolution**

ORICORIO
(POM-POM STYLE)

Does not evolve

001-100

101-200

201-300

401-442

443-500

501-600

701-800

801-898

# ORICORIO

## PA'U STYLE

It relaxes its opponents with its elegant dancing. When they let their guard down, it showers them with psychic energy.

| Dancing Pokémon | |
|---|---|
| POKÉDEX NO. | **741** |
| TYPE | Psychic, Flying |
| ABILITY | Dancer |
| HEIGHT | 2'00" |
| WEIGHT | 7.5 lbs |

### Description

This Oricorio has sipped pink nectar. It gets so caught up in its dancing that it sometimes doesn't hear its Trainer's orders.

### Special Moves

Revelation Dance, Agility, Captivate

**Evolution**

ORICORIO
[PA'U STYLE]

Does not evolve

# ORICORIO

## SENSU STYLE

It charms its opponents with its refined dancing. When they let their guard down, it places a curse on them that will bring on their demise.

| Dancing Pokémon | |
|---|---|
| POKÉDEX NO. | **741** |
| TYPE | Ghost, Flying |
| ABILITY | Dancer |
| HEIGHT | 2'00" |
| WEIGHT | 7.5 lbs |

## Description

This Oricorio has sipped purple nectar. Some dancers use its graceful, elegant dancing as inspiration.

## Special Moves

Revelation Dance, Teeter Dance, Helping Hand

**Evolution**

ORICORIO
(SENSU STYLE)

Does not evolve

001-100
101-200
201-300
401-442
443-500
501-600
701-800
801-898

# ORICORIO

**BAILE STYLE**

It wins the hearts of its enemies with its passionate dancing and then uses the opening it creates to burn them up with blazing flames.

## Dancing Pokémon

| POKÉDEX NO. | **741** |
|---|---|
| TYPE | Fire, Flying |
| ABILITY | Dancer |
| HEIGHT | 2'00" |
| WEIGHT | 7.5 lbs |

### Description

This Oricorio has drunk red nectar. If its Trainer gives the wrong order, this passionate Pokémon becomes fiercely angry.

### Special Moves

Revelation Dance, Air Cutter, Roost

**Evolution**  Does not evolve

ORICORIO
(BAILE STYLE)

# CUTIEFLY

Nectar and pollen are its favorite fare. You can find Cutiefly hovering around Gossifleur,* trying to get some of Gossifleur's pollen.

| Bee Fly Pokémon | |
|---|---|
| POKÉDEX NO. | 742 |
| TYPE | Bug, Fairy |
| ABILITY | Shield Dust, Honey Gather |
| HEIGHT | 0'04" |
| WEIGHT | 0.4 lbs |

## Description

An opponent's aura can tell Cutiefly what that opponent's next move will be. Then Cutiefly can glide around the attack and strike back.

## Special Moves

Absorb, Fairy Wind, Sweet Scent

**Evolution**

CUTIEFLY → RIBOMBEE

*Gossifleur: A Pokémon you'll find on page 451.

349

# RIBOMBEE

It makes pollen puffs from pollen and nectar. The puffs' effects depend on the type of ingredients and how much of each one is used.

| Bee Fly Pokémon | |
|---|---|
| POKÉDEX NO. | **743** |
| TYPE | Bug, Fairy |
| ABILITY | Shield Dust, Honey Gather |
| HEIGHT | 0'08" |
| WEIGHT | 1.1 lbs |

## Description

It can predict the weather based on moisture levels and wind direction. Ribombee only reveals itself when there are a few clear days in a row.

## Special Moves

Pollen Puff, Struggle Bug, Stun Spore

Evolution

 →

CUTIEFLY        RIBOMBEE

# ROCKRUFF

## Puppy Pokémon

| POKÉDEX NO. | 744 |
|---|---|
| **TYPE** | Rock |
| **ABILITY** | Keen Eye, Vital Spirit, Own Tempo |
| **HEIGHT** | 1'08" |
| **WEIGHT** | 20.3 lbs |

This Pokémon intimidates opponents by striking the ground with the rocks on its neck. The moment an opponent flinches, Rockruff attacks.

### Description

This Pokémon can bond very strongly with its Trainer, but it also has a habit of biting. Raising a Rockruff for a long time can be challenging.

### Special Moves

Bite, Rock Tomb, Rock Throw

**Evolution**

ROCKRUFF

LYCANROC (DUSK FORM)

LYCANROC (MIDDAY FORM)

LYCANROC (MIDNIGHT FORM)

001-100
101-200
201-300
401-442
443-500
501-600
701-800
801-898

# LYCANROC

## DUSK FORM*

### Wolf Pokémon

| POKÉDEX NO. | **745** |
|---|---|
| TYPE | Rock |
| ABILITY | Tough Claws |
| HEIGHT | 2'07" |
| WEIGHT | 55.1 lbs |

### Description

This form of Lycanroc is normally calm and quiet. Once a battle begins, however, this Pokémon displays a ferocious fighting spirit.

These Pokémon have both calm and ferocious qualities. Their temperamental nature makes them a difficult species to raise.

### Special Moves

Crush Claw, Accelerock, Howl

Evolution

ROCKRUFF → LYCANROC (DUSK FORM)

*Lycanroc (Dusk Form) will only evolve from a special Rockruff with the ability of Own Tempo.

# LYCANROC

## MIDDAY FORM

This Lycanroc is calm and cautious. The rocks jutting from its mane are razor sharp.

| Wolf Pokémon | |
|---|---|
| **POKÉDEX NO.** | **745** |
| TYPE | Rock |
| ABILITY | Keen Eye, Sand Rush |
| HEIGHT | 2'07" |
| WEIGHT | 55.1 lbs |

## Description

With swift movements, this Pokémon gradually backs its prey into a corner. Lycanroc's fangs are always aimed toward opponents' weak spots.

## Special Moves

Sucker Punch, Accelerock, Stone Edge

## Evolution

ROCKRUFF

LYCANROC
[MIDDAY FORM]

001-100
101-200
201-300
401-442
443-500
501-600
701-800
801-898

# LYCANROC

## MIDNIGHT FORM

It's invigorated by powerful opponents—the stronger the better. A full-force headbutt from one of these Lycanroc can shatter giant boulders.

## Wolf Pokémon

| POKÉDEX NO. | 745 |
| --- | --- |
| TYPE | Rock |
| ABILITY | Keen Eye, Vital Spirit |
| HEIGHT | 3'07" |
| WEIGHT | 55.1 lbs |

### Description

This form of Lycanroc is reckless. It charges headlong at its opponents, attacking without any care about what injuries it might receive.

### Special Moves

Counter, Stealth Rock, Leer

**Evolution**

ROCKRUFF → LYCANROC (MIDNIGHT FORM)

# WISHIWASHI

## SOLO FORM

Individually, they're incredibly weak. It's by gathering up into schools that they're able to confront opponents.

| Small Fry Pokémon | |
|---|---|
| POKÉDEX NO. | **746** |
| TYPE | Water |
| ABILITY | Schooling |
| HEIGHT | 0'08" |
| WEIGHT | 0.7 lbs |

### Description

When it senses danger, its eyes tear up. The sparkle of its tears signals other Wishiwashi to gather.

### Special Moves

Water Gun, Aqua Ring, Tearful Look

**Evolution**  Does not evolve

WISHIWASHI
(SOLO FORM)

001-100
101-200
201-300
401-442
443-500
501-600
701-800
801-898

# WISHIWASHI

## SCHOOL FORM

On their own, they're very weak. But when Wishiwashi pool their power together in a school, they become a demon of the sea.

| Small Fry Pokémon | |
|---|---|
| **POKÉDEX NO.** | **746** |
| **TYPE** | Water |
| **ABILITY** | Schooling |
| **HEIGHT** | 26'11" |
| **WEIGHT** | 173.3 lbs |

### Description

When facing tough opponents, they get into formation. But if they get wounded in battle, they'll scatter and become solitary again.

### Special Moves

Hydro Pump, Brine, Beat Up

**Evolution**

WISHIWASHI
(SCHOOL FORM)

Does not evolve

# MAREANIE

Aside from its head, its body parts regenerate quickly if they're cut off. After a good night's sleep, Mareanie is back to normal.

## Brutal Star Pokémon

| | |
|---|---|
| POKÉDEX NO. | **747** |
| TYPE | Poison, Water |
| ABILITY | Limber, Merciless |
| HEIGHT | 1'04" |
| WEIGHT | 17.6 lbs |

### Description

The first symptom of its sting is numbness. The next is an itching sensation so intense that it's impossible to resist the urge to claw at your skin.

### Special Moves

Poison Sting, Venoshock, Pin Missile

### Evolution

 ➡

MAREANIE          TOXAPEX

001-100
101-200
201-300
401-442
443-500
501-600
701-800
801-898

# TOXAPEX

Within the poison sac in its body is a poison so toxic that Pokémon as large as Wailord* will still be suffering three days after it first takes effect.

## Brutal Star Pokémon

| POKÉDEX NO. | **748** |
|---|---|
| TYPE | Poison, Water |
| ABILITY | Limber, Merciless |
| HEIGHT | 2'04" |
| WEIGHT | 32.0 lbs |

### Description

With its 12 legs, it creates a dome to shelter within. The flow of the tides doesn't affect Toxapex in there, so it's very comfortable.

### Special Moves

Baneful Bunker, Venom Drench, Liquidation

**Evolution**

MAREANIE

TOXAPEX

*Wailord: A Pokémon you'll find in volume 1.

# MUDBRAY

Loads weighing up to 50 times as much as its own body weight pose no issue for this Pokémon. It's skilled at making use of mud.

| Donkey Pokémon | |
|---|---|
| **POKÉDEX NO.** | **749** |
| TYPE | Ground |
| ABILITY | Own Tempo, Stamina |
| HEIGHT | 3'03" |
| WEIGHT | 242.5 lbs |

## Description

It eats dirt to create mud and smears this mud all over its feet, giving it the grip needed to walk on rough terrain without slipping.

## Special Moves

Mud-Slap, Rock Smash, Mega Kick

001-100
101-200
201-300
401-442
443-500
501-600
701-800
801-898

**Evolution**

 →

MUDBRAY        MUDSDALE

# MUDSDALE

Mudsdale has so much stamina that it could carry over 10 tons across the Galar region without rest or sleep.

| Draft Horse Pokémon | |
|---|---|
| POKÉDEX NO. | **750** |
| TYPE | Ground |
| ABILITY | Own Tempo, Stamina |
| HEIGHT | 8'02" |
| WEIGHT | 2028.3 lbs |

## Description

Mud that hardens around a Mudsdale's legs sets harder than stone. It's so hard that it allows this Pokémon to scrap a truck with a single kick.

## Special Moves

Heavy Slam, High Horsepower, Stomp

**Evolution**

MUDBRAY

MUDSDALE

# DEWPIDER

It forms a water bubble at the rear of its body and then covers its head with it. Meeting another Dewpider means comparing water-bubble sizes.

## Water Bubble Pokémon

| POKÉDEX NO. | **751** |
| --- | --- |
| TYPE | Water, Bug |
| ABILITY | Water Bubble |
| HEIGHT | 1'00" |
| WEIGHT | 8.8 lbs |

### Description

Dewpider normally lives underwater. When it comes onto land in search of food, it takes water with it in the form of a bubble on its head.

### Special Moves

Bubble Beam, Infestation, Bub Bite

Evolution   ➡

DEWPIDER                ARAQUANID

001-100
101-200
201-300
401-442
443-500
501-600
701-800
801-898

# ARAQUANID

It launches water bubbles with its legs, drowning prey within the bubbles. This Pokémon can then take its time to savor its meal.

| Water Bubble Pokémon | |
|---|---|
| POKÉDEX NO. | **752** |
| TYPE | Water, Bug |
| ABILITY | Water Bubble |
| HEIGHT | 5'11" |
| WEIGHT | 180.8 lbs |

### Description

It acts as a caretaker for Dewpider, putting them inside its bubble and letting them eat any leftover food.

### Special Moves

Liquidation, Crunch, Leech Life

**Evolution**

DEWPIDER

→

ARAQUANID

# FOMANTIS

During the day, Fomantis basks in sunlight and sleeps peacefully. It wakes and moves around at night.

## Sickle Grass Pokémon

| POKÉDEX NO. | 753 |
|---|---|
| TYPE | Grass |
| ABILITY | Leaf Guard |
| HEIGHT | 1'00" |
| WEIGHT | 3.3 lbs |

### Description

When bathed in sunlight, this Pokémon emits a pleasantly sweet scent, which causes bug Pokémon to gather around it.

### Special Moves

Fury Cutter, Sunny Day, Sweet Scent

**Evolution**

FOMANTIS

⇒

LURANTIS

001-100
101-200
201-300
401-442
443-500
501-600
701-800
801-898

# LURANTIS

The petals on this Pokémon's arms are thin and super sharp, and they can fire laser beams if Lurantis gathers light first.

## Bloom Sickle Pokémon

| POKÉDEX NO. | 754 |
|---------|---------|
| TYPE | Grass |
| ABILITY | Leaf Guard |
| HEIGHT | 2'11" |
| WEIGHT | 40.8 lbs |

### Description

This Pokémon resembles a beautiful flower. A properly raised Lurantis will have gorgeous, brilliant colors.

### Special Moves

Petal Blizzard, Solar Blade, Night Slash

### Evolution

 FOMANTIS ➡  LURANTIS

# MORELULL

Morelull live in forests that stay dark even during the day. They scatter flickering spores that put enemies to sleep.

## Illuminating Pokémon

| POKÉDEX NO. | 755 |
|---|---|
| TYPE | Grass, Fairy |
| ABILITY | Effect Spore, Illuminate |
| HEIGHT | 0'08" |
| WEIGHT | 3.3 lbs |

### Description

Pokémon living in the forest eat the delicious caps on Morelull's head. The caps regrow overnight.

### Special Moves

Absorb, Sleep Powder, Confuse Ray

**Evolution**

 ➡

MORELULL　　SHIINOTIC

001-100
101-200
201-300
401-442
443-500
501-600
151-100
701-800
801-898

# SHIINOTIC

Its flickering spores lure in prey and put them to sleep. Once this Pokémon has its prey snoozing, it drains their vitality with its fingertips.

## Illuminating Pokémon

| | |
|---|---|
| **POKÉDEX NO.** | **756** |
| **TYPE** | Grass, Fairy |
| **ABILITY** | Effect Spore, Illuminate |
| **HEIGHT** | 3'03" |
| **WEIGHT** | 25.4 lbs |

### Description

If you see a light deep in a forest at night, don't go near. Shiinotic will make you fall fast asleep.

### Special Moves

Spore, Moonblast, Dream Eater

**Evolution**

MORELULL → SHIINOTIC

# SALANDIT

This sneaky Pokémon will slink behind its prey and immobilize it with poisonous gas before the prey even realizes Salandit is there.

| Toxic Lizard Pokémon | |
|---|---|
| POKÉDEX NO. | **757** |
| TYPE | Poison, Fire |
| ABILITY | Corrosion |
| HEIGHT | 2'00" |
| WEIGHT | 10.6 lbs |

### Description

Its venom sacs produce a fluid that this Pokémon then heats up with the flame in its tail. This process creates Salandit's poisonous gas.

### Special Moves

Poison Gas, Nasty Plot, Venoshock

**Evolution**

SALANDIT

SALAZZLE (FEMALE ONLY)

001-100
101-200
201-300
401-442
443-500
501-600
701-800
801-898

# SALAZZLE

The winner of competitions between Salazzle is decided by which one has the most male Salandit with it.

| Toxic Lizard Pokémon | |
|---|---|
| POKÉDEX NO. | **758** |
| TYPE | Poison, Fire |
| ABILITY | Corrosion |
| HEIGHT | 3'11" |
| WEIGHT | 48.9 lbs |

### Description

Only female Salazzle exist. They emit a gas laden with pheromones to captivate male Salandit.

### Special Moves

Fire Lash, Poison Fang, Incinerate

**Evolution**

SALANDIT (FEMALE ONLY) → SALAZZLE

# STUFFUL

The way it protects itself by flailing its arms may be an adorable sight, but stay well away. This is flailing that can snap thick tree trunks.

| Flailing Pokémon | |
|---|---|
| POKÉDEX NO. | **759** |
| TYPE | Normal, Fighting |
| ABILITY | Klutz, Fluffy |
| HEIGHT | 1'08" |
| WEIGHT | 15.0 lbs |

### Description

Its fluffy fur is a delight to pet, but carelessly reaching out to touch this Pokémon could result in painful retaliation.

### Special Moves

Tackle, Brutal Swing, Baby-Doll Eyes

**Evolution**

 ➡

STUFFUL      BEWEAR

# BEWEAR

The moves it uses to take down its prey would make a martial artist jealous. It tucks subdued prey under its arms to carry them to its nest.

| Strong Arm Pokémon | |
|---|---|
| POKÉDEX NO. | **760** |
| TYPE | Normal, Fighting |
| ABILITY | Klutz, Fluffy |
| HEIGHT | 6'11" |
| WEIGHT | 297.6 lbs |

### Description

Once it accepts you as a friend, it tries to show its affection with a hug. Letting it do that is dangerous—it could easily shatter your bones.

### Special Moves

Bind, Hammer Arm, Superpower

**Evolution**

STUFFUL

BEWEAR

# BOUNSWEET

Its body gives off a sweet, fruity scent that is extremely appetizing to bird Pokémon.

| Fruit Pokémon | |
|---|---|
| **POKÉDEX NO.** | **761** |
| TYPE | Grass |
| ABILITY | Oblivious, Leaf Guard |
| HEIGHT | 1'00" |
| WEIGHT | 7.1 lbs |

## Description

When under attack, it secretes a sweet and delicious sweat. But the scent only calls more enemies to it.

## Special Moves

Splash, Play Nice, Magical Leaf

001-100
101-200
201-300
401-442
443-500
501-600
701-800
801-898

**Evolution**

BOUNSWEET → STEENEE → TSAREENA

# STEENEE

Any Corvisquire* that pecks at this Pokémon will be greeted with a smack from its sepals,** followed by a sharp kick.

| Fruit Pokémon | |
|---|---|
| **POKÉDEX NO.** | **762** |
| **TYPE** | Grass |
| **ABILITY** | Oblivious, Leaf Guard |
| **HEIGHT** | 2'04" |
| **WEIGHT** | 18.1 lbs |

### Description

As it twirls like a dancer, a sweet smell spreads out around it. Anyone who inhales the scent will feel a surge of happiness.

### Special Moves

Razor Leaf, Rapid Spin, Flail

**Evolution**

BOUNSWEET

STEENEE

TSAREENA

*Corvisquire: A Pokémon you'll find on page 442. **Sepal: A small green leaf.

# TSAREENA

A kick from the hardened tips of this Pokémon's legs leaves a wound in the opponent's body and soul that will never heal.

| Fruit Pokémon | |
|---|---|
| **POKÉDEX NO.** | **763** |
| TYPE | Grass |
| ABILITY | Leaf Guard, Queenly Majesty |
| HEIGHT | 3'11" |
| WEIGHT | 47.2 lbs |

### Description

This feared Pokémon has long, slender legs and a cruel heart. It shows no mercy as it stomps on its opponents.

### Special Moves

Trop Kick, High Jump Kick, Stomp

**Evolution**

BOUNSWEET

STEENEE

TSAREENA

001-100
101-200
201-300
401-442
443-500
501-600
701-800
801-898

# COMFEY

Comfey picks flowers with its vine and decorates itself with them. For some reason, flowers won't wither once they're attached to a Comfey.

## Posy Picker Pokémon

| POKÉDEX NO. | 764 |
| --- | --- |
| TYPE | Fairy |
| ABILITY | Flower Veil, Triage |
| HEIGHT | 0'04" |
| WEIGHT | 0.7 lbs |

### Description

These Pokémon smell very nice. All Comfey wear different flowers, so each of these Pokémon has its own individual scent.

### Special Moves

Petal Dance, Petal Blizzard, Grass Knot

### Evolution

COMFEY

Does not evolve

# ORANGURU

It knows the forest inside and out. If it comes across a wounded Pokémon, Oranguru will gather medicinal herbs to treat it.

| Sage Pokémon | |
|---|---|
| **POKÉDEX NO.** | **765** |
| TYPE | Normal, Psychic |
| ABILITY | Inner Focus, Telepathy |
| HEIGHT | 4'11" |
| WEIGHT | 167.6 lbs |

### Description

With waves of its fan—made from leaves and its own fur—Oranguru skillfully gives instructions to other Pokémon.

### Special Moves

Instruct, Psychic, Zen Headbutt

**Evolution**

ORANGURU

Does not evolve

001-100
101-200
201-300
401-442
443-500
501-600
701-800
801-898

# PASSIMIAN

Passimian live in groups of about 20, with each member performing an assigned role. Through cooperation, the group survives.

## Teamwork Pokémon

| POKÉDEX NO. | 766 |
|---|---|
| TYPE | Fighting |
| ABILITY | Receiver |
| HEIGHT | 6'07" |
| WEIGHT | 182.5 lbs |

### Description

Displaying amazing teamwork, they follow the orders of their boss as they all help out in the search for their favorite berries.

### Special Moves

Fling, Giga Impact, Close Combat

Evolution

PASSIMIAN

Does not evolve

# WIMPOD

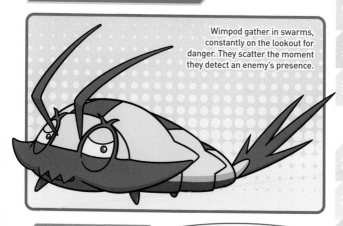

Wimpod gather in swarms, constantly on the lookout for danger. They scatter the moment they detect an enemy's presence.

| Turn Tail Pokémon | |
|---|---|
| POKÉDEX NO. | **767** |
| TYPE | Bug, Water |
| ABILITY | Wimp Out |
| HEIGHT | 1'08" |
| WEIGHT | 26.5 lbs |

### Description

It's nature's cleaner—it eats anything and everything, including garbage and rotten things. The ground near its nest is always clean.

### Special Moves

Struggle Bug, Sand Attack, Defense Curl

**Evolution**

WIMPOD ➡ GOLISOPOD

001-100
101-200
201-300
401-442
443-500
501-600
701-800
801-898

# GOLISOPOD

It will do anything to win, taking advantage of every opening and finishing opponents off with the small claws on its front legs.

## Hard Scale Pokémon

| POKÉDEX NO. | 768 |
|---|---|
| TYPE | Bug, Water |
| ABILITY | Emergency Exit |
| HEIGHT | 6'07" |
| WEIGHT | 238.1 lbs |

### Description

Its claws, which it can extend and retract at will, are its greatest weapons. Golisopod is sometimes accompanied by Wimpod.

### Special Moves

First Impression, Liquidation, Rock Smash

**Evolution**

WIMPOD

GOLISOPOD

# SANDYGAST

Sandygast mainly inhabits beaches. It takes control of anyone who puts their hand into its mouth, forcing them to make its body bigger.

| Sand Heap Pokémon | |
|---|---|
| POKÉDEX NO. | **769** |
| TYPE | Ghost, Ground |
| ABILITY | Water Compaction |
| HEIGHT | 1'08" |
| WEIGHT | 154.3 lbs |

### Description

Born from a sand mound playfully built by a child, this Pokémon embodies the grudges of the departed.

### Special Moves

Harden, Mega Drain, Shore Up

**Evolution**

SANDYGAST

PALOSSAND

# PALOSSAND

Palossand is known as the Beach Nightmare. It pulls its prey down into the sand by controlling the sand itself, and then it sucks out their souls.

## Sand Castle Pokémon

| | |
|---|---|
| **POKÉDEX NO.** | **770** |
| **TYPE** | Ghost, Ground |
| **ABILITY** | Water Compaction |
| **HEIGHT** | 4'03" |
| **WEIGHT** | 551.2 lbs |

### Description

This Pokémon lives on beaches, but it hates water. Palossand can't maintain its castle-like shape if it gets drenched by a heavy rain.

### Special Moves

Earth Power, Sand Tomb, Shore Up

**Evolution**

SANDYGAST

PALOSSAND

# PYUKUMUKU

**Sea Cucumber Pokémon**

| POKÉDEX NO. | 771 |
| --- | --- |
| **TYPE** | Water |
| **ABILITY** | Innards Out |
| **HEIGHT** | 1'00" |
| **WEIGHT** | 2.6 lbs |

001-100
101-200
201-300
401-442
443-500
501-600
701-800
801-898

### Description

It's covered in a slime that keeps its skin moist, allowing it to stay on land for days without drying up.

It lives in warm, shallow waters. If it encounters a foe, it will spit out its internal organs as a means to punch them.

### Special Moves

Counter, Recover, Soak

**Evolution**  Does not evolve

PYUKUMUKU

# TYPE: NULL

## Synthetic Pokémon

| POKÉDEX NO. | **772** |
|---|---|
| TYPE | Normal |
| ABILITY | Battle Armor |
| HEIGHT | 6'03" |
| WEIGHT | 265.7 lbs |

A Pokémon weapon developed for a specific mission, it went berserk during an experiment, so it was cryogenically frozen.

### Description

It was modeled after a mighty Pokémon of myth. The mask placed upon it limits its power in order to keep it under control.

### Special Moves

Crush Claw, Double Hit, Take Down

Evolution  ➡

TYPE: NULL     SILVALLY

# SILVALLY

| | |
|---|---|
| **Synthetic Pokémon** | |
| **POKÉDEX NO.** | **773** |
| **TYPE** | Normal |
| **ABILITY** | RKS System |
| **HEIGHT** | 7'07" |
| **WEIGHT** | 221.6 lbs |

001-100
101-200
201-300
401-442
443-500
501-600
601-700
701-800
801-898

The final factor needed to release this Pokémon's true power was a strong bond with a Trainer it trusts.

### Description

A solid bond of trust between this Pokémon and its Trainer awakened the strength hidden within Silvally. It can change its type at will.

### Special Moves

Multi-Attack, Tri Attack, Imprison

**Evolution**

TYPE: NULL      SILVALLY

# RKS SYSTEM

Silvally uses its ability, RKS System, to change its type and body color depending on the Memory it is holding.

**Dark Type**

Dark Memory

**Rock Type**

Rock Memory

**Psychic Type**

Psychic Memory

**Fighting Type**

Fighting Memory

**Grass Type**

Grass Memory

**Ghost Type**

Ghost Memory

**Ice Type**

Ice Memory

**Ground Type**

Ground Memory

## Electric Type
Electric Memory

## Poison Type
Poison Memory

## Dragon Type
Dragon Memory

## Steel Type
Steel Memory

## Flying Type
Flying Memory

## Fairy Type
Fairy Memory

## Fire Type
Fire Memory

## Water Type
Water Memory

## Bug Type
Bug Memory

001-100

101-200

201-300

401-442

443-500

501-600

701-800

801-898

# MINIOR

## Meteor Pokémon

| | |
|---|---|
| **POKÉDEX NO.** | **774** |
| **TYPE** | Rock, Flying |
| **ABILITY** | Shields Down |
| **HEIGHT** | 1'00" |
| **WEIGHT** | 88.2 lbs |

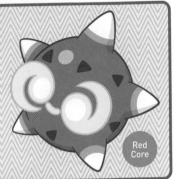

Red Core

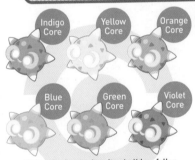

Indigo Core
Yellow Core
Orange Core
Blue Core
Green Core
Violet Core

This is its form when its shell has fallen off. The color of its core depends on the materials that made up the food it ate.

### Description

Places where Minior fall from the night sky are few and far between, with Alola being one of the precious few.

### Special Moves

Swift, Ancient Power, Self-Destruct

### Evolution

MINIOR

Does not evolve

# KOMALA

It stays asleep from the moment it's born. When it falls into a deep sleep, it stops moving altogether.

| Drowsing Pokémon | |
|---|---|
| **POKÉDEX NO.** | **775** |
| TYPE | Normal |
| ABILITY | Comatose |
| HEIGHT | 1'04" |
| WEIGHT | 43.9 lbs |

### Description

It remains asleep from birth to death as a result of the sedative properties of the leaves that form its diet.

### Special Moves

Wood Hammer, Rapid Spin, Yawn

**Evolution**

KOMALA

Does not evolve

001-100
101-200
201-300
401-442
443-500
501-600
701-800
801-898

# TURTONATOR

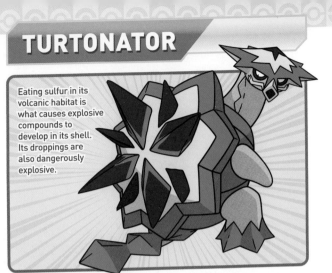

Eating sulfur in its volcanic habitat is what causes explosive compounds to develop in its shell. Its droppings are also dangerously explosive.

| Blast Turtle Pokémon | |
|---|---|
| POKÉDEX NO. | **776** |
| TYPE | Fire, Dragon |
| ABILITY | Shell Armor |
| HEIGHT | 6'07" |
| WEIGHT | 467.4 lbs |

## Description

Explosive substances coat the shell on its back. Enemies that dare attack it will be blown away by an immense detonation.

## Special Moves

Shell Trap, Explosive, Incinerate

Evolution

TURTONATOR

Does not evolve

# TOGEDEMARU

## Roly-Poly Pokémon

| POKÉDEX NO. | **777** |
|---|---|
| **TYPE** | Electric, Steel |
| **ABILITY** | Lightning Rod, Iron Barbs |
| **HEIGHT** | 1'00" |
| **WEIGHT** | 7.3 lbs |

With the long hairs on its back, this Pokémon takes in electricity from other electric Pokémon. It stores what it absorbs in an electric sac.

## Description

When it's surprised or agitated, the 14 fur spikes on its back will stand up involuntarily.

## Special Moves

Nuzzle, Pin Missile, Spark

**Evolution**   Does not evolve

TOGEDEMARU

001-100
101-200
201-300
401-442
443-500
501-600
701-800
801-898

# MIMIKYU

## Disguise Pokémon

| POKÉDEX NO. | 778 |
| --- | --- |
| **TYPE** | Ghost, Fairy |
| **ABILITY** | Disguise |
| **HEIGHT** | 0'08" |
| **WEIGHT** | 1.5 lbs |

There was a scientist who peeked under Mimikyu's old rag in the name of research. The scientist died of a mysterious disease.

### Description

It wears a rag fashioned into a Pikachu costume in an effort to look less scary. Unfortunately, the costume only makes it creepier.

### Special Moves

Shadow Sneak, Shadow Claw, Wood Hammer

**Evolution**

Does not evolve

MIMIKYU
(DISGUISED FORM)

# MIMIKYU

**BUSTED FORM**

Its disguise made from an old rag allowed it to avoid an attack, but the impact broke the neck of the disguise. Now everyone knows it's a Mimikyu.

## Disguise Pokémon

| POKÉDEX NO. | **778** |
|---|---|
| TYPE | Ghost, Fairy |
| ABILITY | Disguise |
| HEIGHT | 0'08" |
| WEIGHT | 1.5 lbs |

### Description

There will be no forgiveness for any who reveal that it was pretending to be Pikachu. It will bring the culprit down, even at the cost of its own life.

### Special Moves

Shadow Sneak, Baby-Doll Eyes, Double Team

**Evolution**

**MIMIKYU**
(BUSTED FORM)

Does not evolve

001-100
101-200
201-300
401-442
443-500
501-600
701-800
801-898

# BRUXISH

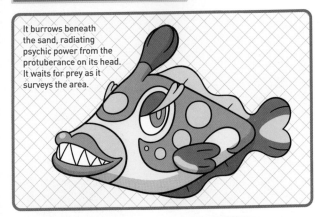

It burrows beneath the sand, radiating psychic power from the protuberance on its head. It waits for prey as it surveys the area.

| Gnash Teeth Pokémon | |
|---|---|
| **POKÉDEX NO.** | **779** |
| TYPE | Water, Psychic |
| ABILITY | Strong Jaw, Dazzling |
| HEIGHT | 2'11" |
| WEIGHT | 41.9 lbs |

## Description

Its skin is thick enough to fend off Mareanie's* spikes. With its robust teeth, Bruxish crunches up the spikes and eats them.

## Special Moves

Psychic Fangs, Crunch, Screech

**Evolution**

BRUXISH

Does not evolve

 *Mareanie: A Pokémon you'll find on page 357.

# DRAMPA

Drampa is a kind and friendly Pokémon—up until it's angered. When that happens, it stirs up a gale and flattens everything around.

| Placid Pokémon | |
|---|---|
| **POKÉDEX NO.** | **780** |
| **TYPE** | Normal, Dragon |
| **ABILITY** | Sap Sipper, Berserk |
| **HEIGHT** | 9'10" |
| **WEIGHT** | 407.9 lbs |

### Description

The mountains it calls home are nearly two miles in height. On rare occasions, it descends to play with the children living in the towns below.

### Special Moves

Dragon Pulse, Fly, Extrasensory

**Evolution**

DRAMPA

Does not evolve

001-100
101-200
201-300
401-442
443-500
501-600
701-800
801-898

# DHELMISE

After lowering its anchor, it waits for its prey. It catches large Wailord* and drains their life-force.

## Sea Creeper Pokémon

| POKÉDEX NO. | 781 |
|---|---|
| TYPE | Ghost, Grass |
| ABILITY | Steelworker |
| HEIGHT | 12'10" |
| WEIGHT | 463.0 lbs |

### Description

After a piece of seaweed merged with debris from a sunken ship, it was reborn as this ghost Pokémon.

### Special Moves

Anchor Shot, Giga Drain, Whirlpool

### Evolution

DHELMISE

Does not evolve

*Wailord: A Pokémon you'll find in volume 1.

# JANGMO-O

They learn to fight by smashing their head scales together. The dueling strengthens both their skills and their spirits.

| Scaly Pokémon | |
|---|---|
| **POKÉDEX NO.** | **782** |
| TYPE | Dragon |
| ABILITY | Soundproof, Bulletproof |
| HEIGHT | 2'00" |
| WEIGHT | 65.5 lbs |

## Description

Jangmo-o strikes its scales to communicate with others of its kind. Its scales are actually fur that's become as hard as metal.

## Special Moves

Tackle, Leer, Dragon Tail

**Evolution**

JANGMO-O → HAKAMO-O → KOMMO-O

001-100
101-200
201-300
401-442
443-500
501-600
701-800
801-898

# HAKAMO-O

The scaleless, scarred parts of its body are signs of its strength. It shows them off to defeated opponents.

## Scaly Pokémon

| POKÉDEX NO. | **783** |
|---|---|
| **TYPE** | Dragon, Fighting |
| **ABILITY** | Soundproof, Bulletproof |
| **HEIGHT** | 3'11" |
| **WEIGHT** | 103.6 lbs |

### Description

Before attacking its enemies, it clashes its scales together and roars. Its sharp claws shred the opposition.

### Special Moves

Dragon Claw, Dragon Dance, Iron Defense

**Evolution**

JANGMO-O

HAKAMO-O

KOMMO-O

# KOMMO-O

Certain ruins have paintings of ancient warriors wearing armor made of Kommo-o scales.

| Scaly Pokémon | |
|---|---|
| POKÉDEX NO. | **784** |
| TYPE | Dragon, Fighting |
| ABILITY | Soundproof, Bulletproof |
| HEIGHT | 5'03" |
| WEIGHT | 172.4 lbs |

## Description

It clatters its tail scales to unnerve opponents. This Pokémon will battle only those who stand steadfast in the face of this display.

## Special Moves

Clanging Scales, Clangorous Soul, Boomburst

**Evolution**

JANGMO-O

HAKAMO-O

KOMMO-O

001-100
101-200
201-300
401-442
443-500
501-600
701-800
801-898

# TAPU KOKO

## Land Spirit Pokémon

| POKÉDEX NO. | **785** |
| --- | --- |
| TYPE | Electric, Fairy |
| ABILITY | Electric Surge |
| HEIGHT | 5'11" |
| WEIGHT | 45.2 lbs |

The lightning-wielding guardian deity of Melemele.* Tapu Koko is brimming with curiosity and appears before people from time to time.

### Description

Although it's called a guardian deity, if a person or Pokémon puts it in a bad mood, it will become a malevolent deity and attack.

### Special Moves

Wild Charge, Shock Wave, Charge

### Evolution

TAPU KOKO

Does not evolve

*Melemele: An island in the Alola region.

# TAPU LELE

| Land Spirit Pokémon | |
|---|---|
| **POKÉDEX NO.** | **786** |
| TYPE | Psychic, Fairy |
| ABILITY | Psychic Surge |
| HEIGHT | 3'11" |
| WEIGHT | 41.0 lbs |

001-100
101-200
201-300
401-442
443-500
501-600
701-800
801-898

It heals the wounds of people and Pokémon by sprinkling them with its sparkling scales. This guardian deity is worshipped on Akala.*

### Description

Although it's called a guardian deity, Tapu Lele is devoid of guilt about its cruel disposition and can be described as nature incarnate.

### Special Moves

Psyshock, Moonblast, Tickle

**Evolution**

**TAPU LELE**

Does not evolve

---

*Akala: An island in the Alola region.

# TAPU BULU

## Land Spirit Pokémon

| POKÉDEX NO. | **787** |
|---|---|
| **TYPE** | Grass, Fairy |
| **ABILITY** | Grassy Surge |
| **HEIGHT** | 6'03" |
| **WEIGHT** | 100.3 lbs |

It makes ringing sounds with its tail to let others know where it is, avoiding unneeded conflicts. This guardian deity of Ula'ula* controls plants.

### Description

Although it's called a guardian deity, it's violent enough to crush anyone it sees as an enemy.

### Special Moves

Horn Leech, Wood Hammer, Megahorn

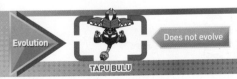

**Evolution**    TAPU BULU    Does not evolve

*Ula'ula: An island in the Alola region.

# TAPU FINI

Land Spirit Pokémon

| POKÉDEX NO. | **788** |
| --- | --- |
| TYPE | Water, Fairy |
| ABILITY | Misty Surge |
| HEIGHT | 4'03" |
| WEIGHT | 46.7 lbs |

001-100
101-200
201-300
401-442
443-500
501-600
701-800
801-898

## Description

Although it's called a guardian deity, terrible calamities sometimes befall those who recklessly approach Tapu Fini.

This guardian deity of Poni Island* manipulates water. Because it lives deep within a thick fog, it came to be both feared and revered.

## Special Moves

Hydro Pump, Heal Pulse, Surf

Evolution

TAPU FINI

Does not evolve

---

*Poni: An island in the Alola region.

# COSMOG

| | |
|---|---|
| **Nebula Pokémon** | |
| **POKÉDEX NO.** | **789** |
| **TYPE** | Psychic |
| **ABILITY** | Unaware |
| **HEIGHT** | 0'08" |
| **WEIGHT** | 0.2 lbs |

Cosmog is very curious but not very cautious, often placing itself in danger. If things start to look dicey, it teleports away.

## Description

This Pokémon came from another universe. Its gaseous body is so light that even a gentle breeze can blow it away.

## Special Moves

Splash,
Teleport

**Evolution**

COSMOG → COSMOEM → SOLGALEO   LUNALA

# COSMOEM

The absorption of starlight fuels this Pokémon's growth. The shell that encases it is harder than any known material.

## Protostar Pokémon

| POKÉDEX NO. | **790** |
|---|---|
| TYPE | Psychic |
| ABILITY | Sturdy |
| HEIGHT | 0'04" |
| WEIGHT | 2204.4 lbs |

### Description

It sucks in dust from the air at an astounding rate, frantically building up energy within its core as preparation for evolution.

### Special Moves

Cosmic Power, Teleport

Evolution

COSMOG

COSMOEM

SOLGALEO

LUNALA

001-100
101-200
201-300
401-442
443-500
501-600
701-800
801-898

# SOLGALEO

## Sunne Pokémon

| POKÉDEX NO. | **791** |
|---|---|
| **TYPE** | Psychic, Steel |
| **ABILITY** | Full Metal Body |
| **HEIGHT** | 11'02" |
| **WEIGHT** | 507.1 lbs |

Radiant Sun Phase

Solgaleo was once known as the Beast That Devours the Sun. Energy in the form of light radiates boundlessly from it.

### Description

When light radiates from its body, this Pokémon could almost appear to be the sun. It will dispel any darkness and light up the world.

### Special Moves

Sunsteel Strike, Metal Burst, Noble Roar

Evolution

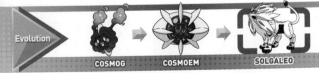

COSMOG → COSMOEM → SOLGALEO

# LUNALA

| | |
|---|---|
| **Moone Pokémon** | |
| **POKÉDEX NO.** | **792** |
| **TYPE** | Psychic, Ghost |
| **ABILITY** | Shadow Shield |
| **HEIGHT** | 13'01" |
| **WEIGHT** | 264.6 lbs |

### Description

Known as the Beast That Calls the Moon, this Pokémon lives by taking in any and all light and converting it into its own energy.

**Full Moon Phase**

It steals the light from its surroundings and then becomes the full moon, showering its own light across the night sky.

### Special Moves

Moongeist Beam, Moonblast, Dream Eater

**Evolution**

COSMOG → COSMOEM → LUNALA

# NIHILEGO

A life form from another world, it was dubbed an Ultra Beast and is thought to produce a strong neurotoxin.

| Parasite Pokémon | |
|---|---|
| **POKÉDEX NO.** | **793** |
| TYPE | Rock, Poison |
| ABILITY | Beast Boost |
| HEIGHT | 3'11" |
| WEIGHT | 122.4 lbs |

### Description

It appeared in this world from an Ultra Wormhole. Nihilego appears to be a parasite that lives by feeding on people and Pokémon.

### Special Moves

Acid Spray, Stealth Rock, Toxic Spikes

**Evolution**  NIHILEGO — Does not evolve

# BUZZWOLE

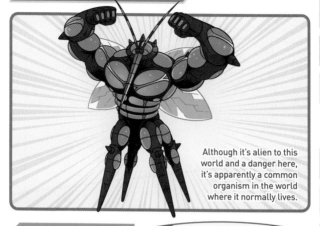

Although it's alien to this world and a danger here, it's apparently a common organism in the world where it normally lives.

| Swollen Pokémon | |
| --- | --- |
| POKÉDEX NO. | **794** |
| TYPE | Bug, Fighting |
| ABILITY | Beast Boost |
| HEIGHT | 7'10" |
| WEIGHT | 735.5 lbs |

## Description

Buzzwole goes around showing off its abnormally swollen muscles. It is one kind of Ultra Beast.

## Special Moves

Focus Punch, Dynamic Punch, Superpower

Evolution

BUZZWOLE

Does not evolve

001-100
101-200
201-300
401-442
443-500
501-600
701-800
801-898

# PHEROMOSA

Although it's alien to this world and a danger here, it's apparently a common organism in the world where it normally lives.

## Lissome Pokémon

| POKÉDEX NO. | 795 |
|---|---|
| TYPE | Bug, Fighting |
| ABILITY | Beast Boost |
| HEIGHT | 5'11" |
| WEIGHT | 55.1 lbs |

### Description

A life form that lives in another world, its body is thin and supple, but it also possesses great power.

### Special Moves

High Jump Kick, Speed Swap, Stomp

**Evolution**  Does not evolve

PHEROMOSA

# XURKITREE

001-100
101-200
201-300
401-442
443-500
501-600
701-800
801-898

**Glowing Pokémon**

| | |
|---|---|
| **POKÉDEX NO.** | **796** |
| **TYPE** | Electric |
| **ABILITY** | Beast Boost |
| **HEIGHT** | 12'06" |
| **WEIGHT** | 220.5 lbs |

Although it's alien to this world and a danger here, it's apparently a common organism in the world where it normally lives.

## Description

They've been dubbed Ultra Beasts. Some of them stand unmoving, like trees, with their arms and legs stuck into the ground.

## Special Moves

Zap Cannon, Thunderbolt, Magnet Rise

**Evolution**   Does not evolve

XURKITREE

# CELESTEELA

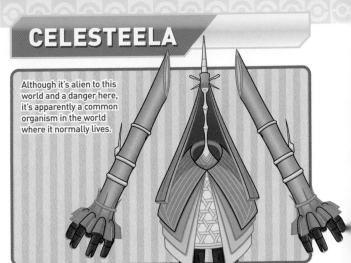

Although it's alien to this world and a danger here, it's apparently a common organism in the world where it normally lives.

## Launch Pokémon

| POKÉDEX NO. | 797 |
| --- | --- |
| TYPE | Steel, Flying |
| ABILITY | Beast Boost |
| HEIGHT | 30'02" |
| WEIGHT | 2204.4 lbs |

### Description

One of the dangerous Ultra Beasts, high energy readings can be detected coming from both of its huge arms.

### Special Moves

Flash Cannon, Heavy Slam, Iron Defense

Evolution   Does not evolve

CELESTEELA

# KARTANA

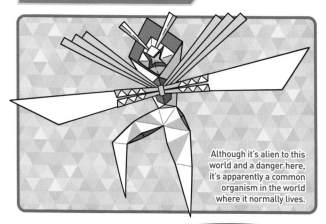

Although it's alien to this world and a danger here, it's apparently a common organism in the world where it normally lives.

| Drawn Sword Pokémon | |
|---|---|
| **POKÉDEX NO.** | **798** |
| TYPE | Grass, Steel |
| ABILITY | Beast Boost |
| HEIGHT | 1'00" |
| WEIGHT | 0.2 lbs |

### Description

This Ultra Beast's body, which is as thin as paper, is like a sharpened sword.

### Special Moves

Cut, Sacred Sword, Air Cutter

Evolution

KARTANA

Does not evolve

001-100
101-200
201-300
401-442
443-500
501-600
701-800
801-898

# GUZZLORD

Although it's alien to this world and a danger here, it's apparently a common organism in the world where it normally lives.

| Junkivore Pokémon | |
|---|---|
| POKÉDEX NO. | **799** |
| TYPE | Dark, Dragon |
| ABILITY | Beast Boost |
| HEIGHT | 18'01" |
| WEIGHT | 1957.7 lbs |

## Description

An unknown life form called an Ultra Beast. It may be constantly hungry—it is certainly always devouring something.

## Special Moves

Dragon Rush, Giga Impact, Swallow

**Evolution**  GUZZLORD Does not evolve

# NECROZMA

### Prism Pokémon

| POKÉDEX NO. | **800** |
|---|---|
| TYPE | Psychic |
| ABILITY | Prism Armor |
| HEIGHT | 7'10" |
| WEIGHT | 507.1 lbs |

It needs light to survive, and it goes on a rampage seeking it out. Its laser beams will cut anything to pieces.

### Description

It survives by absorbing light. After a long time spent slumbering underground, impurities accumulated within it, causing its body to darken.

### Special Moves

Prismatic Laser, Power Gem, Night Slash

**Evolution**
NECROZMA

Does not evolve

001-100
101-200
201-300
401-442
663-700
501-600
701-800
801-898

# NECROZMA

**ULTRA NECROZMA**

## Prism Pokémon

| POKÉDEX NO. | **800** |
|---|---|
| **TYPE** | Psychic, Dragon |
| **ABILITY** | Neuroforce |
| **HEIGHT** | 24'07" |
| **WEIGHT** | 507.1 lbs |

### Description

This is its form when it has absorbed overwhelming light energy. It fires laser beams from all over its body.

The light pouring out from all over its body affects living things and nature, impacting them in various ways.

### Special Moves

Photon Geyser, Metal Claw, Slash

**Evolution**  Does not evolve

NECROZMA
(ULTRA NECROZMA)

# NECROZMA

## DUSK MANE NECROZMA

### Prism Pokémon

| POKÉDEX NO. | **800** |
|---|---|
| TYPE | Psychic, Steel |
| ABILITY | Prism Armor |
| HEIGHT | 12'06" |
| WEIGHT | 1014.1 lbs |

001-100
101-200
201-300
401-442
443-500
501-600
701-800
801-898

### Description

Necrozma has attached itself to Solgaleo.* It siphons away its host's limitless energy, exploiting that energy to fuel a rampage.

When it dominates Solgaleo, it takes on this form. It's a vicious Pokémon, mangling prey with its many claws—including those on its back.

### Special Moves

Sunsteel Strike, Charge Beam, Iron Defense

**Evolution**

NECROZMA
(DUSK MANE NECROZMA)

Does not evolve

*Solgaleo: A Pokémon you'll find on page 404.

# NECROZMA

## DAWN WINGS NECROZMA

### Prism Pokémon

| POKÉDEX NO. | **800** |
|---|---|
| **TYPE** | Psychic, Ghost |
| **ABILITY** | Prism Armor |
| **HEIGHT** | 13'09" |
| **WEIGHT** | 771.6 lbs |

Necrozma has subjugated Lunala entirely, forcing the unfortunate Pokémon to emit its light energy for Necrozma to consume.

### Description

When Necrozma latches onto Lunala,* it becomes vicious, seeing enemies everywhere it looks. It will burn the world with lasers.

### Special Moves

Moongeist Beam, Psycho Cut, Night Slash

**Evolution**  Does not evolve

NECROZMA
[DAWN WINGS NECROZMA]

*Lunala: A Pokémon you'll find on page 405.

# MAGEARNA

**Artificial Pokémon**

| POKÉDEX NO. | **801** |
|---|---|
| **TYPE** | Steel, Fairy |
| **ABILITY** | Soul-Heart |
| **HEIGHT** | 3'03" |
| **WEIGHT** | 177.5 lbs |

## Description

Built roughly 500 years ago by a scientist, the part called the Soul-Heart is the actual life form.

It synchronizes its consciousness with others to understand their feelings. This faculty makes it useful for taking care of people.

## Special Moves

Fleur Cannon, Gear Up, Zap Cannon

**Evolution**

MAGEARNA | Does not evolve

001-100
101-200
201-300
401-442
443-500
501-600
701-800
801-898

# MARSHADOW

## Gloomdweller Pokémon

| POKÉDEX NO. | **802** |
|---|---|
| **TYPE** | Fighting, Ghost |
| **ABILITY** | Technician |
| **HEIGHT** | 2'04" |
| **WEIGHT** | 48.9 lbs |

By slipping into the shadows of a martial arts master and copying their movements, this Pokémon learned the ultimate techniques.

### Description

This Pokémon can conceal itself in any shadow, so it went undiscovered for a long time.

### Special Moves

Spectral Thief, Force Palm, Close Combat

---

**Evolution**   Does not evolve

MARSHADOW

# POIPOLE

## Poison Pin Pokémon

| POKÉDEX NO. | **803** |
|---|---|
| TYPE | Poison |
| ABILITY | Beast Boost |
| HEIGHT | 2'00" |
| WEIGHT | 4.0 lbs |

001-100
101-200
201-300
401-442
443-500
501-600
701-800
801-898

### Description

This Ultra Beast is well enough liked to be chosen as a first partner in its own world.

An Ultra Beast that lives in a different world, it cackles wildly as it sprays its opponents with poison from the needles on its head.

### Special Moves

Acid, Venoshock, Fury Attack

**Evolution**

 ➡

POIPOLE          NAGANADEL

# NAGANADEL

| | |
|---|---|
| **POKÉDEX NO.** | **804** |
| **TYPE** | Poison, Dragon |
| **ABILITY** | Beast Boost |
| **HEIGHT** | 11'10" |
| **WEIGHT** | 330.7 lbs |

One kind of Ultra Beast, it fires a glowing, venomous liquid from its needles. This liquid is also immensely adhesive.

### Description

It stores large amounts of poisonous liquid inside its body. It is one of the organisms known as Ultra Beasts.

### Special Moves

Air Cutter, Dragon Rush, Fell Stinger

**Evolution**

POIPOLE

NAGANADEL

420

# STAKATAKA

It appeared from an Ultra Wormhole. Each one appears to be made up of many life forms stacked one on top of each other.

| Rampart Pokémon | |
|---|---|
| **POKÉDEX NO.** | **805** |
| TYPE | Rock, Steel |
| ABILITY | Beast Boost |
| HEIGHT | 18'01" |
| WEIGHT | 1807.8 lbs |

### Description

When stone walls started moving and attacking, the brute's true identity was this mysterious life form, which brings to mind an Ultra Beast.

### Special Moves

Rock Blast, Magnet Rise, Iron Defense

Evolution  Does not evolve

STAKATAKA

001-100
101-200
201-300
401-442
443-500
501-600
601-700
701-800
801-898

# BLACEPHALON

It slithers toward people. Then, without warning, it triggers the explosion of its own head. It's apparently one kind of Ultra Beast.

## Fireworks Pokémon

| POKÉDEX NO. | **806** |
|---|---|
| TYPE | Fire, Ghost |
| ABILITY | Beast Boost |
| HEIGHT | 5'11" |
| WEIGHT | 28.7 lbs |

### Description

An Ultra Beast that appeared from an Ultra Wormhole, it causes explosions, then takes advantage of opponents' surprise to rob them of their vitality.

### Special Moves

Mind Blown, Night Shade, Fire Blast

Evolution

BLACEPHALON

Does not evolve

# ZERAORA

| | |
|---|---|
| **Thunderclap Pokémon** | |
| **POKÉDEX NO.** | **807** |
| TYPE | Electric |
| ABILITY | Volt Absorb |
| HEIGHT | 4'11" |
| WEIGHT | 98.1 lbs |

001-100
101-200
201-300
401-442
443-500
501-600
701-800
801-898

### Description

It runs as fast as lightning strikes, shredding its opponents with its high-voltage claws.

Electricity sparks from the pads on its limbs. Wherever Zeraora runs, lightning flashes and thunder echoes.

### Special Moves

Plasma Fists,
Power-Up Punch, Hone Claws

**Evolution**  Does not evolve

ZERAORA

# MELTAN

| Hex Nut Pokémon | |
|---|---|
| **POKÉDEX NO.** | **808** |
| TYPE | Steel |
| ABILITY | Magnet Pull |
| HEIGHT | 0'08" |
| WEIGHT | 17.6 lbs |

It dissolves and eats metal. Circulating liquid metal within its body is how it generates energy.

### Description

They live as a group, but when the time comes, one strong Meltan will absorb all the others and evolve.

### Special Moves

Thunder Shock, Thunder Wave, Flash Cannon

**Evolution**

MELTAN → MELMETAL

# MELMETAL

### Hex Nut Pokémon

| | |
|---|---|
| **POKÉDEX NO.** | **809** |
| **TYPE** | Steel |
| **ABILITY** | Iron Fist |
| **HEIGHT** | 8'02" |
| **WEIGHT** | 1763.7 lbs |

001-100
101-200
201-300
401-442
443-500
501-600
601-700
701-800
801-898

Centrifugal force is behind the punches of Melmetal's heavy hex-nut arms. Melmetal is said to deliver the strongest punches of all Pokémon.

### Description

At the end of its life span, Melmetal will rust and fall apart. The small shards left behind will eventually be reborn as Meltan.

### Special Moves

Double Iron Bash, Flash Cannon, Protect

**Evolution**

MELTAN

MELMETAL

# MELMETAL

## GIGANTAMAX FORM

It can send electric beams streaking out from the hole in its belly. The beams' tremendous energy can vaporize an opponent in one shot.

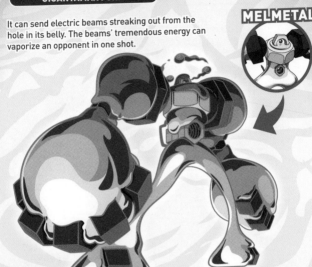

MELMETAL

### Description

In a distant land, there are legends of a cyclopean giant. In fact, the giant was a Melmetal that was flooded with Gigantamax energy.

### Special Moves

G-Max Meltdown

| Hex Nut Pokémon | |
|---|---|
| **POKÉDEX NO.** | **809** |
| TYPE | Steel |
| ABILITY | Iron Fist |
| HEIGHT | 82'00"+ |
| WEIGHT | ??? lbs |

# GROOKEY

### Chimp Pokémon

| POKÉDEX NO. | **810** |
|---|---|
| TYPE | Grass |
| ABILITY | Overgrow |
| HEIGHT | 1'00" |
| WEIGHT | 11.0 lbs |

001-100
101-200
201-300
401-442
443-500
501-600
701-800
801-898

### Description

It attacks with rapid beats of its stick. As it strikes with amazing speed, it gets more and more pumped.

When it uses its special stick to strike up a beat, the sound waves produced carry revitalizing energy to the plants and flowers in the area.

### Special Moves

Slam, Razor Leaf, Branch Poke

**Evolution**

GROOKEY

THWACKEY

RILLABOOM

# THWACKEY

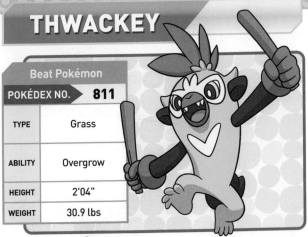

**Beat Pokémon**

| POKÉDEX NO. | **811** |
| --- | --- |
| **TYPE** | Grass |
| **ABILITY** | Overgrow |
| **HEIGHT** | 2'04" |
| **WEIGHT** | 30.9 lbs |

## Description

The faster a Thwackey can beat out a rhythm with its two sticks, the more respect it wins from its peers.

When it's drumming out rapid beats in battle, it gets so caught up in the rhythm that it won't even notice that it's already knocked out its opponent.

## Special Moves

Double Hit, Knock Off, Screech

**Evolution**

GROOKEY → THWACKEY → RILLABOOM

# RILLABOOM

**Drummer Pokémon**

| POKÉDEX NO. | **812** |
|---|---|
| TYPE | Grass |
| ABILITY | Overgrow |
| HEIGHT | 6'11" |
| WEIGHT | 198.4 lbs |

001-100
101-200
201-300
401-442
443-500
501-600
781-800
801-898

By drumming, it taps into the power of its special tree stump. The roots of the stump follow its direction in battle.

### Description

The one with the best drumming techniques becomes the boss of the troop. It has a gentle disposition and values harmony among its group.

### Special Moves

Drum Beating, Boomburst, Endeavor

**Evolution**

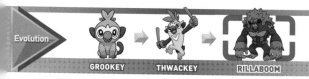

GROOKEY → THWACKEY → RILLABOOM

# RILLABOOM

RILLABOOM

Gigantamax energy has caused Rillaboom's stump to grow into a drum set that resembles a forest.

## Drummer Pokémon

| POKÉDEX NO. | 812 |
|---|---|
| TYPE | Grass |
| ABILITY | Overgrow |
| HEIGHT | 91'10"+ |
| WEIGHT | ??? lbs |

### Description

Rillaboom has become one with its forest of drums and continues to lay down beats that shake all of Galar.

### Special Moves

G-Max Drum Solo

# SCORBUNNY

| Rabbit Pokémon | |
|---|---|
| POKÉDEX NO. | **813** |
| TYPE | Fire |
| ABILITY | Blaze |
| HEIGHT | 1'00" |
| WEIGHT | 9.9 lbs |

001-100
101-200
201-300
401-442
443-500
501-600
701-800
801-898

It has special pads on the backs of its feet, and one on its nose. Once it's raring to fight, these pads radiate tremendous heat.

### Description

A warm-up of running around gets fire energy coursing through this Pokémon's body. Once that happens, it's ready to fight at full power.

### Special Moves

Ember, Quick Attack, Agility

**Evolution**

SCORBUNNY → RABOOT → CINDERACE

# RABOOT

### Rabbit Pokémon

| | |
|---|---|
| POKÉDEX NO. | **814** |
| TYPE | Fire |
| ABILITY | Blaze |
| HEIGHT | 2'00" |
| WEIGHT | 19.8 lbs |

Its thick and fluffy fur protects it from the cold and enables it to use hotter fire moves.

### Description

It kicks berries right off the branches of trees and then juggles them with its feet, practicing its footwork.

### Special Moves

Flame Charge, Counter, Bounce

**Evolution**

SCORBUNNY

RABOOT

CINDERACE

# CINDERACE

### Striker Pokémon

| POKÉDEX NO. | **815** |
| --- | --- |
| TYPE | Fire |
| ABILITY | Blaze |
| HEIGHT | 4'07" |
| WEIGHT | 72.8 lbs |

It's skilled at both offense and defense, and it gets pumped up when it's cheered on. But if it starts showboating,* it could put itself in a tough spot.

### Description

It juggles a pebble with its feet, turning it into a burning soccer ball. Its shots strike opponents hard and leave them scorched.

### Special Moves

Pyro Ball,
Court Change, Feint

001-100
101-200
201-300
401-442
443-500
501-600
701-800
801-898

**Evolution**

SCORBUNNY → RABOOT → CINDERACE

*Showboating: Showing off to attract attention.

# CINDERACE

## GIGANTAMAX FORM

### CINDERACE

Infused with Cinderace's fighting spirit, the gigantic Pyro Ball never misses its targets and completely roasts opponents.

| Striker Pokémon | |
|---|---|
| POKÉDEX NO. | **815** |
| TYPE | Fire |
| ABILITY | Blaze |
| HEIGHT | 88'07"+ |
| WEIGHT | ??? lbs |

### Description

Gigantamax energy can sometimes cause the diameter of this Pokémon's fireball to exceed 300 feet.

### Special Moves

G-Max Fireball

# SOBBLE

| | |
|---|---|
| **Water Lizard Pokémon** | |

| POKÉDEX NO. | **816** |
|---|---|
| TYPE | Water |
| ABILITY | Torrent |
| HEIGHT | 1'00" |
| WEIGHT | 8.8 lbs |

When scared, this Pokémon cries. Its tears pack the chemical punch of 100 onions, and attackers won't be able to resist weeping.

001-100
101-200
201-300
401-442
443-500
501-600
701-800
801-898

## Description

When it gets wet, its skin changes color, and this Pokémon becomes invisible, as if it were camouflaged.

## Special Moves

Growl, Water Gun, Tearful Look

**Evolution**

SOBBLE

DRIZZILE

INTELEON

# DRIZZILE

| Water Lizard Pokémon | |
|---|---|
| **POKÉDEX NO.** | **817** |
| **TYPE** | Water |
| **ABILITY** | Torrent |
| **HEIGHT** | 2'04" |
| **WEIGHT** | 25.4 lbs |

A clever combatant, this Pokémon battles using water balloons created with moisture secreted from its palms.

### Description

Highly intelligent but also very lazy, it keeps enemies out of its territory by laying traps everywhere.

### Special Moves

Water Pulse, U-turn, Soak

**Evolution**

SOBBLE → DRIZZILE → INTELEON

# INTELEON

## Secret Agent Pokémon

| POKÉDEX NO. | **818** |
|---|---|
| **TYPE** | Water |
| **ABILITY** | Torrent |
| **HEIGHT** | 6'03" |
| **WEIGHT** | 99.6 lbs |

001-100
101-200
201-300
401-442
443-500
501-600
701-800
801-898

It has many hidden capabilities, such as fingertips that can shoot water and a membrane on its back that it can use to glide through the air.

### Description

Its nictitating membranes let it pick out foes' weak points so it can precisely blast them with water that shoots from its fingertips at Mach 3.*

### Special Moves

Snipe Shot, Liquidation, Water Pulse

### Evolution

SOBBLE → DRIZZILE → INTELEON

*Mach: A measurement of speed. Mach 1 is the same speed as sound, at 1,125 feet per second.

# INTELEON

## GIGANTAMAX FORM

It has excellent sniping skills. Shooting a berry rolling along nine miles away is a piece of cake for this Pokémon.

INTELEON

| Secret Agent Pokémon | |
|---|---|
| POKÉDEX NO. | **818** |
| TYPE | Water |
| ABILITY | Torrent |
| HEIGHT | 131'03"+ |
| WEIGHT | ??? lbs |

### Description

Gigantamax Inteleon's Water Gun move fires at Mach 7.* As the Pokémon takes aim, it uses the crest on its head to gauge wind and temperature.

### Special Moves

G-Max Hydrosnipe

*Mach: A measurement of speed. Mach 1 is the same speed as sound, at 1,125 feet per second.

# SKWOVET

001-100
101-200
201-300
401-442
443-500
501-600
701-800
801-898

## Cheeky Pokémon

| POKÉDEX NO. | **819** |
| --- | --- |
| TYPE | Normal |
| ABILITY | Cheek Pouch |
| HEIGHT | 1'00" |
| WEIGHT | 5.5 lbs |

### Description

It eats berries nonstop—a habit that has made it more resilient than it looks. It'll show up on farms, searching for yet more berries.

### Special Moves

Tail Whip, Bullet Seed, Swallow

Found throughout the Galar region, this Pokémon becomes uneasy if its cheeks are ever completely empty of berries.

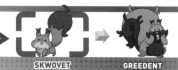

**Evolution**

SKWOVET → GREEDENT

# GREEDENT

**Greedy Pokémon**

| POKÉDEX NO. | 820 |
| --- | --- |

| TYPE | Normal |
| --- | --- |
| ABILITY | Cheek Pouch |
| HEIGHT | 2'00" |
| WEIGHT | 13.2 lbs |

It stashes berries in its tail—so many berries that they fall out constantly. But this Pokémon is a bit slow-witted, so it doesn't notice the loss.

### Description

Common throughout the Galar region, this Pokémon has strong teeth and can chew through the toughest of berry shells.

### Special Moves

Super Fang, Bullet Seed, Covet

**Evolution**

SKWOVET

GREEDENT

# ROOKIDEE

**Tiny Bird Pokémon**

| POKÉDEX NO. | 821 |
|---|---|
| **TYPE** | Flying |
| **ABILITY** | Keen Eye, Unnerve |
| **HEIGHT** | 0'08" |
| **WEIGHT** | 4.0 lbs |

001-100
101-200
201-300
401-442
443-500
501-600
701-800
801-898

Jumping nimbly about, this small-bodied Pokémon takes advantage of even the slightest opportunity to disorient larger opponents.

### Description

It will bravely challenge any opponent, no matter how powerful. This Pokémon benefits from every battle— even a defeat increases its strength a bit.

### Special Moves

Fury Attack, Leer, Hone Claws

**Evolution**

ROOKIDEE    CORVISQUIRE    CORVIKNIGHT

# CORVISQUIRE

| Raven Pokémon | |
|---|---|
| **POKÉDEX NO.** | **822** |
| TYPE | Flying |
| ABILITY | Keen Eye, Unnerve |
| HEIGHT | 2'07" |
| WEIGHT | 35.3 lbs |

The lessons of many harsh battles have taught it how to accurately judge an opponent's strength.

## Description

Smart enough to use tools in battle, these Pokémon have been seen picking up rocks and flinging them or using ropes to wrap up enemies.

## Special Moves

Drill Peck, Scary Face, Fury Attack

Evolution

ROOKIDEE → CORVISQUIRE → CORVIKNIGHT

# CORVIKNIGHT

## Raven Pokémon

| POKÉDEX NO. | **823** |
|---|---|
| **TYPE** | Flying, Steel |
| **ABILITY** | Pressure, Unnerve |
| **HEIGHT** | 7'03" |
| **WEIGHT** | 165.3 lbs |

With their great intellect and flying skills, these Pokémon very successfully act as the Galar region's airborne taxi service.

### Description

This Pokémon reigns supreme in the skies of the Galar region. The black luster of its steel body could drive terror into the heart of any foe.

### Special Moves

Steel Wing, Brave Bird, Iron Defense

**Evolution**

**ROOKIDEE** → **CORVISQUIRE** → **CORVIKNIGHT**

001-100
101-200
201-300
401-442
443-500
501-600
701-800
801-898

# CORVIKNIGHT

## GIGANTAMAX FORM

The eight feathers on its back are called blade birds, and they can launch off its body to attack foes independently.

CORVIKNIGHT

| Raven Pokémon | |
|---|---|
| **POKÉDEX NO.** | **823** |
| TYPE | Flying, Steel |
| ABILITY | Pressure, Unnerve |
| HEIGHT | 45'11"+ |
| WEIGHT | ??? lbs |

### Description

Imbued with Gigantamax energy, its wings can whip up winds more forceful than any hurricane could muster. The gusts blow everything away.

### Special Moves

G-Max Wind Rage

# BLIPBUG

### Larva Pokémon

| | |
|---|---|
| **POKÉDEX NO.** | **824** |
| **TYPE** | Bug |
| **ABILITY** | Compound Eyes, Swarm |
| **HEIGHT** | 1'04" |
| **WEIGHT** | 17.6 lbs |

A constant collector of information, this Pokémon is very smart. Very strong is what it isn't.

### Description

Often found in gardens, this Pokémon has hairs on its body that it uses to assess its surroundings.

### Special Moves

Struggle Bug

001-100

101-200

201-300

401-442

443-500

501-600

601-700

701-800

801-898

**Evolution**

BLIPBUG

DOTTLER

ORBEETLE

# DOTTLER

**Radome Pokémon**

| POKÉDEX NO. | **825** |
|---|---|
| TYPE | Bug, Psychic |
| ABILITY | Compound Eyes, Swarm |
| HEIGHT | 1'04" |
| WEIGHT | 43.0 lbs |

### Description

It barely moves, but it's still alive. Hiding in its shell without food or water seems to have awakened its psychic powers.

As it grows inside its shell, it uses its psychic abilities to monitor the outside world and prepare for evolution.

### Special Moves

Confusion, Light Screen, Struggle Bug

Evolution

 BLIPBUG →  DOTTLER →   ORBEETLE

# ORBEETLE

### Seven Spot Pokémon

| POKÉDEX NO. | 826 |
|---|---|
| **TYPE** | Bug, Psychic |
| **ABILITY** | Swarm, Frisk |
| **HEIGHT** | 1'04" |
| **WEIGHT** | 89.9 lbs |

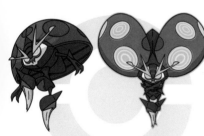

It's famous for its high level of intelligence, and the large size of its brain is proof that it also possesses immense psychic power.

## Description

It emits psychic energy to observe and study what's around it—and what's around it can include things over six miles away.

## Special Moves

Bug Buzz, Psychic, Calm Mind

**Evolution**

BLIPBUG → DOTTLER → ORBEETLE

001-100
101-200
201-300
401-442
443-500
501-600
701-800
801-898

# ORBEETLE

## GIGANTAMAX FORM

If it were to utilize every last bit of its power, it could control the minds of every living being in its vicinity.

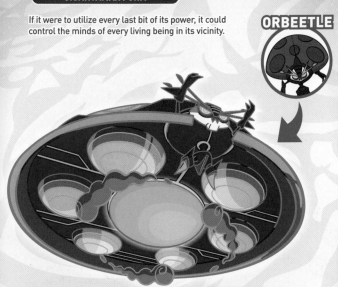

ORBEETLE

## Seven Spot Pokémon

| POKÉDEX NO. | 826 |
|---|---|
| TYPE | Bug, Psychic |
| ABILITY | Swarm, Frisk |
| HEIGHT | 45'11"+ |
| WEIGHT | ??? lbs |

### Description

Its brain has grown to a gargantuan size, as has the rest of its body. This Pokémon's intellect and psychic abilities are overpowering.

### Special Moves

G-Max Gravitas

# NICKIT

**Fox Pokémon**

| POKÉDEX NO. | **827** |
|---|---|
| **TYPE** | Dark |
| **ABILITY** | Run Away, Unburden |
| **HEIGHT** | 2'00" |
| **WEIGHT** | 19.6 lbs |

Cunning and cautious, this Pokémon survives by stealing food from others. It erases its tracks with swipes of its tail as it makes off with its plunder.

### Description

Aided by the soft pads on its feet, it silently raids the food stores of other Pokémon. It survives off its ill-gotten gains.

### Special Moves

Tail Whip, Quick Attack, Nasty Plot

**Evolution**

NICKIT ➡
THIEVUL

001-100
101-200
201-300
401-442
443-500
501-600
701-600
801-898

# THIEVUL

## Fox Pokémon

| | |
|---|---|
| **POKÉDEX NO.** | **828** |
| **TYPE** | Dark |
| **ABILITY** | Run Away, Unburden |
| **HEIGHT** | 3'11" |
| **WEIGHT** | 43.9 lbs |

### Description

It secretly marks potential targets with a scent. By following the scent, it stalks its targets and steals from them when they least expect it.

With a lithe body and sharp claws, it goes around stealing food and eggs. Boltund* is its natural enemy.

### Special Moves

Thief, Tail Slap, Snarl

### Evolution

NICKIT → THIEVUL

*Boltund: A Pokémon you'll find on page 459.

# GOSSIFLEUR

| Flowering Pokémon | |
|---|---|
| **POKÉDEX NO.** | **829** |
| **TYPE** | Grass |
| **ABILITY** | Regenerator, Cotton Down |
| **HEIGHT** | 1'04" |
| **WEIGHT** | 4.9 lbs |

It anchors itself to the ground with its single leg, then basks in the sun. After absorbing enough sunlight, its petals spread as it blooms brilliantly.

001-100
101-200
201-300
401-442
443-500
501-600
601-700
701-800
801-898

### Description

It whirls around in the wind while singing a joyous song. This delightful display has charmed many into raising this Pokémon.

### Special Moves

Leafage, Sweet Scent, Razor Leaf

**Evolution**

GOSSIFLEUR → ELDEGOSS

# ELDEGOSS

| Cotton Bloom Pokémon | |
|---|---|
| **POKÉDEX NO.** | **830** |
| **TYPE** | Grass |
| **ABILITY** | Regenerator, Cotton Down |
| **HEIGHT** | 1'08" |
| **WEIGHT** | 5.5 lbs |

The cotton on the head of this Pokémon can be spun into a glossy, gorgeous yarn—a Galar regional specialty.

### Description

The seeds attached to its cotton fluff are full of nutrients. It spreads them on the wind so that plants and other Pokémon can benefit from them.

### Special Moves

Cotton Spore, Cotton Guard, Synthesis

**Evolution**

**GOSSIFLEUR** →   **ELDEGOSS**

452

# WOOLOO

| | |
|---|---|
| **Sheep Pokémon** | |
| **POKÉDEX NO.** | **831** |
| **TYPE** | Normal |
| **ABILITY** | Run Away, Fluffy |
| **HEIGHT** | 2'00" |
| **WEIGHT** | 13.2 lbs |

If its fleece grows too long, Wooloo won't be able to move. Cloth made with the wool of this Pokémon is surprisingly strong.

### Description

Its curly fleece is such an effective cushion that this Pokémon could fall off a cliff and stand right back up at the bottom, unharmed.

### Special Moves

Tackle, Defense Curl, Double-Edge

**Evolution**

WOOLOO

➡

DUBWOOL

001-100
101-200
201-300
401-442
443-500
501-600
701-800
801-898

# DUBWOOL

| **Sheep Pokémon** | |
|---|---|
| **POKÉDEX NO.** | **832** |
| **TYPE** | Normal |
| **ABILITY** | Steadfast, Fluffy |
| **HEIGHT** | 4'03" |
| **WEIGHT** | 94.8 lbs |

Its majestic horns are meant only to impress the opposite gender. They never see use in battle.

## Description

Weave a carpet from its springy wool, and you end up with something closer to a trampoline. You'll start to bounce the moment you set foot on it.

## Special Moves

Cotton Guard, Guard Swap, Take Down

**Evolution**

WOOLOO

DUBWOOL

# CHEWTLE

## Snapping Pokémon

| POKÉDEX NO. | **833** |
|---|---|
| TYPE | Water |
| ABILITY | Shell Armor, Strong Jaw |
| HEIGHT | 1'00" |
| WEIGHT | 18.7 lbs |

### Description

Apparently the itch of its teething impels it to snap its jaws at anything in front of it.

It starts off battles by attacking with its rock-hard horn, but as soon as the opponent flinches, this Pokémon bites down and never lets go.

### Special Moves

Water Gun, Body Slam, Jaw Lock

**Evolution**

CHEWTLE → DREDNAW

001-100
101-200
201-300
401-442
443-500
501-600
601-700
701-800
801-898

# DREDNAW

**Bite Pokémon**

| | |
|---|---|
| **POKÉDEX NO.** | **834** |
| **TYPE** | Water, Rock |
| **ABILITY** | Shell Armor, Strong Jaw |
| **HEIGHT** | 3'03" |
| **WEIGHT** | 254.6 lbs |

### Description

With jaws that can shear through steel rods, this highly aggressive Pokémon chomps down on its unfortunate prey.

This Pokémon rapidly extends its retractable neck to sink its sharp fangs into distant enemies and take them down.

### Special Moves

Rock Tomb, Crunch, Rock Polish

**Evolution**

CHEWTLE → DREDNAW

# DREDNAW

## GIGANTAMAX FORM

In the Galar region, there's a tale about this Pokémon chewing up a mountain and using the rubble to stop a flood.

**DREDNAW**

001-100
101-200
201-300
401-442
443-500
501-600
701-800
801-898

| Bite Pokémon | |
|---|---|
| POKÉDEX NO. | **834** |
| TYPE | Water, Rock |
| ABILITY | Shell Armor, Strong Jaw |
| HEIGHT | 78'09"+ |
| WEIGHT | ??? lbs |

### Description

It responded to Gigantamax energy by becoming bipedal. First it comes crashing down on foes, and then it finishes them off with its massive jaws.

### Special Moves

G-Max Stonesurge

# YAMPER

## Puppy Pokémon

| | |
|---|---|
| **POKÉDEX NO.** | **835** |
| **TYPE** | Electric |
| **ABILITY** | Ball Fetch |
| **HEIGHT** | 1'00" |
| **WEIGHT** | 29.8 lbs |

This Pokémon is very popular as a herding dog in the Galar region. As it runs, it generates electricity from the base of its tail.

### Description

This gluttonous Pokémon only assists people with their work because it wants treats. As it runs, it crackles with electricity.

### Special Moves

Bite, Nuzzle, Play Rough

Evolution

YAMPER → BOLTUND

# BOLTUND

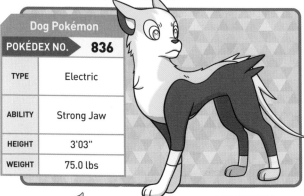

| Dog Pokémon | |
|---|---|
| POKÉDEX NO. | **836** |
| TYPE | Electric |
| ABILITY | Strong Jaw |
| HEIGHT | 3'03" |
| WEIGHT | 75.0 lbs |

001-100
101-200
201-300
401-442
443-500
501-600
601-700
701-800
801-898

### Description

This Pokémon generates electricity and channels it into its legs to keep them going strong. Boltund can run nonstop for three full days.

### Special Moves

Crunch, Charge, Wild Charge

It sends electricity through its legs to boost their strength. Running at top speed, it easily breaks 50 mph.

Evolution

YAMPER → BOLTUND

# ROLYCOLY

Most of its body has the same composition as coal. Fittingly, this Pokémon was first discovered in coal mines about 400 years ago.

| Coal Pokémon | |
|---|---|
| **POKÉDEX NO.** | **837** |
| TYPE | Rock |
| ABILITY | Heatproof, Steam Engine |
| HEIGHT | 1'00" |
| WEIGHT | 26.5 lbs |

## Description

It can race around like a unicycle, even on rough, rocky terrain. Burning coal sustains it.

## Special Moves

Smokescreen, Tackle, Ancient Power

**Evolution**

ROLYCOLY

CARKOL

COALOSSAL

# CARKOL

## Coal Pokémon

| | |
|---|---|
| **POKÉDEX NO.** | **838** |
| **TYPE** | Rock, Fire |
| **ABILITY** | Flame Body, Steam Engine |
| **HEIGHT** | 3'07" |
| **WEIGHT** | 172.0 lbs |

By rapidly rolling its legs, it can travel at over 18 mph. The temperature of the flames it breathes exceeds 1,800 degrees Fahrenheit.

### Description

It forms coal inside its body. Coal dropped by this Pokémon once helped fuel the lives of people in the Galar region.

### Special Moves

Flame Charge, Smack Down, Incinerate

**Evolution**

ROLYCOLY → CARKOL → COALOSSAL

001-100
101-200
201-300
401-442
443-800
501-600
701-800
801-898

# COALOSSAL

| | |
|---|---|
| **Coal Pokémon** | |
| **POKÉDEX NO.** | **839** |
| **TYPE** | Rock, Fire |
| **ABILITY** | Flame Body, Steam Engine |
| **HEIGHT** | 9'02" |
| **WEIGHT** | 684.5 lbs |

While it's engaged in battle, its mountain of coal will burn bright red, sending off sparks that scorch the surrounding area.

### Description

It's usually peaceful, but the vandalism of mines enrages it. Offenders will be incinerated with flames that reach 2,700 degrees Fahrenheit.

### Special Moves

Tar Shot, Burn Up, Rock Polish

**Evolution**

ROLYCOLY

CARKOL

COALOSSAL

# COALOSSAL

## GIGANTAMAX FORM

Its body is a colossal stove. With Gigantamax energy stoking the fire, this Pokémon's flame burns hotter than 3,600 degrees Fahrenheit.

COALOSSAL

001–100

101–200

201–300

401–442

443–500

501–600

601–700

701–800

801–898

| Coal Pokémon | |
|---|---|
| **POKÉDEX NO.** | **839** |
| **TYPE** | Rock, Fire |
| **ABILITY** | Flame Body, Steam Engine |
| **HEIGHT** | 137'10"+ |
| **WEIGHT** | ??? lbs |

### Description

When Galar was hit by a harsh cold wave, this Pokémon served as a giant heating stove and saved many lives.

### Special Moves

G-Max Volcalith

# APPLIN

**Apple Core Pokémon**

| POKÉDEX NO. | 840 |
| --- | --- |
| **TYPE** | Grass, Dragon |
| **ABILITY** | Gluttony, Ripen |
| **HEIGHT** | 0'08" |
| **WEIGHT** | 1.1 lbs |

As soon as it's born, it burrows into an apple. Not only does the apple serve as its food source, but the flavor of the fruit determines its evolution.

### Description

It spends its entire life inside an apple. It hides from its natural enemies, bird Pokémon, by pretending it's just an apple and nothing more.

### Special Moves

Astonish, Withdraw

**Evolution**

APPLIN → FLAPPLE    APPLETUN

# FLAPPLE

## Apple Wing Pokémon

| | |
|---|---|
| **POKÉDEX NO.** | **841** |
| **TYPE** | Grass, Dragon |
| **ABILITY** | Gluttony, Ripen |
| **HEIGHT** | 1'00" |
| **WEIGHT** | 2.2 lbs |

It flies on wings of apple skin and spits a powerful acid. It can also change its shape into that of an apple.

001-100
101-200
201-300
401-442
443-500
501-600
781-800
801-898

## Description

It ate a sour apple, and that induced its evolution. In its cheeks, it stores an acid capable of causing chemical burns.

## Special Moves

Wing Attack, Grav Apple, Fly

**Evolution**

APPLIN → FLAPPLE

# FLAPPLE

## GIGANTAMAX FORM

If it stretches its neck, the strong aroma of its nectar pours out. The scent is so sickeningly sweet that one whiff makes other Pokémon faint.

FLAPPLE

## Apple Wing Pokémon

| POKÉDEX NO. | 841 |
|---|---|
| TYPE | Grass, Dragon |
| ABILITY | Gluttony, Ripen |
| HEIGHT | 78'09"+ |
| WEIGHT | ??? lbs |

### Description

Under the influence of Gigantamax energy, it produces much more sweet nectar, and its shape has changed to resemble a giant apple.

### Special Moves

G-Max Tartness

# APPLETUN

**Apple Nectar Pokémon**

| POKÉDEX NO. | **842** |
| --- | --- |
| TYPE | Grass, Dragon |
| ABILITY | Gluttony, Ripen |
| HEIGHT | 1'04" |
| WEIGHT | 28.7 lbs |

Its body is covered in sweet nectar, and the skin on its back is especially yummy. Children used to have it as a snack.

### Description

Eating a sweet apple caused its evolution. A nectarous scent wafts from its body, luring in the bug Pokémon it preys on.

### Special Moves

Headbutt, Bullet Seed, Dragon Pulse

801-100
101-200
201-300
401-442
443-500
501-600
521-700
701-800
801-898

**Evolution**

APPLIN → APPLETUN

# APPLETUN

## GIGANTAMAX FORM

It blasts its opponents with massive amounts of sweet, sticky nectar, drowning them under the deluge.

APPLETUN

| Apple Nectar Pokémon | |
|---|---|
| **POKÉDEX NO.** | **842** |
| TYPE | Grass, Dragon |
| ABILITY | Gluttony, Ripen |
| HEIGHT | 78'09"+ |
| WEIGHT | ??? lbs |

### Description

Due to Gigantamax energy, this Pokémon's nectar has thickened. The increased viscosity lets the nectar absorb more damage than before.

### Special Moves

G-Max Sweetness

# SILICOBRA

| Sand Snake Pokémon | |
|---|---|
| POKÉDEX NO. | 843 |
| TYPE | Ground |
| ABILITY | Shed Skin, Sand Spit |
| HEIGHT | 7'03" |
| WEIGHT | 16.8 lbs |

## Description

As it digs, it swallows and stores it in its neck pouch. The pouch can hold more than 17 pounds of sand.

It spews sand from its nostrils. While the enemy is blinded, it burrows into the ground to hide.

## Special Moves

Sand Attack, Dig, Coil

**Evolution**

SILICOBRA →  SANDACONDA

001-100
101-200
201-300
401-442
443-500
501-600
701-800
801-898

# SANDACONDA

## Sand Snake Pokémon

| | |
|---|---|
| POKÉDEX NO. | 844 |
| TYPE | Ground |
| ABILITY | Shed Skin, Sand Spit |
| HEIGHT | 12'06" |
| WEIGHT | 144.4 lbs |

Its unique style of coiling allows it to blast sand out of its sand sac more efficiently.

### Description

When it contracts its body, over 220 pounds of sand sprays from its nose. If it ever runs out of sand, it becomes disheartened.

### Special Moves

Glare, Sand Tomb, Skull Bash

---

Evolution

SILICOBRA

SANDACONDA

# SANDACONDA

## GIGANTAMAX FORM

Sand swirls around its body with such speed and power that it could pulverize a skyscraper.

**SANDACONDA**

001-100

101-200

201-300

401-442

443-500

501-600

701-800

801-898

| Sand Snake Pokémon | |
|---|---|
| **POKÉDEX NO.** | **844** |
| **TYPE** | Ground |
| **ABILITY** | Shed Skin, Sand Spit |
| **HEIGHT** | 72'02"+ |
| **WEIGHT** | ??? lbs |

### Description

Its sand pouch has grown to tremendous proportions. More than one million tons of sand now swirl around its body.

### Special Moves

G-Max Sandblast

# CRAMORANT

## Gulp Pokémon

| POKÉDEX NO. | 845 |
| --- | --- |
| TYPE | Flying, Water |
| ABILITY | Gulp Missile |
| HEIGHT | 2'07" |
| WEIGHT | 39.7 lbs |

It's so strong that it can knock out some opponents in a single hit, but it also may forget what it's battling midfight.

### Description

This hungry Pokémon swallows Arrokuda* whole. Occasionally, it makes a mistake and tries to swallow a Pokémon other than its preferred prey.

### Special Moves

Swallow, Spit Up, Hydro Pump

**Evolution**  Does not evolve

CRAMORANT

*Arrokuda: A Pokémon you'll find on page 475.

# CRAMORANT

## GULPING FORM

Cramorant is constantly on the hunt for food along riverbanks. It loves Arrokuda*—when it finds them, it swallows them whole without a thought.

001-100
101-200
201-300
401-442
643-500
501-600
701-800
801-898

| Gulp Pokémon | |
|---|---|
| **POKÉDEX NO.** | **845** |
| TYPE | Flying, Water |
| ABILITY | Gulp Missile |
| HEIGHT | 2'07" |
| WEIGHT | 39.7 lbs |

### Description

Cramorant takes advantage of Arrokuda's frantic thrashing to help spit Arrokuda out at high speed.

### Special Moves

Swallow, Spit Up, Hydro Pump

**Evolution**

CRAMORANT
(GULPING FORM)

Does not evolve

*Arrokuda: A Pokémon you'll find on page 475.

473

# CRAMORANT

## GORGING FORM

The half-swallowed Pikachu* is so startled that it isn't struggling yet, but it's still looking for a chance to strike back.

### Gulp Pokémon

| POKÉDEX NO. | 845 |
| --- | --- |
| TYPE | Flying, Water |
| ABILITY | Gulp Missile |
| HEIGHT | 2'07" |
| WEIGHT | 39.7 lbs |

### Description

This Cramorant has accidentally gotten a Pikachu lodged in its gullet. Cramorant is choking a little, but it isn't really bothered.

### Special Moves

Swallow, Spit Up, Hydro Pump

| Evolution |  CRAMORANT [GORGING FORM] | Does not evolve |
| --- | --- | --- |

*Pikachu: A Pokémon you'll find in volume 1.

# ARROKUDA

| Rush Pokémon | |
|---|---|
| POKÉDEX NO. | **846** |
| TYPE | Water |
| ABILITY | Swift Swim |
| HEIGHT | 1'08" |
| WEIGHT | 2.2 lbs |

001-100

101-200

201-300

401-442

463-500

501-600

701-800

801-898

After it's eaten its fill, its movements become extremely sluggish. That's when Cramorant swallows it up.

### Description

If it sees any movement around it, this Pokémon charges for it straightaway, leading with its sharply pointed jaw. It's very proud of that jaw.

### Special Moves

Aqua Jet, Bite, Agility

**Evolution**

ARROKUDA          BARRASKEWDA

# BARRASKEWDA

## Skewer Pokémon

| | |
|---|---|
| **POKÉDEX NO.** | **847** |
| **TYPE** | Water |
| **ABILITY** | Swift Swim |
| **HEIGHT** | 4'03" |
| **WEIGHT** | 66.1 lbs |

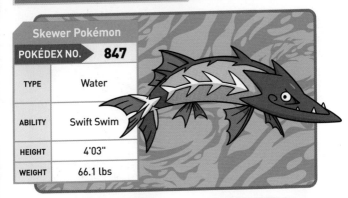

### Description

It spins its tail fins to propel itself, surging forward at speeds of over 100 knots* before ramming prey and spearing into them.

This Pokémon has a jaw that's as sharp as a spear and as strong as steel. Apparently Barraskewda's flesh is surprisingly tasty, too.

### Special Moves

Throat Chop, Dive, Liquidation

**Evolution**

ARROKUDA → BARRASKEWDA

*Knot: A measurement of a ship's speed. One hundred knots is roughly 115 mph.

# TOXEL

| | |
|---|---|
| **Baby Pokémon** | |
| **POKÉDEX NO.** | **848** |
| **TYPE** | Electric, Poison |
| **ABILITY** | Static, Rattled |
| **HEIGHT** | 1'04" |
| **WEIGHT** | 24.3 lbs |

001-100
101-200
201-300
401-442
443-500
501-600
701-800
801-898

It stores poison in an internal poison sac and secretes that poison through its skin. If you touch this Pokémon, a tingling sensation follows.

### Description

It manipulates the chemical makeup of its poison to produce electricity. The voltage is weak, but it can cause a tingling paralysis.

### Special Moves

Nuzzle, Flail, Acid

**Evolution**

TOXEL → TOXTRICITY (AMPED FORM)   TOXTRICITY (LOW KEY FORM)

# TOXTRICITY

**AMPED FORM**

## Punk Pokémon

| POKÉDEX NO. | 849 |
| --- | --- |

| TYPE | Electric, Poison |
| --- | --- |
| ABILITY | Plus, Punk Rock |
| HEIGHT | 5'03" |
| WEIGHT | 88.2 lbs |

### Description

When this Pokémon sounds as if it's strumming a guitar, it's actually clawing at the protrusions on its chest to generate electricity.

This short-tempered and aggressive Pokémon chugs stagnant water to absorb any toxins it might contain.

### Special Moves

Spark, Overdrive, Shock Wave

Evolution

TOXEL

TOXTRICITY
(AMPED FORM)

# TOXTRICITY

LOW KEY FORM

## Punk Pokémon

| POKÉDEX NO. | **849** | |
|---|---|---|
| **TYPE** | Electric, Poison | |
| **ABILITY** | Minus, Punk Rock | |
| **HEIGHT** | 5'03" | |
| **WEIGHT** | 88.2 lbs | |

001-100
101-200
201-300
401-442
443-500
501-600
601-700
701-800
801-898

### Description

As it gulps down stagnant water and generates electricity in its body, a sound like a rhythm played by a bass guitar reverberates all around.

Many youths admire the way this Pokemon listlessly picks fights and keeps its cool no matter what opponent it faces.

### Special Moves

Spark, Acid Spray, Venom Drench

**Evolution**

TOXEL

TOXTRICITY
[LOW KEY FORM]

# TOXTRICITY

## GIGANTAMAX FORM

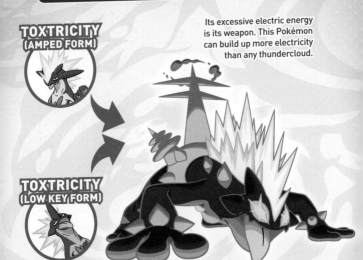

### TOXTRICITY (AMPED FORM)

### TOXTRICITY (LOW KEY FORM)

Its excessive electric energy is its weapon. This Pokémon can build up more electricity than any thundercloud.

| Punk Pokémon | |
|---|---|
| **POKÉDEX NO.** | **849** |
| TYPE | Electric, Poison |
| ABILITY | Amped Form: Plus, Punk Rock Low Key Form: Minus, Punk Rock |
| HEIGHT | 78'09"+ |
| WEIGHT | ??? lbs |

### Description

Out of control after its own poison penetrated its brain, it tears across the land in a rampage, contaminating the earth with toxic sweat.

### Special Moves

G-Max Stun Shock

# SIZZLIPEDE

| | |
|---|---|
| **Radiator Pokémon** | |

| POKÉDEX NO. | **850** |
|---|---|
| **TYPE** | Fire, Bug |
| **ABILITY** | Flash Fire, White Smoke |
| **HEIGHT** | 2'04" |
| **WEIGHT** | 2.2 lbs |

001-100
101-200
201-300
401-442
643-800
501-600
701-800
801-898

### Description

It wraps prey up with its heated body, cooking them in its coils. Once they're well-done, it will voraciously nibble them down to the last morsel.

It stores flammable gas in its body and uses it to generate heat. The yellow sections on its belly get particularly hot.

### Special Moves

Smokescreen, Fire Spin, Fire Lash

**Evolution**

SIZZLIPEDE → CENTISKORCH

481

# CENTISKORCH

**Radiator Pokémon**

| | |
|---|---|
| **POKÉDEX NO.** | **851** |
| **TYPE** | Fire, Bug |
| **ABILITY** | Flash Fire, White Smoke |
| **HEIGHT** | 9'10" |
| **WEIGHT** | 264.6 lbs |

While its burning body is already dangerous on its own, this excessively hostile Pokémon also has large and very sharp fangs.

### Description

When it heats up, its body temperature reaches about 1,500 degrees Fahrenheit. It lashes its body like a whip and launches itself at enemies.

### Special Moves

Flame Wheel, Burn Up, Coil

**Evolution**

SIZZLIPEDE

→

CENTISKORCH

# CENTISKORCH

## GIGANTAMAX FORM

The heat that comes off a Gigantamax Centiskorch may destabilize air currents. Sometimes it can even cause storms.

**CENTISKORCH**

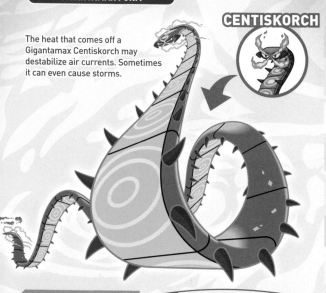

001-100
101-200
201-300
401-442
443-500
501-600
701-800
801-898

| Radiator Pokémon | |
|---|---|
| **POKÉDEX NO.** | **851** |
| TYPE | Fire, Bug |
| ABILITY | Flash Fire, White Smoke |
| HEIGHT | 246'01"+ |
| WEIGHT | ??? lbs |

### Description

Gigantamax energy has evoked a rise in its body temperature, now reaching over 1,800 degrees Fahrenheit. Its heat waves incinerate its enemies.

### Special Moves

G-Max Centiferno

# CLOBBOPUS

**Tantrum Pokémon**

| POKÉDEX NO. | **852** |
| --- | --- |
| **TYPE** | Fighting |
| **ABILITY** | Limber |
| **HEIGHT** | 2'00" |
| **WEIGHT** | 8.8 lbs |

Its tentacles tear off easily, but it isn't alarmed when that happens—it knows they'll grow back. It's about as smart as a three-year-old.

### Description

It's very curious, but its means of investigating things is to try to punch them with its tentacles. The search for food is what brings it onto land.

### Special Moves

Leer, Rock Smash, Brick Break

**Evolution**

CLOBBOPUS → GRAPPLOCT

# GRAPPLOCT

| | |
|---|---|
| **Jujitsu Pokémon** | |
| **POKÉDEX NO.** | **853** |
| TYPE | Fighting |
| ABILITY | Limber |
| HEIGHT | 5'03" |
| WEIGHT | 86.0 lbs |

A body made up of nothing but muscle makes the grappling moves this Pokémon performs with its tentacles tremendously powerful.

### Description

Searching for an opponent to test its skills against, it emerges onto land. Once the battle is over, it returns to the sea.

### Special Moves

Octolock, Submission, Octazooka

---

**Evolution**

CLOBBOPUS → GRAPPLOCT

001-100
101-200
201-300
401-442
443-500
501-600
701-800
801-898

# SINISTEA

## PHONY FORM

| Black Tea Pokémon | |
|---|---|
| POKÉDEX NO. | **854** |
| TYPE | Ghost |
| ABILITY | Weak Armor |
| HEIGHT | 0'04" |
| WEIGHT | 0.4 lbs |

The Phony Form is fake. It does not have a stamp on the bottom.

The teacup in which this Pokémon makes its home is a famous piece of antique tableware. Many forgeries are in circulation.

### Description

This Pokémon is said to have been born when a lonely spirit possessed a cold, leftover cup of tea.

### Special Moves

Giga Drain, Shadow Ball, Astonish

**Evolution**

SINISTEA
(PHONY FORM)

POLTEAGEIST
(PHONY FORM)

# SINISTEA

**ANTIQUE FORM**

| Black Tea Pokémon | |
|---|---|
| **POKÉDEX NO.** | **854** |
| TYPE | Ghost |
| ABILITY | Weak Armor |
| HEIGHT | 0'04" |
| WEIGHT | 0.4 lbs |

The Antique Form is authentic. It has a stamp of authenticity on the bottom.

The swirl pattern in this Pokémon's body is its weakness. If it gets stirred, the swirl loses its shape, and Sinistea gets dizzy.

### Description

It absorbs the life force of those who drink it. It waits patiently, but opportunities are fleeting—it tastes so bad that it gets spat out immediately.

### Special Moves

Giga Drain, Shadow Ball, Astonish

**Evolution**

**SINISTEA**
(ANTIQUE FORM)

**POLTEAGEIST**
(ANTIQUE FORM)

001-100

101-200

201-300

401-442

443-500

501-600

701-800

801-898

# POLTEAGEIST

## PHONY FORM

| Black Tea Pokémon | |
|---|---|
| **POKÉDEX NO.** | **855** |
| TYPE | Ghost |
| ABILITY | Weak Armor |
| HEIGHT | 0'08" |
| WEIGHT | 0.9 lbs |

The Phony Form is fake. It does not have a stamp on the bottom.

Leaving leftover black tea unattended is asking for this Pokémon to come along and pour itself into it, turning the tea into a new Polteageist.

## Description

This species lives in antique teapots. Most pots are forgeries, but on rare occasions, an authentic work is found.

## Special Moves

Teatime, Shadow Ball, Aromatic Mist

**Evolution**

SINISTEA
(PHONY FORM)

POLTEAGEIST
(PHONY FORM)

# POLTEAGEIST

## ANTIQUE FORM

### Black Tea Pokémon

| POKÉDEX NO. | **855** |
|---|---|
| **TYPE** | Ghost |
| **ABILITY** | Weak Armor |
| **HEIGHT** | 0'08" |
| **WEIGHT** | 0.9 lbs |

The Antique Form is authentic. It has a stamp of authenticity on the bottom.

When angered, it launches tea from its body at the offender's mouth. The tea causes strong chills if swallowed.

### Description

Trainers Polteageist trusts will be allowed to experience its distinctive flavor and aroma firsthand by sampling just a tiny bit of its tea.

### Special Moves

Teatime, Shadow Ball, Aromatic Mist

**Evolution**

SINISTEA
(ANTIQUE FORM)

➡️

POLTEAGEIST
(ANTIQUE FORM)

001-100
101-200
201-300
401-442
443-500
501-600
701-800
801-898

# HATENNA

Calm Pokémon

| POKÉDEX NO. | 856 |
| --- | --- |

| | |
| --- | --- |
| TYPE | Psychic |
| ABILITY | Anticipation, Healer |
| HEIGHT | 1'04" |
| WEIGHT | 7.5 lbs |

### Description

Via the protrusion on its head, it senses other creatures' emotions. If you don't have a calm disposition, it will never warm up to you.

If this Pokémon senses a strong emotion, it will run away as fast as it can. It prefers areas without people.

### Special Moves

Confusion, Psybeam, Disarming Voice

Evolution

HATENNA → HATTREM → HATTERENE

# HATTREM

Serene Pokémon

| POKÉDEX NO. | **857** |
| --- | --- |
| TYPE | Psychic |
| ABILITY | Anticipation, Healer |
| HEIGHT | 2'00" |
| WEIGHT | 10.6 lbs |

### Description

No matter who you are, if you bring strong emotions near this Pokémon, it will silence you violently.

Using the braids on its head, it pummels foes to get them to quiet down. One blow from those braids would knock out a professional boxer.

### Special Moves

Brutal Swing, Play Nice, Psybeam

Evolution

HATENNA

HATTREM

HATTERENE

001-100
101-200
201-300
401-2
443-500
501-600
701-800
801-898

# HATTERENE

### Silent Pokémon

| POKÉDEX NO. | 858 |
| --- | --- |
| TYPE | Psychic, Fairy |
| ABILITY | Anticipation, Healer |
| HEIGHT | 6'11" |
| WEIGHT | 11.2 lbs |

## Description

It emits psychic power strong enough to cause headaches as a deterrent to the approach of others.

If you're too loud around it, you risk being torn apart by the claws on its tentacle. This Pokémon is also known as the Forest Witch.

## Special Moves

Psycho Cut, Magic Powder, Brutal Swing

Evolution

HATENNA → HATTREM → HATTERENE

# HATTERENE

## GIGANTAMAX FORM

### HATTERENE

Beams like lightning shoot down from its tentacles. It's known to some as the Raging Goddess.

| Silent Pokémon | |
|---|---|
| **POKÉDEX NO.** | **858** |
| TYPE | Psychic, Fairy |
| ABILITY | Anticipation, Healer |
| HEIGHT | 85'04"+ |
| WEIGHT | ??? lbs |

### Description

This Pokémon can read the emotions of creatures over 30 miles away. The minute it senses hostility, it goes on the attack.

### Special Moves

G-Max Smite

001-100
101-200
201-300
401-442
443-500
501-600
701-800
801-898

# IMPIDIMP

| | Wily Pokémon | |
|---|---|---|
| **POKÉDEX NO.** | **859** | |
| **TYPE** | Dark, Fairy | |
| **ABILITY** | Frisk, Prankster | |
| **HEIGHT** | 1'04" | |
| **WEIGHT** | 12.1 lbs | |

It sneaks into people's homes, stealing things and feasting on the negative energy of the frustrated occupants.

### Description

Through its nose, it sucks in the emanations produced by people and Pokémon when they feel annoyed. It thrives off this negative energy.

### Special Moves

Confide, Nasty Plot, Sucker Punch

**Evolution**

IMPIDIMP → MORGREM → GRIMMSNARL

# MORGREM

001–100
101–200
201–300
401–242
443–500
501–600
701–800
801–898

**Devious Pokémon**

| | |
|---|---|
| **POKÉDEX NO.** | **860** |
| **TYPE** | Dark, Fairy |
| **ABILITY** | Frisk, Prankster |
| **HEIGHT** | 2'07" |
| **WEIGHT** | 27.6 lbs |

With sly cunning, it tries to lure people into the woods. Some believe it to have the power to make crops grow.

### Description

When it gets down on all fours as if to beg for forgiveness, it's trying to lure opponents in so that it can stab them with its spear-like hair.

### Special Moves

False Surrender, Dark Pulse, Fake Out

**Evolution**

 →  →

IMPIDIMP     MORGREM     GRIMMSNARL

# GRIMMSNARL

### Bulk Up Pokémon

| POKÉDEX NO. | 861 |
|---|---|
| TYPE | Dark, Fairy |
| ABILITY | Frisk, Prankster |
| HEIGHT | 4'11" |
| WEIGHT | 134.5 lbs |

Its hairs work like muscle fibers. When its hairs unfurl, they latch on to opponents, ensnaring them as tentacles would.

### Description

With the hair wrapped around its body helping to enhance its muscles, this Pokémon can overwhelm even Machamp.*

### Special Moves

Spirit Break, Hammer Arm, Swagger

Evolution

IMPIDIMP → MORGREM → GRIMMSNARL

496    *Machamp: A Pokémon you'll find in volume 1.

# GRIMMSNARL

## GIGANTAMAX FORM

**GRIMMSNARL**

Gigantamax energy has caused more hair to sprout all over its body. With the added strength, it can jump over the world's tallest building.

001-100
101-200
201-300
401-442
443-500
501-600
701-800
801-898

| Bulk Up Pokémon | |
|---|---|
| POKÉDEX NO. | **861** |
| TYPE | Dark, Fairy |
| ABILITY | Frisk, Prankster |
| HEIGHT | 105'00"+ |
| WEIGHT | ??? lbs |

### Description

By transforming its leg hair, this Pokémon delivers power-packed drill kicks that can bore huge holes in Galar's terrain.

### Special Moves

G-Max Snooze

497

# OBSTAGOON

| Blocking Pokémon | |
|---|---|
| POKÉDEX NO. | **862** |
| TYPE | Dark, Normal |
| ABILITY | Guts, Reckless |
| HEIGHT | 5'03" |
| WEIGHT | 101.4 lbs |

## Description

Its voice is staggering in volume. Obstagoon has a tendency to take on a threatening posture and shout—this move is known as Obstruct.

It evolved after experiencing numerous fights. While crossing its arms, it lets out a shout that would make any opponent flinch.

## Special Moves

Obstruct, Snarl, Taunt

**Evolution**

ZIGZAGOON
(GALARIAN FORM)

LINOONE
(GALARIAN FORM)

OBSTAGOON

# PERRSERKER

001-100
101-200
201-300
401-442
443-500
501-600
701-800
801-898

| Viking Pokémon | |
|---|---|
| **POKÉDEX NO.** | **863** |
| **TYPE** | Steel |
| **ABILITY** | Battle Armor, Tough Claws |
| **HEIGHT** | 2'07" |
| **WEIGHT** | 61.7 lbs |

### Description

What appears to be an iron helmet is actually hardened hair. This Pokémon lives for the thrill of battle.

After many battles, it evolved dangerous claws that come together to form daggers when extended.

### Special Moves

Iron Head, Metal Claw, Fake Out

**Evolution**

MEOWTH (GALARIAN FORM) → PERRSERKER

# CURSOLA

**Coral Pokémon**

| POKÉDEX NO. | 864 |
|---|---|
| TYPE | Ghost |
| ABILITY | Weak Armor |
| HEIGHT | 3'03" |
| WEIGHT | 0.9 lbs |

Its shell is overflowing with its heightened otherworldly energy. The ectoplasm serves as protection for this Pokémon's core spirit.

### Description

Be cautious of the ectoplasmic body surrounding its soul. You'll become stiff as stone if you touch it.

### Special Moves

Strength Sap, Perish Song, Curse

**Evolution**

CORSOLA (GALARIAN FORM) → CURSOLA

# SIRFETCH'D

### Wild Duck Pokémon

| POKÉDEX NO. | 865 |
|---|---|
| **TYPE** | Fighting |
| **ABILITY** | Steadfast |
| **HEIGHT** | 2'07" |
| **WEIGHT** | 257.9 lbs |

After deflecting attacks with its hard leaf shield, it strikes back with its sharp leek stalk. The leek stalk is both weapon and food.

## Description

Only Farfetch'd that have survived many battles can attain this evolution. When this Pokémon's leek withers, it will retire from combat.

## Special Moves

Meteor Assault, Brave Bird, Iron Defense

**Evolution**

FARFETCH'D
(GALARIAN FORM)

SIRFETCH'D

001-100
101-200
201-300
401-442
443-500
501-600
701-800
801-898

# MR. RIME

**Comedian Pokémon**

| | |
|---|---|
| **POKÉDEX NO.** | **866** |
| **TYPE** | Ice, Psychic |
| **ABILITY** | Tangled Feet, Screen Cleaner |
| **HEIGHT** | 4'11" |
| **WEIGHT** | 128.3 lbs |

Its amusing movements make it very popular. It releases its psychic power from the pattern on its belly.

### Description

It's highly skilled at tap dancing. It waves its cane of ice in time with its graceful movements.

### Special Moves

Freeze-Dry, Teeter Dance, Mimic

**Evolution**

MIME JR.

MR. MIME
(GALARIAN FORM)

MR. RIME

# RUNERIGUS

### Grudge Pokémon

| POKÉDEX NO. | 867 |
|---|---|

| TYPE | Ground, Ghost |
|---|---|
| ABILITY | Wandering Spirit |
| HEIGHT | 5'03" |
| WEIGHT | 146.8 lbs |

### Description

Never touch its shadowlike body, or you'll be shown the horrific memories behind the picture carved into it.

A powerful curse was woven into an ancient painting. After absorbing the spirit of a Yamask,* the painting began to move.

### Special Moves

Shadow Claw, Mean Look, Curse

001-100
101-200
201-300
401-442
443-500
501-600
701-800
801-898

Evolution

YAMASK
(GALARIAN FORM)

RUNERIGUS

*Yamask: A Pokémon you'll find on page 148.

# MILCERY

**Cream Pokémon**

| POKÉDEX NO. | 868 |
|---|---|
| TYPE | Fairy |
| ABILITY | Sweet Veil |
| HEIGHT | 0'08" |
| WEIGHT | 0.7 lbs |

This Pokémon was born from sweet-smelling particles in the air. Its body is made of cream.

## Description

They say that any patisserie* visited by Milcery is guaranteed success and good fortune.

## Special Moves

Aromatic Mist, Draining Kiss, Attract

**Evolution**

MILCERY → ALCREMIE

*Patisserie: A pastry shop.

# ALCREMIE

| Cream Pokémon | |
|---|---|
| **POKÉDEX NO.** | **869** |
| TYPE | Fairy |
| ABILITY | Sweet Veil |
| HEIGHT | 1'00" |
| WEIGHT | 1.1 lbs |

001-100
101-200
201-300
401-442
443-500
501-600
701-800
801-898

When Alcremie is content, the cream it secretes from its hands becomes sweeter and richer.

### Description

When it trusts a Trainer, it will treat them to berries it's decorated with cream.

### Special Moves

Decorate, Dazzling Gleam, Acid Armor

**Evolution**

MILCERY → ALCREMIE

# ALCREMIE FORMS

Alcremie's evolved form will change depending on what it was holding and how it was evolved from Milcery. The color of its body and the sweet on its head are different.

## Vanilla Cream

| Strawberry Sweet | Berry Sweet | Love Sweet | Clover Sweet | Flower Sweet | Star Sweet | Ribbon Sweet |
| --- | --- | --- | --- | --- | --- | --- |

## Matcha Cream

| Strawberry Sweet | Berry Sweet | Love Sweet | Clover Sweet | Flower Sweet | Star Sweet | Ribbon Sweet |
| --- | --- | --- | --- | --- | --- | --- |

## Caramel Swirl

| Strawberry Sweet | Berry Sweet | Love Sweet | Clover Sweet | Flower Sweet | Star Sweet | Ribbon Sweet |
| --- | --- | --- | --- | --- | --- | --- |

## Lemon Cream

| Strawberry Sweet | Berry Sweet | Love Sweet | Clover Sweet | Flower Sweet | Star Sweet | Ribbon Sweet |
| --- | --- | --- | --- | --- | --- | --- |

## Ruby Cream

| Strawberry Sweet | Berry Sweet | Love Sweet | Clover Sweet | Flower Sweet | Star Sweet | Ribbon Sweet |

## Salted Cream

| Strawberry Sweet | Berry Sweet | Love Sweet | Clover Sweet | Flower Sweet | Star Sweet | Ribbon Sweet |

## Ruby Swirl

| Strawberry Sweet | Berry Sweet | Love Sweet | Clover Sweet | Flower Sweet | Star Sweet | Ribbon Sweet |

## Mint Cream

| Strawberry Sweet | Berry Sweet | Love Sweet | Clover Sweet | Flower Sweet | Star Sweet | Ribbon Sweet |

## Rainbow Swirl

| Strawberry Sweet | Berry Sweet | Love Sweet | Clover Sweet | Flower Sweet | Star Sweet | Ribbon Sweet |

001-100
101-200
201-300
401-442
443-500
501-600
601-700
701-800
801-898

# ALCREMIE

## GIGANTAMAX FORM

Cream pours endlessly from this Pokémon's body. The cream stiffens when compressed by an impact. A harder impact results in harder cream.

**ALCREMIE**

| Cream Pokémon | |
|---|---|
| POKÉDEX NO. | **869** |
| TYPE | Fairy |
| ABILITY | Sweet Veil |
| HEIGHT | 98'05"+ |
| WEIGHT | ??? lbs |

## Description

It launches swarms of missiles, each made of cream and loaded with 100,000 calories. Get hit by one of these, and your head will swim.

## Special Moves

G-Max Finale

# FALINKS

001-100
101-200
201-300
-442
443-600
501-600
701-800
801-898

## Formation Pokémon

| POKÉDEX NO. | **870** |
|---|---|
| TYPE | Fighting |
| ABILITY | Battle Armor |
| HEIGHT | 9'10" |
| WEIGHT | 136.7 lbs |

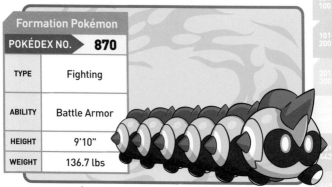

### Description

Five of them are troopers, and one is the brass. The brass's orders are absolute.

The six of them work together as one Pokémon. Teamwork is also their battle strategy, and they constantly change their formation as they fight.

### Special Moves

First Impression, No Retreat, Megahorn

Evolution

Does not evolve

FALINKS

# PINCURCHIN

Sea Urchin Pokémon

| POKÉDEX NO. | 871 |
|---|---|
| TYPE | Electric |
| ABILITY | Lightning Rod |
| HEIGHT | 1'00" |
| WEIGHT | 2.2 lbs |

### Description

It stores electricity in each spine. Even if one gets broken off, it still continues to emit electricity for at least three hours.

It feeds on seaweed, using its teeth to scrape it off rocks. Electric current flows from the tips of its spines.

### Special Moves

Spark, Zing Zap, Charge

Evolution

PINCURCHIN

Does not evolve

# SNOM

| | |
|---|---|
| **Worm Pokémon** | |
| **POKÉDEX NO.** | **872** |
| **TYPE** | Ice, Bug |
| **ABILITY** | Shield Dust |
| **HEIGHT** | 1'00" |
| **WEIGHT** | 8.4 lbs |

001-100
101-200
201-300
401-442
443-500
501-600
701-800
801-898

It spits out thread imbued with a frigid sort of energy and uses it to tie its body to branches, disguising itself as an icicle while it sleeps.

### Description

It eats snow that piles up on the ground. The more snow it eats, the bigger and more impressive the spikes on its back grow.

### Special Moves

Struggle Bug, Powder Snow

**Evolution**

 →

SNOM        FROSMOTH

# FROSMOTH

**Frost Moth Pokémon**

| POKÉDEX NO. | **873** |
| --- | --- |
| **TYPE** | Ice, Bug |
| **ABILITY** | Shield Dust |
| **HEIGHT** | 4'03" |
| **WEIGHT** | 92.6 lbs |

It shows no mercy to any who desecrate fields and mountains. It will fly around on its icy wings, causing a blizzard to chase offenders away.

### Description

Icy scales fall from its wings like snow as it flies over fields and mountains. The temperature of its wings is less than -290 degrees Fahrenheit.

### Special Moves

Icy Wind, Aurora Beam, Hail

**Evolution**

SNOM → FROSMOTH

# STONJOURNER

It stands in grasslands, watching the sun's descent from zenith to horizon. This Pokémon has a talent for delivering dynamic kicks.

001-100
101-200
201-300
401-442
443-500
501-600
701-800
801-898

## Big Rock Pokémon

| POKÉDEX NO. | 874 |
|---|---|
| TYPE | Rock |
| ABILITY | Power Spot |
| HEIGHT | 8'02" |
| WEIGHT | 1146.4 lbs |

### Description

Once a year, on a specific date and at a specific time, they gather out of nowhere and form up in a circle.

### Special Moves

Rock Slide, Stone Edge, Wide Guard

Evolution

STONJOURNER

Does not evolve

513

# EISCUE

## ICE FACE

### Penguin Pokémon

| | |
|---|---|
| POKÉDEX NO. | **875** |
| TYPE | Ice |
| ABILITY | Ice Face |
| HEIGHT | 4'07" |
| WEIGHT | 196.2 lbs |

### Description

It drifted in on the flow of ocean waters from a frigid place. It keeps its head iced constantly to make sure it stays nice and cold.

This Pokémon keeps its heat-sensitive head cool with ice. It fishes for its food, dangling its single hair into the sea to lure prey.

### Special Moves

Freeze-Dry, Aurora Veil, Blizzard

**Evolution**    Does not evolve

**EISCUE**
[ICE FACE]

# EISCUE

NOICE FACE

Penguin Pokémon

| POKÉDEX NO. | **875** |
|---|---|
| TYPE | Ice |
| ABILITY | Ice Face |
| HEIGHT | 4'07" |
| WEIGHT | 196.2 lbs |

The ice covering this Pokémon's face has shattered, revealing a slightly worried expression that many people are enamored with.

### Description

The hair on its head connects to the surface of its brain. When this Pokémon has something on its mind, its hair chills the air around it.

### Special Moves

Surf, Weather Ball, Icy Wind

**Evolution**

EISCUE
(NOICE FACE)

Does not evolve

001-100
101-200
201-300
401-442
443-500
501-600
601-700
701-800
801-898

# INDEEDEE

## MALE

| Emotion Pokémon | |
|---|---|
| POKÉDEX NO. | **876** |
| TYPE | Psychic, Normal |
| ABILITY | Synchronize, Own Tempo |
| HEIGHT | 2'11" |
| WEIGHT | 61.7 lbs |

Through its horns, it can pick up the emotions of creatures around it. Positive emotions are the source of its strength.

### Description

It uses the horns on its head to sense the emotions of others. Males will act as valets for those they serve, looking after their every need.

### Special Moves

Psychic, Encore, Power Split

**Evolution**

INDEEDEE
[MALE]

Does not evolve

# INDEEDEE

**FEMALE**

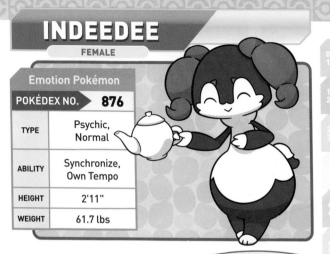

| Emotion Pokémon | |
|---|---|
| **POKÉDEX NO.** | **876** |
| **TYPE** | Psychic, Normal |
| **ABILITY** | Synchronize, Own Tempo |
| **HEIGHT** | 2'11" |
| **WEIGHT** | 61.7 lbs |

001-100
101-200
201-300
401-442
443-500
501-600
601-700
701-800
801-898

These intelligent Pokémon touch horns with each other to share information between them.

### Description

They diligently serve people and Pokémon so they can gather feelings of gratitude. The females are particularly good at babysitting.

### Special Moves

Healing Wish, Helping Hand, Disarming Voice

**Evolution**

**INDEEDEE**
**(FEMALE)**

Does not evolve

# MORPEKO

## FULL BELLY MODE

| Two-Sided Pokémon | |
|---|---|
| POKÉDEX NO. | **877** |
| TYPE | Electric, Dark |
| ABILITY | Hunger Switch |
| HEIGHT | 1'00" |
| WEIGHT | 6.6 lbs |

It carries electrically roasted seeds with it as if they're precious treasures. No matter how much it eats, it always gets hungry again in short order.

### Description

As it eats the seeds stored up in its pocket-like pouches, this Pokémon is not just satisfying its constant hunger. It's also generating electricity.

### Special Moves

Aura Wheel, Bullet Seed, Spark

Evolution

MORPEKO
(FULL BELLY MODE)

Does not evolve

# MORPEKO

## HANGRY MODE

### Two-Sided Pokémon

| POKÉDEX NO. | **877** |
| --- | --- |
| TYPE | Electric, Dark |
| ABILITY | Hunger Switch |
| HEIGHT | 1'00" |
| WEIGHT | 6.6 lbs |

Hunger hormones affect its temperament. Until its hunger is appeased, it gets up to all manner of evil deeds.

### Description

Intense hunger drives it to extreme violence, and the electricity in its cheek sacs has converted into a Dark-type energy.

### Special Moves

Aura Wheel, Leer, Crunch

001-100
101-200
201-300
401-442
443-500
501-600
701-800
801-898

Evolution

MORPEKO
(HANGRY MODE)

Does not evolve

# CUFANT

Copperderm Pokémon

| POKÉDEX NO. | 878 |
|---|---|

| TYPE | Steel |
|---|---|
| ABILITY | Sheer Force |
| HEIGHT | 3'11" |
| WEIGHT | 220.5 lbs |

### Description

It digs up the ground with its trunk. It's also very strong, being able to carry loads of over five tons without any problem at all.

If a job requires serious strength, this Pokémon will excel at it. Its copper body tarnishes in the rain, turning a vibrant green color.

### Special Moves

Dig, Bulldoze, Iron Head

Evolution

CUFANT → COPPERAJAH

# COPPERAJAH

| | |
|---|---|
| **Copperderm Pokémon** | |
| **POKÉDEX NO.** | **879** |
| **TYPE** | Steel |
| **ABILITY** | Sheer Force |
| **HEIGHT** | 9'10" |
| **WEIGHT** | 1433.0 lbs |

These Pokémon live in herds. Their trunks have incredible grip strength, strong enough to crush giant rocks into powder.

## Description

They came over from another region long ago and worked together with humans. Their green skin is resistant to water.

## Special Moves

Heavy Slam, Strength, High Horsepower

001-100
101-200
201-300
401-442
443-500
501-600
701-800
801-898

**Evolution**

CUFANT → COPPERAJAH

# COPPERAJAH

## GIGANTAMAX FORM

### COPPERAJAH

After this Pokémon has Gigantamaxed, its massive nose can utterly demolish large structures with a single smashing blow.

| Copperderm Pokémon | |
|---|---|
| **POKÉDEX NO.** | **879** |
| **TYPE** | Steel |
| **ABILITY** | Sheer Force |
| **HEIGHT** | 75'06"+ |
| **WEIGHT** | ??? lbs |

### Description

So much power is packed within its trunk that if it were to unleash that power, the resulting blast could level mountains and change the landscape.

### Special Moves

G-Max Steelsurge

# DRACOZOLT

### Fossil Pokémon

| POKÉDEX NO. | **880** |
|---|---|
| TYPE | Electric, Dragon |
| ABILITY | Volt Absorb, Hustle |
| HEIGHT | 5'11" |
| WEIGHT | 418.9 lbs |

The powerful muscles in its tail generate its electricity. Compared to its lower body, its upper half is entirely too small.

### Description

In ancient times, it was unbeatable thanks to its powerful lower body, but it went extinct anyway after it depleted all its plant-based food sources.

### Special Moves

Bolt Beak, Aerial Ace, Discharge

**Evolution**

DRACOZOLT

Does not evolve

001-100
101-200
201-300
401-442
443-500
501-600
701-800
801-898

# ARCTOZOLT

**Fossil Pokémon**

| POKÉDEX NO. | **881** |
|---|---|
| **TYPE** | Electric, Ice |
| **ABILITY** | Static, Volt Absorb |
| **HEIGHT** | 7'07" |
| **WEIGHT** | 330.7 lbs |

The shaking of its freezing upper half is what generates its electricity. It has a hard time walking around.

## Description

This Pokémon lived on prehistoric seashores and was able to preserve food with the ice on its body. It went extinct because it moved so slowly.

## Special Moves

Bolt Beak, Freeze-Dry, Blizzard

**Evolution**   ARCTOZOLT — Does not evolve

# DRACOVISH

| Fossil Pokémon | |
|---|---|
| **POKÉDEX NO.** | **882** |
| **TYPE** | Water, Dragon |
| **ABILITY** | Water Absorb, Strong Jaw |
| **HEIGHT** | 7'07" |
| **WEIGHT** | 474.0 lbs |

### Description

Powerful legs and jaws made it the apex predator of its time. Its own overhunting of its prey was what drove it to extinction.

Its mighty legs are capable of running at speeds exceeding 40 mph, but this Pokémon can't breathe unless it's underwater.

### Special Moves

Fishious Rend, Dragon Pulse, Dragon Rush

**Evolution**   Does not evolve

DRACOVISH

001-100
101-200
201-300
401-442
443-500
501-600
701-800
801-898

# ARCTOVISH

## Fossil Pokémon

| POKÉDEX NO. | **883** |
|---|---|
| **TYPE** | Water, Ice |
| **ABILITY** | Water Absorb, Ice Body |
| **HEIGHT** | 6'07" |
| **WEIGHT** | 385.8 lbs |

### Description

The skin on its face is impervious to attack, but the breathing difficulties made this Pokémon go extinct anyway.

### Special Moves

Fishious Rend, Icicle Crash, Freeze-Dry

Though it's able to capture prey by freezing its surroundings, it has trouble eating the prey afterward because its mouth is on top of its head.

**Evolution**  Does not evolve

ARCTOVISH

# DURALUDON

## Alloy Pokémon

| | |
|---|---|
| **POKÉDEX NO.** | **884** |
| **TYPE** | Steel, Dragon |
| **ABILITY** | Light Metal, Heavy Metal |
| **HEIGHT** | 5'11" |
| **WEIGHT** | 88.2 lbs |

### Description

Its body resembles polished metal, and it's both lightweight and strong. The only drawback is that it rusts easily.

### Special Moves

Metal Burst, Dragon Claw, Iron Defense

The special metal ithat composes its body is very light, so this Pokémon has considerable agility. It lives in caves because it dislikes the rain.

**Evolution**

DURALUDON

Does not evolve

001-100
101-200
201-300
401-442
443-500
501-600
701-800
801-898

# DURALUDON

It's grown to resemble a skyscraper. Parts of its towering body glow due to a profusion of energy.

**DURALUDON**

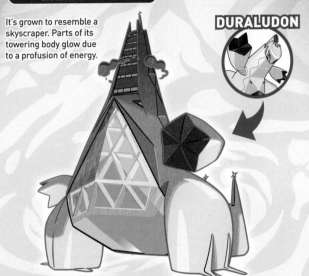

## Alloy Pokémon

| POKÉDEX NO. | 884 |
|---|---|
| TYPE | Steel, Dragon |
| ABILITY | Light Metal, Heavy Metal |
| HEIGHT | 141'01"+ |
| WEIGHT | ??? lbs |

### Description

The hardness of its cells is exceptional, even among Steel types. It also has a body structure that's resistant to earthquakes.

### Special Moves

G-Max Depletion

# DREEPY

**Lingering Pokémon**

| POKÉDEX NO. | **885** |
|---|---|
| TYPE | Dragon, Ghost |
| ABILITY | Clear Body, Infiltrator |
| HEIGHT | 1'08" |
| WEIGHT | 4.4 lbs |

001-100
101-200
201-300
401-442
443-500
501-600
701-800
801-898

## Description

After being reborn as a ghost Pokémon, Dreepy wanders the areas it used to inhabit back when it was alive in the prehistoric seas.

If this weak Pokémon is by itself, a mere child could defeat it. But if Dreepy has friends to help it train, it can evolve and become much stronger.

## Special Moves

Quick Attack, Astonish, Infestation

**Evolution**

DREEPY → DRAKLOAK → DRAGAPULT

# DRAKLOAK

Caretaker Pokémon

| POKÉDEX NO. | 886 |
| --- | --- |
| TYPE | Dragon, Ghost |
| ABILITY | Clear Body, Infiltrator |
| HEIGHT | 4'07" |
| WEIGHT | 24.3 lbs |

Without a Dreepy to place on its head and care for, it gets so uneasy it'll try to substitute any Pokémon it finds for the missing Dreepy.

### Description

It's capable of flying faster than 120 mph. It battles alongside Dreepy and dotes on them until they successfully evolve.

### Special Moves

Dragon Pulse, Dragon Dance, Hex

Evolution

DREEPY → DRAKLOAK → DRAGAPULT

# DRAGAPULT

Stealth Pokémon

| POKÉDEX NO. | 887 |
| --- | --- |
| TYPE | Dragon, Ghost |
| ABILITY | Clear Body, Infiltrator |
| HEIGHT | 9'10" |
| WEIGHT | 110.2 lbs |

### Description

When it isn't battling, it keeps Dreepy in the holes on its horns. Once a fight starts, it launches the Dreepy like supersonic missiles.

Apparently the Dreepy inside Dragapult's horns eagerly look forward to being launched out at Mach* speeds.

### Special Moves

Dragon Darts, Take Down, Phantom Force

001-100
101-200
201-300
401-442
443-500
501-600
701-800
801-898

| Evolution | | |
| --- | --- | --- |
| DREEPY | DRAKLOAK | DRAGAPULT |

*Mach: A measurement of speed. Mach 1 is the same speed as sound, at 1,125 feet per second.

# ZACIAN

## HERO OF MANY BATTLES

### Warrior Pokémon

| | |
|---|---|
| POKÉDEX NO. | **888** |
| TYPE | Fairy |
| ABILITY | Intrepid Sword |
| HEIGHT | 9'02" |
| WEIGHT | 242.5 lbs |

### Description

This Pokémon has slumbered for many years. Some say it's Zamazenta's* elder sister—others say the two Pokémon are rivals.

Known as a legendary hero, this Pokémon absorbs metal particles, transforming them into a weapon it uses in battle.

### Special Moves

Sacred Sword, Iron Head, Howl

**Evolution**  Does not evolve

**ZACIAN**
(HERO OF MANY BATTLES)

*Zamazenta: A Pokémon you'll find on page 534.

# ZACIAN

## CROWNED SWORD

### Warrior Pokémon

| POKÉDEX NO. | **888** |
| --- | --- |
| TYPE | Fairy, Steel |
| ABILITY | Intrepid Sword |
| HEIGHT | 9'02" |
| WEIGHT | 782.6 lbs |

001-
100

101-
200

201-
300

401-
442

443-
500

501-
600

701-
800

801-
898

### Description

Able to cut down anything with a single strike, it became known as the Fairy King's Sword, and it inspired awe in friend and foe alike.

### Special Moves

Behemoth Blade, Giga Impact, Slash

Now armed with a weapon it used in ancient times, this Pokémon needs only a single strike to fell even Gigantamax Pokémon.

| Evolution | | Does not evolve |
| --- | --- | --- |

ZACIAN
(CROWNED SWORD)

# ZAMAZENTA

**HERO OF MANY BATTLES**

## Warrior Pokémon

| | |
|---|---|
| **POKÉDEX NO.** | **889** |
| **TYPE** | Fighting |
| **ABILITY** | Dauntless Shield |
| **HEIGHT** | 9'06" |
| **WEIGHT** | 463.0 lbs |

In times past, it worked together with a king of the people to save the Galar region. It absorbs metal that it then uses in battle.

### Description

This Pokémon slept for eons while in the form of a statue. It was asleep for so long, people forgot that it ever existed.

### Special Moves

Metal Burst, Moonblast, Iron Defense

**Evolution**

ZAMAZENTA
(HERO OF MANY BATTLES)

Does not evolve

# ZAMAZENTA

### CROWNED SHIELD

## Warrior Pokémon

| POKÉDEX NO. | **889** |
|---|---|
| **TYPE** | Fighting, Steel |
| **ABILITY** | Dauntless Shield |
| **HEIGHT** | 9'06" |
| **WEIGHT** | 1730.6 lbs |

Now that it's equipped with its shield, it can shrug off impressive blows, including the attacks of Dynamax* Pokémon.

### Description

Its ability to deflect any attack led to it being known as the Fighting Master's Shield. It was feared and respected by all.

### Special Moves

Behemoth Bash, Iron Head, Iron Defense

**Evolution**   Does not evolve

### ZAMAZENTA
(CROWNED SHIELD FORM)

*Dynamax: A phenomenon where a Pokémon turns into a giant size. This occurs in certain areas of the Galar region.

001-100
101-200
201-300
401-442
443-500
501-600
701-800
801-898

# ETERNATUS

| | |
|---|---|
| **Gigantic Pokémon** | |
| **POKÉDEX NO.** | **890** |
| **TYPE** | Poison, Dragon |
| **ABILITY** | Pressure |
| **HEIGHT** | 65'07" |
| **WEIGHT** | 2094.4 lbs |

It was inside a meteorite that fell 20,000 years ago. There seems to be a connection between this Pokémon and the Dynamax* phenomenon.

## Description

The core on its chest absorbs energy emanating from the lands of the Galar region. This energy is what allows Eternatus to stay active.

## Special Moves

Eternabeam, Dynamax Cannon

**Evolution**

Does not evolve

**ETERNATUS**

*Dynamax: A phenomenon where a Pokémon turns into a giant size. This occurs in certain areas of the Galar region.

# KUBFU

| Wushu Pokémon | |
|---|---|
| **POKÉDEX NO.** | **891** |
| TYPE | Fighting |
| ABILITY | Inner Focus |
| HEIGHT | 2'00" |
| WEIGHT | 26.5 lbs |

001-100
101-200
201-300
401-442
443-500
501-600
701-800
801-898

If Kubfu pulls the long white hair on its head, its fighting spirit heightens and power wells up from the depths of its belly.

### Description

Kubfu trains hard to perfect its moves. The moves it masters will determine which form it takes when it evolves.

### Special Moves

Brick Break, Focus Energy, Dynamic Punch

**Evolution**

KUBFU

URSHIFU
(SINGLE STRIKE STYLE)

URSHIFU
(RAPID STRIKE STYLE)

# URSHIFU

**SINGLE STRIKE STYLE**

| Wushu Pokémon | |
|---|---|
| **POKÉDEX NO.** | **892** |
| **TYPE** | Fighting, Dark |
| **ABILITY** | Unseen Fist |
| **HEIGHT** | 6'03" |
| **WEIGHT** | 231.5 lbs |

This form of Urshifu is a strong believer in the one-hit KO. Its strategy is to leap in close to foes and land a devastating blow with a hardened fist.

### Description

Inhabiting the mountains of a distant region, this Pokémon races across sheer cliffs, training its legs and refining its moves.

### Special Moves

Wicked Blow, Focus Punch, Detect

**Evolution**

KUBFU

URSHIFU
(SINGLE STRIKE STYLE)

# URSHIFU

## SINGLE STRIKE STYLE / GIGANTAMAX FORM

### URSHIFU (SINGLE STRIKE STYLE)

001-100
101-200
201-300
401-442
443-500
501-600
701-800
801-898

The energy released by this Pokémon's fist forms shock waves that can blow away Dynamax* Pokémon in just one hit.

| Wushu Pokémon | |
|---|---|
| **POKÉDEX NO.** | **892** |
| **TYPE** | Fighting, Dark |
| **ABILITY** | Unseen Fist |
| **HEIGHT** | 95'02"+ |
| **WEIGHT** | ??? lbs |

### Description

People call it the embodiment of rage. It's said that this Pokémon's terrifying expression and shout will rid the world of malevolence.

### Special Moves

G-Max One Blow

*Dynamax: A phenomenon where a Pokémon turns into a giant size. This occurs in certain areas of the Galar region.

# URSHIFU
## RAPID STRIKE STYLE

| Wushu Pokémon | |
|---|---|
| POKÉDEX NO. | **892** |
| TYPE | Fighting, Water |
| ABILITY | Unseen Fist |
| HEIGHT | 6'03" |
| WEIGHT | 231.5 lbs |

This form of Urshifu is a strong believer in defeating foes by raining many blows down on them. Its strikes are nonstop, flowing like a river.

## Description

It's believed that this Pokémon modeled its fighting style after the flow of a river—sometimes rapid, sometimes calm.

## Special Moves

Surging Strikes, Aqua Jet, Detect

**Evolution**

 →

KUBFU　　　URSHIFU
(RAPID STRIKE STYLE)

# URSHIFU

**RAPID STRIKE STYLE / GIGANTAMAX FORM**

001-100

101-200

201-300

401-442

443-500

501-600

701-800

801-898

## URSHIFU (RAPID STRIKE STYLE)

All it takes is a glare from this Pokémon to take the lives of those with evil in their hearts—or so they say.

| Wushu Pokémon | |
|---|---|
| POKÉDEX NO. | **892** |
| TYPE | Fighting, Water |
| ABILITY | Unseen Fist |
| HEIGHT | 85'04"+ |
| WEIGHT | ??? lbs |

### Description

As it waits for the right moment to unleash its Gigantamax power, this Pokémon maintains a perfect one-legged stance. It won't even twitch.

### Special Moves

G-Max Rapid Flow

541

# ZARUDE

**Rogue Monkey Pokémon**

| POKÉDEX NO. | 893 |
|---|---|
| **TYPE** | Dark, Grass |
| **ABILITY** | Leaf Guard |
| **HEIGHT** | 5'11" |
| **WEIGHT** | 154.3 lbs |

Once the vines on Zarude's body tear off, they become sources of nutrients in the soil. This helps the plants of the forest grow.

### Description

Within dense forests, this Pokémon lives in a pack with others of its kind. It's incredibly aggressive, and the other Pokémon of the forest fear it.

### Special Moves

Jungle Healing, Power Whip, Swagger

Evolution

ZARUDE

Does not evolve

# REGIELEKI

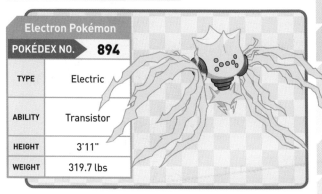

### Electron Pokémon

| POKÉDEX NO. | **894** |
| --- | --- |
| **TYPE** | Electric |
| **ABILITY** | Transistor |
| **HEIGHT** | 3'11" |
| **WEIGHT** | 319.7 lbs |

001-100

101-200

201-300

401-442

443-500

501-600

701-800

801-898

This Pokémon is a cluster of electrical energy. It's said that removing the rings on Regieleki's body will unleash the Pokémon's latent power.

### Description

Its entire body is made up of a single organ that generates electrical energy. Regieleki is capable of creating all Galar's electricity.

### Special Moves

Thunder Cage, Zap Cannon, Extreme Speed

**Evolution**   Does not evolve

REGIELEKI

# REGIDRAGO

**Dragon Orb Pokémon**

| POKÉDEX NO. | 895 |
|---|---|
| TYPE | Dragon |
| ABILITY | Dragon's Maw |
| HEIGHT | 6'11" |
| WEIGHT | 440.9 lbs |

### Description

Its body is composed of crystallized dragon energy. Regidrago is said to have the powers of every dragon Pokémon.

An academic theory proposes that Regidrago's arms were once the head of an ancient dragon Pokémon. The theory remains unproven.

### Special Moves

Dragon Energy, Hyper Beam, Vice Grip

**Evolution**  Does not evolve

REGIDRAGO

# GLASTRIER

## Wild Horse Pokémon

| POKÉDEX NO. | 896 |
| --- | --- |

| TYPE | Ice |
| --- | --- |
| ABILITY | Chilling Neigh |
| HEIGHT | 7'03" |
| WEIGHT | 1763.7 lbs |

Glastrier has tremendous physical strength, and the mask of ice covering its face is 100 times harder than diamond.

### Description

Glastrier emits intense cold from its hooves. It's also a belligerent Pokémon—anything it wants, it takes by force.

### Special Moves

Icicle Crash, Avalanche, Mist

Evolution  Does not evolve

GLASTRIER

# SPECTRIER

Swift Horse Pokémon

| POKÉDEX NO. | **897** |
|---|---|
| **TYPE** | Ghost |
| **ABILITY** | Grim Neigh |
| **HEIGHT** | 6'07" |
| **WEIGHT** | 98.1 lbs |

### Description

It probes its surroundings with all its senses save one—it doesn't use its sense of sight. Spectrier's kicks are said to separate soul from body.

### Special Moves

Shadow Ball, Nasty Plot, Haze

As it dashes through the night, Spectrier absorbs the life force of sleeping creatures. It craves silence and solitude.

Evolution

SPECTRIER

 Does not evolve

# CALYREX

## King Pokémon

| POKÉDEX NO. | 898 |
| --- | --- |

| TYPE | Psychic, Grass |
| --- | --- |
| ABILITY | Unnerve |
| HEIGHT | 3'07" |
| WEIGHT | 17.0 lbs |

### Description

Calyrex is a merciful Pokémon, capable of providing healing and blessings. It reigned over the Galar region in times of yore.

### Special Moves

Psychic, Giga Drain, Future Sight

Calyrex is known in legend as a king that ruled over Galar in ancient times. It has the power to cause hearts to mend and plants to spring forth.

Evolution

Does not evolve

CALYREX

001-100
101-200
201-300
401-442
443-500
501-600
701-800
801-898

# CALYREX

### ICE RIDER CALYREX

## High King Pokémon

| POKÉDEX NO. | 898 |
| --- | --- |
| TYPE | Psychic, Ice |
| ABILITY | As One |
| HEIGHT | 7'10" |
| WEIGHT | 1783.8 lbs |

It's said that this Pokémon once moved a large forest—and all the Pokémon living there—to a new location overnight.

### Description

According to lore, this Pokémon showed no mercy to those who got in its way, yet it would heal its opponents' wounds after battle.

### Special Moves

Glacial Lance, Icicle Crash, Stomp

Evolution  Does not evolve

CALYREX
(ICE RIDER CALYREX)

# CALYREX

## SHADOW RIDER CALYREX

| High King Pokémon | |
|---|---|
| POKÉDEX NO. | **898** |
| TYPE | Psychic, Ghost |
| ABILITY | As One |
| HEIGHT | 7'10" |
| WEIGHT | 118.2 lbs |

001-100
101-200
201-300
401-442
443-500
501-600
701-800
801-898

Legend says that by using its power to see all events, from past to future, this Pokémon saved the creatures of a forest from a meteorite strike.

### Description

It's said that Calyrex and a Pokémon that had bonded with it ran all across the Galar region to bring green to the wastelands.

### Special Moves

Astral Barrage, Giga Drain, Hex

**Evolution**

Does not evolve

CALYREX
[SHADOW RIDER CALYREX]

# POKÉ BALL GUIDE

**There are many kinds of Poké Balls that can be used against wild Pokémon. Each ball has a different effect!**

**POKÉ BALL**

A ball used to capture a wild Pokémon.

**GREAT BALL**

A ball that has a better chance of capturing a Pokémon than a Poké Ball.

**ULTRA BALL**

A ball that has a greater chance of capturing a Pokémon than a Great Ball.

**MASTER BALL**

An amazing ball that will catch any wild Pokémon without fail.

**PREMIER BALL**

A rare ball made in commemoration of some event.

**CHERISH BALL**

A very rare ball made in commemoration of some event.

**HEAL BALL**

A remedial ball that eliminates any status conditions and heals the captured Pokémon's wounds.

**NET BALL**

A ball that works well on Water- and Bug-type Pokémon.

**DUSK BALL**

A ball that makes it easier to capture Pokémon at night and inside caves.

**NEST BALL**

A ball that works better on lower-level Pokémon.

**QUICK BALL**

A ball that has a high catch rate if you use it at the beginning of a battle.

**TIMER BALL**

A ball that is more effective the more turns you spend in battle.

**REPEAT BALL**

A ball that is more effective on Pokémon you've caught before.

**DIVE BALL**

A ball that is effective on Pokémon that live underwater.

**LUXURY BALL**

A ball that makes the captured Pokémon grow more friendly.

**SAFARI BALL**

A special ball that is only used in the Safari Zone.

**BEAST BALL**

A unique ball that has a better catch rate for capturing an Ultra Beast.

**LURE BALL**

A Poké Ball for catching Pokémon hooked by a rod when fishing.

**LEVEL BALL**

A ball for catching Pokémon that are of a lower level than your own Pokémon.

**MOON BALL**

A ball that is effective against Pokémon that evolve with the Moon Stone.

**HEAVY BALL**

A Poké Ball for catching very heavy Pokémon.

**FAST BALL**

A ball effective for catching fast Pokémon.

**FRIEND BALL**

A Poké Ball that makes the captured Pokémon more friendly.

**LOVE BALL**

A ball that is effective at catching Pokémon that are the opposite gender of your Pokémon.

*This only covers the major Poké Balls.

# ALPHABETICAL INDEX

Use this index to locate your favorite Pokémon from each volume! The index is listed alphabetically by the Pokémon's name, with the volume number and page number next to it.

ALPHABETICAL INDEX

**The Complete Pokémon Pocket Guide**
Volume 2

*VIZ Media Edition*

**Editing/Writing (Original Japanese Edition):** Takuma Kaede
**Translation (VIZ Media Edition):** Tetsuichiro Miyaki
**English Adaptation (VIZ Media Edition):** Christine Hunter
**Design (Original Japanese Edition):** Yuriko Naito, Yu Ishimoto
**Design (VIZ Media Edition):** Paul Padurariu
**Editor (VIZ Media Edition):** Joel Enos

Special thanks to Trish Ledoux and Wendy Hoover at The Pokémon
Company International.

The stories, characters, and incidents mentioned in this publication
are entirely fictional.

Library of Congress Cataloging-in-Publication data available.

Printed in China

Published by VIZ Media, LLC
P.O. Box 77010
San Francisco, CA 94107

10 9 8 7 6 5 4 3 2 1
First printing, May 2024

**PARENTAL ADVISORY**
POKÉMON: THE COMPLETE POKÉMON
POCKET GUIDE is rated A and is suitable
for readers of all ages.
ratings.viz.com
RATED A ALL AGES